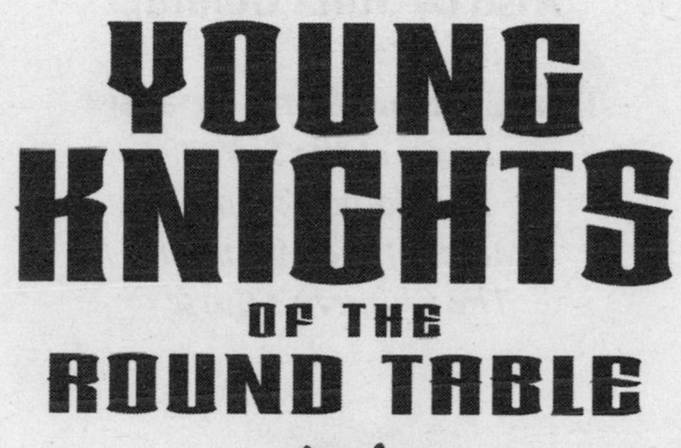
YOUNG
KNIGHTS
OF THE
ROUND TABLE

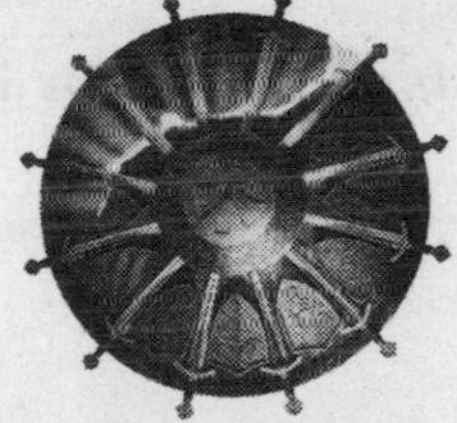

**Also by Julia Golding**

**The Companions Quartet**

*Secret of the Sirens*
*The Gorgon's Gaze*
*Mines of the Minotaur*
*The Chimera's Curse*

*

*The Ship Between the Worlds*
*Dragonfly*
*The Glass Swallow*
*Wolf Cry*

# YOUNG KNIGHTS OF THE ROUND TABLE

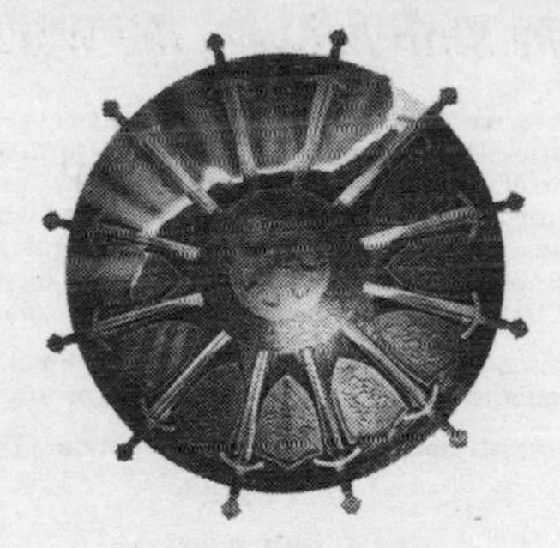

Julia Golding

OXFORD
UNIVERSITY PRESS

Great Clarendon Street, Oxford OX2 6DP
Oxford University Press is a department of the University of Oxford.
It furthers the University's objective of excellence in research, scholarship,
and education by publishing worldwide in

Oxford New York

Auckland Cape Town Dar es Salaam Hong Kong Karachi
Kuala Lumpur Madrid Melbourne Mexico City Nairobi
New Delhi Shanghai Taipei Toronto

With offices in

Argentina Austria Brazil Chile Czech Republic France Greece
Guatemala Hungary Italy Japan Poland Portugal Singapore
South Korea Switzerland Thailand Turkey Ukraine Vietnam



First published 2013



British Library Cataloguing in Publication Data

Data available

ISBN: 978-0-19-273222-4
3 5 7 9 10 8 6 4 2

Printed in Great Britain
Paper used in the production of this book is a natural,
recyclable product made from wood grown in sustainable forests.
The manufacturing process conforms to the environmental
regulations of the country of origin.

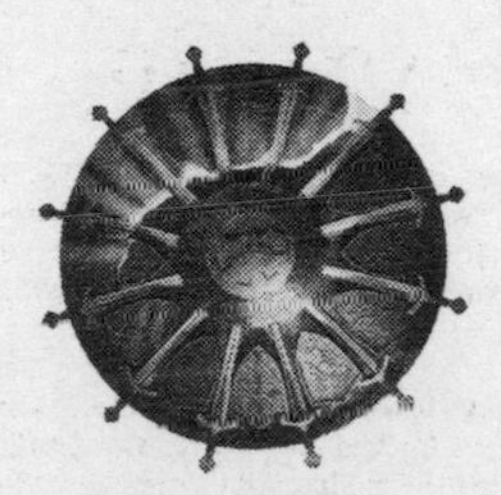

*For Toby and Edward*

With thanks to Andrew Briggs, the real Professor of Nanomaterials at Oxford University, for his fascinating insights into the wilder end of science. I would hazard you did not know, Andrew, that Feys were behind it all. Also my thanks to Professor Ulrike Tillmann of the Mathematical Institute, Oxford University, for telling me about her work on extra dimensions while we shared a school run. I dedicate dimension number seven—the home of all lost things—to you! And a special thank you to Natalia and Tomislav for waiting so long.

# Chapter 1

Humans are the enemy.

Tightening the straps on his leather armguards, Rick glanced up at the motto of Dark Lore House. The words filled him with determination to overcome his human blood and be the best warrior the Fey could train.

'All right, changelings, the sergeant is late,' Rick called to the others. 'Let's do the usual patterns. One-on-one with staffs. Target practice for archers. Blade drill for swords. No magic.'

His classmates groaned, but most settled into their routines as they had been taught.

Rick was proud to call himself a changeling, the name the Fey gave to abandoned children rescued over the centuries from Earth. Taken to Avalon, as the Fey parallel world was known, they were being created into an elite band of warriors. They would eventually be sent back to Earth and get their revenge on mankind. The Fey expected them to be single-minded about their task, which explained why he and his classmates were going through their weapons drill in the indoor combat arena even though their instructor, Sergeant Rotgut, a beefy ogre with a voice like a rusty saw, was late.

Beyond late.

An hour over at least—and that was unheard of in the strict regime of Dark Lore. All the staff had been called at dawn to an emergency meeting in Commander Morgan La Faye's office. Something serious must be going on but as usual the students were the last to know.

As the oldest student, Rick was in charge but he had no illusions that he was in control. While he might feel like a big brother to the younger children, only a few of them showed any signs of appreciating his attempts to care for them.

'Edgar, go easy with that staff: it's only practice.' The stocky medieval peasant lad tapped his forehead, gesturing he understood. Ahmed, the little Arabian boy who was his partner, heaved a sigh of relief. At least those two listened to him. That left just another ninety-seven who did not.

Rick took his sword to practise strikes on the straw dummy of a human knight at the far end of the spacious wooden 'O'. Between fight patterns, he looked up at the Round Table that hung on the wall opposite the motto. Its great circular top was made of the finest oak and covered with intricate carving, each name embellished with the coat of arms of the knight's house. Unlike its glory days in Camelot, it was now marred by a split down the middle where its power had been broken. The Table was the chief trophy won by the Fey in their war against King Arthur and his warriors when the humans had attacked Avalon. The Fey had hung it there as a reminder to the changelings that, one day soon, they too should defeat their human enemies.

Below the Table were the 'most wanted' portraits of the men who used to sit around it. They stretched in a long line: Sir Galahad, Sir Gawain, Sir Lancelot—their names were legend but the people long since eliminated, a point emphasized by the great red cross Commander Morgan had scrawled over their pictures. Of the human criminals, only two remained alive: Arthur, in exile on an island here in Avalon; and Merlin, who was still on the run somewhere in the human world.

Settling into the rhythm of his sword drill, Rick chewed over what emergency could detain Sergeant Rotgut. In all Rick's thirteen years in Dark Lore, he had not known it happen before. It could be a test. The teacher could be observing, expecting someone to break ranks. Stepping out of line meant punishment—and, as the most severe penalty was being fed to dragons in the annual Fey Games, none of them wanted to risk it. Instead, they all stuck to their routines, watching the silver dandelion clock lose its seeds until it reached the bare point that marked the end of the session.

All except one. Santiago Dulac, known as Tiago, had got bored with archery and begun juggling arrows to amuse his little black and white dog. On the short side, Tiago was one of those with mixed parentage—half human, half Dark Folk, as the various species in Avalon were known collectively. With the caramel-toned skin, and long black hair of his Aztec mother, his magical inheritance was declared most clearly by his silvery eyes, a colour only seen among the Mage Fey. The Mage were a rebellious, persecuted race, sharing a common ancestry with the dominant Fey, but they had long ago branched off to evolve a different temperament and slighter stature. With this unusual background, it was hardly surprising that Tiago was a loner, his world being just him and his dog.

The spirit of rebellion was spreading through the room. Other changelings were giving up, deciding Rotgut really wasn't going to show.

'Hey, Tabitha, did you hear?' called Roxy Topley, a girl with a mass of reddish-gold hair. Roxy came originally from Old Ireland, and was a year or two younger than Rick. It was no surprise to Rick that she was one of the first to chance stopping for a chat.

'Hear what?' Tabitha was a plainly dressed, serious child from seventeenth century America and the last person who would break rules, unless she happened to be standing next to the rebel Roxy.

Rick cleared his throat. 'Roxy: there're still fifteen minutes to go.'

Roxy rolled her eyes at Tabitha. 'Ignore Mr Play-it-by-the-rules over there. There's a new batch of changelings in the nursery—special delivery by the king's messengers.'

Tabitha shook her head sadly. 'I thought King Oberon had stopped rescuing the children thrown away by the humans. Doesn't he think there are too many of us already?'

Dark Lore was home to more than a hundred rejected human children rescued over time—one year in Avalon was a century on Earth. Rick had been the first; now he had to share his room with three other boys. It was getting very crowded.

Roxy shrugged. 'Apparently not. Seems like people on Earth are being as evil as ever—abandoning their kids like they did us. I just don't get it: what did we ever do to them?'

Roxy's complaint stirred up unhappy memories for all of the changelings. Rick touched his neck torc, waking his golden snake, Aethel, from her spell of immobility. She wound her gleaming serpentine body down his arm and curved round to blink emerald eyes at him.

Rick returned the look.

With a flick of those stone-bright eyes at their surroundings, the snake realized he had woken her in time for weapons practice, her least favourite activity. She began to slip off Rick's wrist, weaving in the air in search of another perch.

'Watch it! Keep your familiar under control, Rick.' Roxy pulled Tabitha further away from him.

'Get a grip, Roxy. Aethel's not going to attack.'

Roxy followed the serpent suspiciously with her eyes. 'Tabitha's scared of snakes.'

Tabitha nudged Roxy. 'Rox, I'm not scared.'

Which meant Roxy was. Aethel swayed in the air, still undecided if she wanted to risk a bout of sweaty sword fighting. She paused, flickered her tongue at Roxy, then finally returned to coil around Rick's throat. Rick grinned, pleased by her choice—Aethel was the only family he had, even if she was a cowardly magical serpent.

He stroked her neck. 'Leave my snake out of it,

Roxy. At least I don't go round plagued by a flock of robins.'

Roxy folded her arms. Many inches shorter than him, it must bug her that she had to look up to glare. 'They are not a plague.'

'Says the girl who is never without their twigs in her hair.'

She gave a sniff and turned her back on him. Changelings were very sensitive about any criticism of the familiars, or special creatures, who adopted them.

Ten minutes to go before the next lesson: Feysyks with the pixie scientist, Doctor Purl-E. Any delay was welcome as Rick hated the subject. Action was more his thing. He flexed his palm around the hilt of his sword, going through battle readiness drill. High ground, low ground, blind spots. Yes, he had them all covered. Other than Aethel, the sword had been the one possession the Fey had brought with him when they rescued him from the late eighth century. Perhaps they knew even then that they were going to train him as a swordsman. Aethel, in necklace form, had been in his cradle and been carried away in the blanket that wrapped him. He was luckier than most changelings. They usually arrived in Avalon with nothing but the clothes they were in at the time they were sold or abandoned.

Just when he thought he had things back under control, the session went pear-shaped.

'Stuff this. *Adios, amigos,* I'm outta here.' Tiago waved cheerfully to the changelings going through their drill, unworried that he was cutting class early. Bob trotted behind, little tail held aloft like a flag semaphoring his good nature.

Rick was about to call Tiago back, but the words died on his tongue. The mushrooms that decorated the leaf carpet on the floor of the arena abruptly began blooming and shrivelling with unnatural speed—popping up and down like colourful umbrellas on a showery day.

'Whoa!' He jumped aside as a huge toadstool erupted by his left foot with a puff of purple spores. 'Hey, Ed, look at that!'

Abandoning his staff practice, Edgar scrambled on to a bench. 'Troll farts, Rick, that's not right.'

'That's what I thought.' Rick studied the arena in closer detail. Morgan rearranged Dark Lore periodically like someone shuffling a deck and building a new house of cards, fitting the magical illusion to her whim. This month she had made the arena into a forest clearing, walls of tightly packed trunks, ivy hangings and earthen floor. It seemed to be shivering. The changelings had always been moved out when the illusion changed—far too dangerous to be inside. Should they evacuate?

That was the moment the dragon roar fire alarm went off.

The floor tipped, separating Rick from Edgar as they tumbled down opposite sides of the divide. Rick rolled over and over, unable to stop. This was no ordinary change: the arena was collapsing. A major magic malfunction was underway.

Rick grabbed on to a trunk but it went soft in his hands and melted like chocolate on a hot plate. He could hear screams and shouts for help but now a great wall of what had been floor cut him off from the others. Bursts of magic rocketed through the arena, blasts of white light. Sliding out of an open door, he ended up in a passageway. Scrambling to his feet, he tried to run along it but it kept wriggling and writhing. He found he was at one point jogging along the ceiling until it reverted and he came crashing down to what was once more the floor. Pulling himself up, he staggered around a corner, straight into Roxy, Tiago, and Bob. He got a mouthful of Roxy's long hair as she catapulted into his arms. Bob saved himself from tipping into the new chasm that yawned before them by catching on to Rick's trouser leg with his teeth. Tiago scooped the dog up just before Bob fell into the bubbling superheated magic below.

Rick moved them all back from the crack in the floor. 'Roxy, where's Tabitha and the others?'

Roxy rubbed a skinned elbow. 'She got through a window but it melted before I could follow. Tiago and I got stuck behind. How are we going to get out?'

Rick started back towards the arena, but Tiago pulled him in the opposite direction. 'No exit that way, *amigo*. I've tried all the doors but they seem to lead into some kind of magical gunk.'

'What about the Feysyks tower?'

Tiago started running. 'Worth a try—if we stay here much longer we'll be fried.'

A spray of hot magic erupted from the wall, coating everything in its path.

Shielding his face with his forearm, Rick led the way along a corridor and up a spiral stone staircase to the tower above the arena. A great circular room of the same dimensions as the arena below, its walls were lined with books, chemicals, and equipment. In order to keep the tests pure, the laboratory was sealed off from the magic that powered the illusions in the rest of the building.

'So what the hex is going on?' Roxy asked as she searched along the shelves for anything that would help them get out. Tiago and Bob rooted in a trunk at the far side, throwing out long forgotten apparatus and old exam papers.

'No idea.' Rick unbolted and pushed a shuttered window wide. His heart plummeted: they were far too high above ground to survive jumping and soon the Feysyks tower would sink like a melting iceberg into the bubbling sea of magic that had once been the rest of Dark Lore.

'First the instructors hide away in a special meeting,' Roxy said, 'and then the building explodes. Troll's breath—I can't find anything that I can transform into a rope!'

'Hey, how about these instead?' Tiago threw three ancient harnesses at their feet.

Roxy pounced on the nearest and shook it out. It looked like a very large, very damaged set of dragonfly wings. 'What are they?'

'My guess: sycacopter, experimental prototype.' Tiago was already pulling on his. It was far too big—probably made for an ogre test pilot. In recent years, the Dark Folk had started using these flying harnesses modelled on seed pods and powered by magic to travel across Avalon.

Rick grabbed the final set which had only one wing. Great. 'Do you think this will work? They aren't as sleek as the real thing.'

'That's why I think they were prototypes.'

'He means rejects,' glossed Roxy unhelpfully.

A droplet of magic squeezed through a hairline crack in the floor, sizzling as it ate its way across the tiles to the Kemystery cupboard. Definitely time to move.

'Only one way to find out if they fly.' Tiago climbed on to the windowledge. 'Pass Bob to me.'

Rick struggled with an armful of snapping, terrified terrier as Bob howled and tried to scramble free.

*'Tranquilo, amigo,'* crooned Tiago. *'Hasta la vista!'* Then he jumped.

Roxy screamed. 'Did they crash?'

In answer, Tiago reappeared a stone's throw from the window, bobbing erratically up and down in the loose grip of his harness like a rabbit in the claws of a storm-battered eagle.

Bang! Frap-frap! Crash! Roxy and Rick dived for the windowledge. The seeping magic had reached the cupboard and reacted with the first potion it came across, setting off a chain of explosions. Red sparks blasted past Rick's ear, stinging his cheek and setting Roxy's hair smouldering.

'Go!' He launched her with a shove, following immediately afterwards as a roar of flame chased them off the ledge.

'Noooo!' His single wing whirred frantically, powered by his magic, but it spun him in the wrong direction, intent on screwing him into the side of the tower. He bounced off stone and ricocheted away. The high wrought-iron fence surrounding Dark Lore now appeared before him like a net that this shuttlecock-boy would not clear.

Just before he smashed into it, his shoulder harness was snagged by Roxy's foot. She heaved him up just enough to avoid the spikes on top of the fence, but could not prevent them both crashing in full view of the party arriving at the gate.

# Chapter 2

'Thanks, Roxy,' Rick panted. Aethel was quivering with terror on his wrist. 'I'm sorry to put you through that, Legless. We're safe now. Go back to sleep.'

'Rick?' muttered Roxy, staring at something just behind him. 'I wouldn't say we were safe.'

'*Maldito!*' Tiago landed heavily beside them, clutching Bob to his chest.

'What are you doing here?'

Rick went still, his wing flapping feebly against the dirt. He had to be hallucinating. He could have sworn he heard the voice of the commander of Dark Lore.

Morgan La Faye spoke again—but not to the changelings. 'I apologize, your majesty, I do not normally let them run wild like this. It won't happen again.'

'The breakdown in your control over the humans merely proves the urgency of the situation, commander.' The voice that replied was deep, like the toll of a warning bell.

There was no sound from Roxy and Tiago. Bracing himself, Rick rolled on to his back and found himself staring up at a male Fey with dusky bronze skin and startling white hair. Mesmerizing almond-shaped blue eyes returned his gaze. Rick didn't need to see the ice-diamond crown and silver robes to know he was looking at Oberon, the Fey King, the most beautiful and powerful being in Avalon. They had crashed by the Dew Track station, where the king and his entourage had just alighted from their carriage, a beautiful craft made of a bubble of silvery magic. The king must have come to inspect the disaster site. Rick was pinned to the ground by icicles of dread, so cold was the atmosphere surrounding his sovereign.

They were in so much trouble.

The king turned away. 'I see from the state of your camp, Morgan, that the power has been restored as mysteriously and suddenly as it was cut. Our enemies only managed to half-destroy it. What is going on? The shocks have been felt throughout my realm, but the centre of the trouble is here. Nowhere else has the damage been as extreme.'

Struggling against his paralysing awe, Rick pulled himself to his feet and turned to look back at Dark Lore. The tower they had escaped from in the middle of the training centre resembled a half-melted candle—turrets slumping down the white stone walls, a new moat of bubbling magic surrounding what was left. He could see the Fey-syks instructor, Doctor Purl-E, visible thanks to his crop of silver-green hair, dancing at the margin of the gunk, reversing the spell-damage. The other changelings had made it as far as the parade ground and were being marshalled by the troll guards so a head count could be made. Pixie nurses were erecting a shelter for the very youngest charges, the new arrivals Roxy had mentioned. As far as he could tell, it looked as if all of them had survived.

Oberon frowned. 'I will not stand for this!' Droplets of magic ran from his fingertips to the ground with a hiss of power. The grass blackened in the cold bite of his potency. 'Send a team to the Other Side immediately, Morgan.'

Morgan bowed. 'Of course, sire. Whom do you wish me to send?'

'The humans—it is what you have trained them for. Or are you telling me you have not performed your task adequately and none of them are ready?'

Morgan's lips thinned into a bitter line. 'Of course not, sire. All my warriors are well trained.'

Oberon's gaze swept over Rick as if he were a piece of dubious dirt picked up on the royal shoe. 'Then these three should suffice. If they have learned to infiltrate and be accepted among their own people as well as they have absorbed their combat skills, then they are our best hope that we can extract the truth from the human world. I want answers—and I want them today.'

Morgan bowed. 'Yes, your majesty.'

'But you know what I feel about the changelings. They must have people we can trust with them to watch them.'

'I have two handlers in mind already, sir, two of your own feygents.'

'Good. I expect regular reports.' The king turned back to Rick, Roxy, and Tiago. 'Name those responsible for this attack on the power supply to my realm and you will be rewarded; fail and you will be removed. From existence.' He dismissed them with a flick of his silky grey robes and stalked off to inspect the damage. His ogre bodyguards pounded by, a squeak of leather, rattle of weapons, and stench of sweat. Finely clad, perfumed advisers hurried on their heels.

'Report to my office,' Morgan ordered, then quickly followed the king.

Rick, Roxy, and Tiago waited anxiously in Morgan's temporary headquarters set up in a pavilion next to the melted building.

'I don't like this,' muttered Roxy, prowling between two tent posts like a golden tiger in a too-small cage. If she had had a tail it would be whipping to and fro with anger.

'Come on, Roxy!' said Rick. 'It's our big chance. The humans on the Other Side have to be stopped. If they are attacking Avalon, like the knights of the Round Table did before, then it's our right to defend ourselves. Just think what damage the humans did in, what? *half an hour,* by choking off our power supply!'

Roxy wrinkled her nose. 'I've no problem with that, Rick. It's just that now we've got to go and live among humans over in the other world. Oberon said "infiltrate", not fight. We all know how vicious people over there are.'

Rick now understood her pacing. 'Troll spit, I hadn't thought what it would mean. He did say that, didn't he?' They had been allowed access to some human books and moving images called 'television' to pick up the modern way of speaking but only after the most shocking bits had been censored by the Fey. The ideas in a few of the story books Rick had read hadn't sounded too bad: he liked the concept of love, loyalty, friendship; but one look at human history had shown him that these were ideals that never made it beyond the page. Like Roxy, he was expecting to be appalled by his first exposure to unedited human behaviour.

The flaps to the tent were thrust open and Morgan swept into the room.

The changelings stood to attention.

'You may sit.' Morgan gestured to a bench in the middle of the tent.

Rick sank on to his low seat between Tiago and Roxy, feeling at even greater disadvantage on the floor at the commander's feet. Not that she needed anything to reinforce her authority. At seven feet tall, with a gleaming fall of ebony hair and milk-white skin, Morgan was striking in any company. Her face was a perfect oval, her lips blood red, her eyes a vivid green. Her high-collared black jacket was embroidered with lightning bolts on the lapel, a reminder that she was capable of zapping you with the real thing when she was angry. She looked somewhere between twenty and thirty in human years, but she was centuries older. Dark Folk could live to at least three thousand, longer for some very ancient species.

Morgan took out three files from her desk drawer; they had been written on iridescent paper made of butterfly wings, a different colour for each of them. She flicked through the pages of the scarlet folder. 'Elfric Halfdane. You are one of our older warriors—our first. You were taken, when was it?'

'AD 790, sir.' Morgan insisted on being called 'sir'; anyone calling her 'mistress' or 'my lady' did not last long in her training camp.

She nodded. 'Exactly. Thirteen of our years ago in Avalon but over a millennium for the humans. You were a noble son of the royal family of Mercia when you were thrown out. What has become of your royal house now, Elfric?'

Rick's throat tightened painfully, anger at the humans choking him. 'I don't know, sir. No doubt they got what they deserved.'

Morgan studied him closely, sensing his distress, but human feelings were incomprehensible to the Dark Folk. 'I will tell you. Your royal hall is under a car park. Your blood descendants—the family of your brothers and sisters who were left on Earth—are now scattered across the globe. None of them remember you. None of them cared what happened to you.

'Your trainers say that you are one of their most gifted warriors. You have been here long enough to have gained the capacity to manage a huge amount of magical power.' That was true: when Rick looked inside himself he could feel the magic pulsing in his chest like a second heart, hot and potent. 'But they mention also that you are stubborn and at times disobedient.'

Rick swallowed his protest that he'd always tried to obey unless he thought he would harm another student. There were no excuses in Avalon.

Morgan closed the file. 'Obstinacy is bred in your bones so you will be watched for any sign of slacking in your duty to King Oberon.'

'Yes, sir.'

She gave him a chilling smile. 'You remind me of Arthur Pendragon.'

Revolted to be compared to one of the human terrorists he despised, Rick shot to his feet. 'I am nothing like him, sir!'

'Sit down, soldier. See, he was exactly like you: proud, certain he could defeat his enemies. But I showed him, did I not?'

King Arthur was currently imprisoned on an island in a far-flung corner of Avalon, thinking he would one day be released and summoned back to the human world in its hour of greatest need. All the Dark Folk and the changelings knew that would never happen as his jail was too secure, but Arthur persisted in his hope, polishing his armour daily to be ready. Morgan was the Fey who had put him there.

'But I'm not the same as him—really I'm not. Please, I want my chance. I was thrown away by my family and you saved me. I can do this.'

'Hmm. We shall see.' Morgan focused on her next recruit, flicking open an emerald green folder. 'Roxy Topley. Brought here as an infant but raised for years out of my control by a band of wandering pixies.'

It was Roxy's turn to look worried. 'Yes, sir.'

'We know they taught you unusual skills so I will overlook this blot on your record. Prove my trust in your abilities is justified.'

Roxy nodded, a very subdued response for her. Rick guessed she wasn't as eager to go on a mission as he was. She had not trained for as many years as he had so maybe she did not feel ready.

The last file was silver-blue.

'Santiago Dulac, half-human, half-Mage Fey. That is a dangerous combination, Master Dulac.'

Bob whined somewhere in the tent. Rick spotted him hiding under a tapestry, paws peeping out of the bottom edge. The little canine familiar had infiltrated the pavilion through the daring but rather direct method of excavating a socking great big hole.

Intent on her task, Morgan paid no attention to the noise. 'Mage Fey have been suspect ever since King Oberon defeated Malduc of Misty Lake and took control of Avalon from him. The Mage were crushed but those sharing their blood will never be trusted. Still, you have skills that complement those of your team mates so I will allow you to try them out on this quest. You already know what will happen if you fail.'

Tiago's expression was blank. Whatever he was thinking, he was keeping it to himself.

Rick glanced at his companions but none of them looked as if they were about to ask the necessary questions. It was up to him as usual. 'What exactly is the problem you want us to sort out, sir? We understand that the power supply to Dark Lore was cut, but what's that got to do with the human world?'

Morgan flicked her wrist and one side of the pavilion rose up like a curtain, revealing the woods that surrounded Dark Lore and a view of the distant white-capped mountains, edges sharp against the cobalt blue sky. That was as much of Avalon as Rick had ever seen. He had heard tales of this world's incredible beauty and advanced organic technology; seen pictures of Oberon's huge palace of white towers spreading like a coral reef at the centre of his kingdom; the pale sandy beaches of the Land Under the Sea, with its pink starfish basking on crystal rocks; the endless forests of Deepdene where the leaves were copper, bronze, and gold in summer, making a burnished carpet in winter. The land was criss-crossed with soaring Dew Track, a network linking all the key places in the realm. The station for Dark Lore lay just beyond the gates, bubbles of magic sitting on silver rails, ready to carry Fey messengers at high speed to their destination like glass balls in an enormous marble run. Sycacopters (the final model—not prototypes) buzzed in the sky transporting those who preferred air to the rollercoaster ride of the Dew Track. Rick wished he had their freedom.

Morgan gestured to the view. 'The wonders of Avalon exist thanks to the power we draw from the human world. The humans have been attacking the power exchange between Avalon and Earth, putting all this at risk. The worst has been felt here but other sites have experienced disruption. If it carries on, we will have to declare open war on humanity.'

Rick felt a surge of excitement, a hunger for battle. If the humans cut off the energy drawn from the living and growing things of Earth, Fey magic would cease to work. The Dark Folk would be doomed. He'd fight to stop that with everything in his power.

'The task given to you is to prevent such a costly war,' continued Morgan. 'You must identify those responsible so we can deal with them in secret.'

'Who's doing it, sir, and why?' asked Roxy, deciding to join the discussion.

'If we knew the answer, we would not send you but a Fey elimination squad. No, we need you to go undercover as ordinary humans and discover the culprits. It was what we trained you for. We know where the centre of the disturbance is—the ring that powers the magic of Dark Lore—but we do not know exactly how it was done, or who is behind the plot.'

'A Fey power ring, sir?'

'Yes, soldier. The ring is located in a city called Oxford in the centre of England. Created early in the days of ring technology, it sits at a junction between many other supplies—like a key fortress in a network of defences. An attack there is both clever and extremely dangerous—if you take control of that one, it gives you access to all the others.' Morgan steepled her fingers, thinking the matter through. 'We should have seen the threat earlier but nothing has disturbed the rings for centuries so we let down our guard. The Fey in charge of surveillance has already been sent to the dragons.'

'Do we know who is likely to be behind it?' asked Rick, preferring not to dwell on the unlucky Fey.

'The last time the exchange was threatened was when Arthur was at the height of his power. You have been told in your Feysyks lessons that if his knights sat at the Round Table, they were able to disrupt the flow and take our power. They used their stolen magic to repel our counterattack. King Oberon believes we should look for someone who is trying to re-establish the Round Table in modern times.'

'So,' said Rick carefully. You never wanted to say too much around the commander. 'Our job is to hunt down the new knights of the Round Table in this place, Oxford, and stop them before they destroy Avalon?'

'Exactly. Our intelligence suggests that recruitment will begin among the youth, as Arthur Pendragon did before. I'm placing you in one of the biggest pools of raw young talent, close to the centre of the trouble.'

'What kind of place, sir? A training camp for knights?'

'A *school*, Elfric. Have you not been listening in your briefing sessions? Young people do not train openly as knights these days; they go to these so-called educational establishments and are mollycoddled into useless creatures with few practical skills. We are not so lax at Dark Lore. You will infiltrate and discover who there is active in the new Round Table and use them to lead you to the chief plotters.'

'Yes, sir.' Rick's initial excitement faded as he took a more realistic view of the task. They were so doomed. Three untried warriors sent to take on dangerous knights in the world peopled by evil humans: what could possibly go wrong?

Just about everything.

# Chapter 3

Linette Kwan sat at the back of the English room in Isis Comprehensive School, flicking deftly through her planner. She half-listened while Miss Milton introduced some old poems. It was always important to appear to attend even if your mind was juggling many thoughts.

'Legendary heroes, Arthur and his knights have reappeared time and time again in songs and stories.' The little sparrow-like teacher smiled at her class as she clicked through her slides on the whiteboard. Magnificent colourful knights and ladies now rode across the boring classroom wall. Ah, this was intriguing. Linette sat up straighter. 'They are far from straightforward characters.

Lancelot—sometimes the hero, but often going badly wrong. Galahad, the perfect, swoon-worthy knight with a spiritual side. Gawain, the impulsive one, up for a challenge. And then there are the stranger figures. For example, there is always a wounded Fisher King figure in Arthurian legend.'

The boy on the next table belched loudly. Linette sighed. What a shame there were no heroes any more, just rather uninspiring teenagers with stomach-churning habits.

The door opened and a tall, fair-haired boy walked into the classroom, closely followed by the Head of Year Nine, Mrs Proudie. Walked? Cancel that: the boy *marched*. Linette had never seen anyone outside a military parade move like him. He was so very perfect, with the most fantastic golden hair, long at the front so that she could only just make out his hazel eyes under the fringe. Other girls noticed too, exchanging wondering looks. He was somehow *older* than the boys in the class, broad across the chest as if he seriously worked out.

Miss Milton paused her presentation and smiled warmly at the newcomer. 'This must be Rick. 9M, this is the new boy I mentioned would be joining us—Rick Halfdane. Welcome to Oxford, Rick.'

Tyler Walsh, sitting two tables away from Linette, snickered. How predictable. The class ringleader, Tyler was almost good-looking if you ignored his sneer. He delighted in tormenting his classmates about foolish things—like being foreign and new to Oxford. Linette did not like him and knew the feeling was mutual.

'Welcome to 9M, Rick. Take a seat,' Miss Milton continued, giving Tyler a quelling stare—which had absolutely no effect.

The new boy gazed around the room as if he'd never seen inside a classroom before, eyes lingering on the walls, the whiteboard, and finally the other students. He appeared to find them fascinating but a little repellent. He was wearing really odd clothes: shirt buttoned up to the collar, jeans with a crease down the front, and a suit jacket. He dressed like somebody's fashion-challenged dad.

'Rick, you can sit down now,' prompted Miss Milton. Linette sensed that, with the snap decision always made about a newcomer, the class had decided as one that he was weird. Even if he was the best-looking boy the girls had seen at Isis. 'Go and sit with Linette,' the teacher pointed to the empty chair next to her,'—she's quite new too—she joined us at the beginning of the year.'

Oh wonderful.

The boy walked carefully between the desks as if afraid of touching them until he reached Linette's table.

'May I sit here?' he asked politely but his body

language shouted hostility. He kept looking behind him. Was he expecting someone to leap on his back and attack?

Linette could feel a humiliating blush warm her cheeks. He spoke as if he was in some nineteenth century frock-and-bonnet drama serial. 'Yes, of course.' She pulled out the chair. She gave him points for not staring too long at her wheelchair—at least no more than he gazed at everything else in the room.

Miss Milton remained standing at the front, trying to regain the form's attention. 'I hope you all make Rick feel at home. You've come from Dark Lore House, right? Where's that exactly?'

Rick stood up again.

You *really* don't need to do that, Linette wanted to tell him, but it seemed he had a terminal case of politeness.

'It is an exclusive private school in the west of England,' he replied carefully. 'I doubt anyone's heard of it, sir—I mean, *miss*.'

Private school. Fabulous. That went down *so* well in this two thousand strong comprehensive. Linette began to feel sorry for him—he was making mistake after mistake and he'd only been in the room a minute.

'My brother, Santiago Dulac, and my sister, Roxy Topley, are in Year Seven.' He spoke as if he was reporting to a commanding officer.

Miss Milton gave a wavering smile. 'Lovely. Different surnames? Must be confusing.' She gave a light laugh, realizing she shouldn't have remarked on it.

'We are . . . ' he paused, 'foundlings. Orphans.'

Linette quickly revised all her ungenerous thoughts about the boy. He must have come from some kind of orphanage, not the mini-Eton she'd been imagining.

Miss Milton clearly decided they'd all learned more than was comfortable about the new boy. 'Well, we're pleased to have you with us, Rick. Just ask any of the form if you have questions. I'm sure they'll be happy to help.'

The bell rang in the corridor. The boy ducked and his hand moved automatically to his side. A gold bracelet dropped below the cuff of his shirt—a quite beautiful snake with two bright green stone eyes. How completely strange.

'No need to be alarmed, Rick: it's just the bell for the next period. Off you go, class.' Miss Milton opened the door for them. 'Linette, show Rick where the Maths room is, will you?'

*Non, merci, I'd really rather not go near to serpent-boy.* 'Of course, miss,' she said. 'This way.' Linette manoeuvred her chair into the aisle and propelled herself forward.

She had nearly turned the corner to the lift when she realized Rick wasn't following her. He was watching the passing students with an expression of . . . well, if she had to name it she would say it was shock.

'Rick, this way!' she called.

'Oh, yes, right.' He jogged to catch up, his bag bouncing on his shoulder. 'Do you all . . . er . . . have parents and family?' he asked. It sounded almost an accusation.

'Yes, naturally, most of us do.' Linette felt really terrible for him.

'So you weren't abandoned.' He twisted the snake bracelet—a nervous habit, she guessed.

'No.' She did not know how to respond to him; he came at everything from such a bizarre direction. 'My parents are both academics in the university: my mother originally from France, my father from Hong Kong, but now we live in Oxford city centre.' Rick looked puzzled. 'My home. With them.'

The lift doors opened, making the boy jump and reach for his side again. He stuck his head inside. 'I've not seen a real one of these before—only on screen. Where does it go?'

How can he have not been in a lift before? Or did he mean one in a school? 'It takes me upstairs; where else could it go? I suppose your last school didn't have one. More schools should have lifts.'

'I didn't think humans would care about helping the weak. I'm surprised they thought of it.'

Rick ushered her in, then amused himself pushing far too many buttons.

'Weak?' Linette almost growled. Had this boy not heard of political correctness?

Eventually they reached the right floor and he stood back to let her go first.

'Sorry, did I say something offensive? I meant those who can't manage without help.'

Linette couldn't wait to get away from him. 'OK, here's the Maths room.' She scooted inside quickly and put her bag next to Theo, the class genius, who sat up front. Rick had to walk up to the back of the class to find a space next to Izzie. It was an unfortunate fact that Izzie was far too heavy-handed with her perfume each morning; most of the class observed a 'no fly zone' around her until it faded after lunch. Linette heard the same polite request to sit down. Two minutes later, the sneezing started. Linette shrugged philosophically and opened her textbook.

It had come as no surprise to Rick that the human teacher in the English lesson was brainwashing her students into thinking Arthur and his men were heroes rather than the terrorists he knew them to be for their attack on Avalon. Her choice of subject could not be a coincidence; it had to be a sign that Morgan was on the right trail; the Round Table had to be actively recruiting at this school.

Rick scanned the students in the lunch hall, trying to work out who he, if he were planning an attack on the Fey realm, would recruit as a knight of the Round Table. So far he had seen nobody who looked anything like his idea of a human warrior—they all slouched and showed no sign of military discipline.

'What would you like, love?' The dinner lady held her spoon up over the metal containers in front of her. Gleaming piles of . . . well, *something* quivered before her.

'Why do you ask?' Rick looked at her suspiciously. She seemed harmless enough, rosy cheeked and plump, but he had been taught to distrust all surface impressions. For all he knew, she could have been trained to kill ten different ways with that utensil.

The woman rolled her eyes. 'Because I can't read your mind.'

That was a relief. Some of the advanced Fey hand-to-hand instructors had developed a skill to pull your next move from your brain before you knew it yourself.

'Hurry up, moron! Haven't got all day,' grumbled the boy behind him, pushing his tray into Rick's back. Rick spun round, snatched the tray and held it up like a shield between them. 'Sheesh, put that down! I was just joking!'

'Now, none of that in my kitchen!' snapped the dinner lady. 'What's it to be—chicken curry, panini or the vegetarian option?'

They had a choice? At Dark Lore they just ate what they were given. Rick found it almost impossible to decide as he had no idea what any of them were. 'I don't know.' He warily handed the tray back to his attacker.

The dinner lady narrowed her eyes at him. He seemed to be annoying her but he wasn't sure what he had done. 'Then why are you in the queue?'

Was that a trick question? 'Because I want something to eat?'

The boy behind him had had enough. 'Give him the panini, Mrs Trumble. He's new.'

She slapped a strange-looking square of bread on a plate and shoved it over to him. It appeared to be leaking some rubbery plastic substance from the side.

'Is this edible?'

'What? Are you criticizing my cooking?' The woman's voice rose an octave. 'Ruddy cheek! Who's your Head of Year?'

'Don't mind him, Mrs Trumble—it's his first day.' The boy pushed him onwards. 'Get away while you still can,' he hissed.

Astounded that the boy was trying to protect him from the woman's inexplicable anger, Rick shuffled on to a second woman sitting at a till. He handed over a card which appeared to do the job of gold in this place and took his tray to find someone with whom he could sit. His orders were to infiltrate so he needed to blend in with the crowd. Ah, there was Linette, the girl from his class, sitting with some friends. Happily, there was a space at their table.

Coming up from behind her, he set his tray down with more clatter than he intended. 'May I join you?'

Linette started in surprise and then quickly put her spoon in her bowl. 'Oh, I am sorry, Rick, I was just going. I have a . . . a library book to return.' She moved away from the table.

The two other girls got up without explanation, leaving Rick alone. Were they shy? Scared of him? Maybe they expected strangers to attack? He couldn't blame them for their caution as that was the kind of behaviour humans exhibited throughout their history.

He looked round the room to see if there were other signs that the students were expecting imminent assault. Oddly, everywhere he turned he saw the cheerful groups, chatting and laughing. They did not seem so very different from the changelings at Dark Lore. Where were the fights, the tormenting, the bullying he had been led to expect from the TV he had seen? The school seemed . . . peaceful. Happy, even.

It had to be an act. Thirteen years of education in Dark Lore—his own experience being abandoned as a baby—these things couldn't be wrong. Humans were the enemy.

Mind made up, he decided not to risk the panini.

Linette left school with Izzie. They stopped to buy a snack at the local newsagent, then sat on a bench in the sunshine. Among the pupils waiting for the northbound Kidlington service at the bus stop on the opposite side of the road was the new boy, standing out like a lion sizing up a herd of zebra.

'What is it with him?' Izzie wondered, snapping open her crisp packet and chomping thoughtfully. 'Kept staring at my pencil case all Maths. He asked if my compasses were a weapon.'

'Me, I feel a little sorry for him.' It was true—she thought he looked completely out of place.

'Really?'

Linette shrugged. The two girls weren't exactly best friends so she did not want to say too much. Sadly, Linette had no close friends yet at Isis. 'Well, at least he's decorative,' Linette offered, forcing herself to think about the boy rather than her own loneliness.

'True, but so . . . I don't know . . . stiff—just weird. And so clever. He outshone Theo in Maths and looked so superior all during the lesson, like he already knew the answers.'

'He did tell Mr Gamal that he'd completed the topic in his old school.'

'Yeah, but would you still get everything right? That's just creepy.'

Linette shook her head, conceding the point.

'Do you think he's a bit . . . ?' Izzie twirled her hands.

'What?'

'Crazy?' Izzie crunched another crisp.

'He's not so bad—just different.'

Izzie suddenly elbowed her in the ribs, drink slopping over the can lid. 'Look, look, that must be his brother and sister—foster whatevers!'

A petite strawberry-blonde girl and a dark-haired boy joined Rick at the stop. They at least slouched and chatted like ordinary teenagers. Only Rick remained upright, giving them a regal nod when they joined him.

'I'll ask my brother, Tomislav, about them.' Izzie chucked the empty packet in the bin. 'He's in Year Seven.'

'Why are you so interested?' Linette was getting uncomfortable. She guessed the three had a sad home life, what with being orphans and having to move to a new city; she didn't want them to become the centre of some school campaign to mock their peculiarities.

Izzie brushed off her jeans. 'Why not? They're new—I'm curious: that's all. See you tomorrow.'

A northbound bus pulled up to collect the passengers. Rick and his brother and sister took seats by themselves at the back, talking with heads close together. A very unexpected trio, Linette mused. Still wondering about them, she rolled to her stop, arriving with pleasing precision at the same time as her bus. She waited for the floor to lower to the kerb level, waved her pass over the ticket reader, and found a space. Rick's reaction when he realized the other students all had parents and homes to go to had been so sad. Perhaps it was mean of her to avoid him? Tomorrow—yes, tomorrow she would try and help him fit in. Not that she was an expert, but even she could identify a loser when she saw one.

Rick opened the door to the semi-detached house the team was renting in Kidlington, a village just north of Oxford. It wasn't really a village in his estimation—the old centre had been overwhelmed by a sprawl of modern housing. From what he had read about the human world, he preferred the style of settlements of his own era with no more than ten houses, healthy herds of sheep and cows, stables for horses—not garages for cars and concrete roads everywhere. Despite all the in-depth briefing he had received in Avalon, the twenty-first century was beyond his comprehension most of the time. Perhaps he shouldn't have avoided so many television sessions? Roxy and Tiago had made sure they went to every one, confessing a fascination with the material they had been shown. As a result, they had adapted a little better to the shock of a modern school full of their enemies.

'Hello, we're back!' he called.

Their two minders came out of the kitchen. Magmell, a male Fey, was still in his dressing gown—a satin quilted affair he'd bought in a gentleman's outfitters in Savile Row. He had dead-straight black hair cut in a sleek short back and sides, wicked dark-brown eyes rimmed by long lashes and milk-white skin. Like all Feys he was breathtakingly handsome to humans, but entirely heartless.

He stifled a yawn. 'Home in one piece then? I'll hear your report at supper.' He had begun to drift to the sofa in the living room to watch more daytime television when their other minder, Shreddie, a pixie female, caught him by the back of his gown.

'We rehearsed this, remember!' she hissed. At four feet nine, she was tall for one of her species; with her golden skin and bright green hair, she looked like a little sun-tanned punk rocker. Playing to that image, she'd dressed in ripped jeans and a T-shirt listing the dates of some pixie band tour on the back. Turning to Roxy, she read the words she'd scribbled on her hand. 'How was your day?'

Roxy glanced at Rick. They'd only met their minders the night before when Morgan had opened the portal from Avalon that delivered them to the fields near the house; they hadn't had a chance to learn much about them yet, other than not to trust Magmell and not leave any valuables near Shreddie. 'Fine.'

Shreddie nodded, as if pleased to have been given the right answer.

'Yes, the school was good,' Rick replied, deciding to expand a little in the interests of making allies of their minders. 'I got on well—achieving top marks in Maths. Most humans are as stupid as we were told to expect.'

The pixie was looking at him with disapproval.

'But I did—I tried really hard!' Rick assured her.

'You'—a pixie forefinger drilled in his chest—'are supposed just to say "fine" and no more. It's not normal for human teenagers to speak to their parents. We have to fit in or our enemies might realize we're here.'

Tiago ambled past and went out into the back garden with a whistle for Bob to follow.

'How do you know what humans say?' Rick asked, feeling a strange sense of disappointment. Playing at families undercover like this had temporarily lulled him into the belief that he might get treated as a son for once.

Shreddie pulled out a book from her handbag. *Raising Teens* was emblazoned on the cover. 'We do this properly or someone will suspect us.'

Even Rick, with his limited experience of the twenty-first century, didn't think a punk mother and a satin-robed father would lull anyone into thinking they were in any way normal. 'OK. Sorry. My day was fine.'

'Have you done your homework?' the pixie asked, retreating into the kitchen.

'We've only just walked through the door!' protested Roxy.

'Oh yes, that's true. I should probably save that question for thirty minutes after you get in.' The pixie made a note on the back of her hand. 'By the way, good answer—you are showing the right level of teenage antagonism. Unlike some.' She glared at Rick.

Magmell once more settled in front of the TV, his long limbs arranged elegantly across the two-seater, leaving no space for anyone else. Shreddie picked up a recipe book and leafed through it, humming to herself.

'We'll . . . er . . . be in the garden,' Rick offered. 'Reviewing our progress.'

'Run along,' chirped the pixie, 'I'm just deciding what to cook for dinner. We've been told our mission is deep cover, so we'll do this properly, fully human and no magic in case someone calls.'

Rick would believe that when he saw it. Telling Dark Folk not to use magic was like telling a fish not to swim.

Roxy and Rick found Tiago perched on top of an old compost bin teaching Bob to jump.

'Come on, boy, you can do it. See—nice stick.' He waved a twig enticingly about six feet off the ground. Bob looked up at it and whined. 'You're just too lazy.'

Bob crouched between his front paws, rump in the air, looking aggrieved.

'Go on, you silly mutt.'

A whine.

'Oh, all right, you win.' Tiago tossed him the stick, which Bob pounced on and shook like a rat.

Rick slid Aethel from his wrist. 'Go and hunt,' he told her.

The snake shimmered into life and slithered off into the undergrowth.

'So, what have we learned so far about recruitment for a new Round Table at Isis?' asked Rick. Despite what he had said to Shreddie, he feared that he had not made the flying start he had wanted. Maybe the others had been luckier.

Roxy raised a hand. 'Shall I go first?'

'Go ahead.'

'I learned zilch. I don't think Morgan really understood how much time we'd have to spend doing teenage stuff when she insisted we enrol in the school like other kids. So far I've not come across a whisper of recruitment in my year. And as for our handlers helping us blend in—well, I think they're crazy.' Roxy pulled herself up into the lower boughs of an old apple tree. 'Their ideas about how humans behave are so random—clearly they need to update their research. You know how Shreddie chose her name?'

'Er, no.'

'She told me this morning. You know how pixie names work? Most end in "E"?'

'Yes, I know.'

'Well, Shreddie's got some unpronounceable pixie name back in Avalon so she decided to pick a human name that was fairly close.'

Rick frowned. 'Doesn't sound human to me.'

Roxy began to giggle. 'That's because she chose it off a supermarket receipt she found. It's a breakfast cereal.'

Flicking dead leaves off the compost bin, Tiago shrugged. 'So what? Someone in my class is called Apple. Perhaps humans have a thing for food names.'

Roxy folded her arms. 'No, they really don't, Tiago. Trust me.'

'She seems the most eager to do a good job at this quest,' Rick commented. 'She might be able to help.'

'I can't imagine why Magmell agreed to come.' Roxy swung her legs to and fro, kicking at the new buds on the bare twigs. 'Not even sure he cares.'

'Oh, he cares,' said Rick. 'Don't be fooled by that lazy act of his. He was ordered here by Oberon.'

'Yeah, Rick's right.' Tiago levitated six snails he'd picked off the compost bin. 'Magmell was an engineer on the Dew Track but made a mistake which caused a spill.'

Roxy flinched. 'Ouch!'

'There was magic everywhere and one very angry Fey courtier. Magmell was told it was this or dragon keeping.'

A shiver went down Rick's spine: no one wanted to end up looking after the king's dragon stable. The job came with a very short life expectancy.

'OK, so our handlers aren't likely to help our quest much but we've got to put up with them. I didn't learn anything conclusive at school either, though Miss Milton needs watching as she mentioned Arthur. Tiago?'

'Nothing, but I think we might have to earn their trust before anyone lets us in on their secrets.'

'True, so we redouble our attempts to gain their friendship.' Rick had a disconcerting recollection of sitting alone at lunchtime but pushed it to one side. 'Tiago, what did Bob find when you sent him to investigate activity around the power ring?'

'He's already filled me in but, before I explain what he found, I need to know how much you two understand about rings.'

It was rather lowering to discover it was probably less than the dog's. 'Not a vast amount,' Rick admitted.

'I know that Avalon doesn't rely just on one generator,' offered Roxy. 'The power rings are scattered all over the place.'

'That's right. They can be found in places with circular structures—natural or manmade—and can be identified by the high levels of inventiveness or imagination found there.'

'Glad one of us understands this stuff,' said Rick.

Tiago huffed in annoyance. 'The exchange! Don't you two listen in Feysyks?'

'Not really,' admitted Rick. 'One of my weakest subjects.'

'And mine,' agreed Roxy. 'Speak, O Genius.'

Tiago ignored her teasing. 'You can't take something into Avalon without giving something back. You have to keep the balance. Take green energy and you have to hand over something the Fey have in abundance—and that is the power of imagination and invention.'

'You're kidding?' Rick shook his head. 'You mean the Dark Folk are responsible for all of that stuff in humans? Art, literature, music?'

'Yes. And Oxford is one of the hotspots. Think of all those writers of fantasy in the Dark Lore library—Lewis Carroll, Tolkien, C. S. Lewis, and Philip Pullman—how else do you think they did it if they hadn't lived so close to a Fey ring?'

Roxy whistled. 'I'm never gonna look at a human brain the same way again—it's a by-product of Fey power.'

'Or you could say green-powered Fey magic is the by-product of human imagination—depends which end of the telescope you are looking through.' Tiago appeared quite happy with the paradox; then again, he always aced in Feysyks. 'The feed to Dark Lore is here—right in the centre of the city.'

'Where?' asked Rick.

'The Radcliffe Camera.' Tiago reached in his pocket and took out a grubby postcard that showed clear signs of having been held in Bob's teeth. The building in the picture looked like a tubby wedding cake decorated with white and gold icing. It was easy to imagine taking a knife and cutting out a huge slab to reveal the filling of scholars and books within. 'It sits in the centre of Oxford University, which is more or less at the centre of England, drawing natural energy from the woods, rivers, and fields. It distributes in return the imaginative powers of the Fey. If you go down, beneath the human storerooms, I guess you'll find a hidden portal leading to the ring.'

Rick scratched his cheek, struggling to picture it. 'Can you describe how the ring works?'

'I'll try. They work in the seventh.'

Rick wrinkled his forehead in confusion. 'Seventh what?'

'Dimension, you dipstick, commonly known as "elsewhere".' Tiago looked annoyed that Rick had failed even to gather this basic fact. 'We feed Fey particles from Avalon into the ring tunnel. They circulate at incredible speeds, colliding with natural elemental energy drawn from Earth. The result is more Fey power—like a kind of cosmic particle breeding programme. Humans have detected the mini-power rings—mushroom circles—but they don't suspect the big ones as yet, though they've been unconsciously mimicking them for some time, what with the Large Hadron Collider—'

'The what?'

'That's a bit beyond you, Rick. You only got a B minus in your last Feysyks assessment.'

'Yeah, rub it in, why don't you?' Rick was anxious to return to the subject of the quest. 'But what about the ring here? How would a new Round Table affect it?'

Tiago's silvery eyes glinted shrewdly. 'I wondered about that myself and I think I worked it out last night. You've noticed this electricity the humans have in the walls?'

'Of course.'

'If you want to draw off the electricity, you add in a new circuit. You can even divert the power away and use it yourself if you want.'

'You mean steal it?'

'Yep. I'm thinking that Merlin worked out a way of breaking into the Fey power exchange and stealing the magic for Arthur and his knights. Morgan talked about the power being taken and I bet it was diverted to Arthur and his men. The Round Table was a great big charger into which they kind of plugged themselves, and hey presto, went away as awesome knights to fight their magical enemies. Otherwise the battle between the Fey and the knights of that Round Table would have all been over in five minutes flat and Arthur no more than a blip in history.'

'OK, I think I get that: the power ring is under the Radcliffe Camera; new knights, led by some magician to rival Merlin, are setting up a Round Table nearby to steal the Fey magic; that is putting Avalon at risk so we have to find them and stop it. What do we do first?' asked Rick.

Tiago chucked Bob another stick. 'One approach is to find the Table itself. As far as I can tell from Bob's report, there is no construction work going on near the ring, no tunnelling or mining. We should look in and under the existing buildings nearby.'

'Makes sense,' agreed Roxy. 'Do we know what a new Round Table will look like?'

'Not exactly. It could be a replica of the one we've all seen at Dark Lore, but I guess that any circular arrangement using the same spells would work.'

'But a Table makes sense?' prompted Rick.

'It's as good a place as any to start—and it has the past success to recommend it to a new generation of knights making a bid to siphon off magic.'

A piercing whistle came from the house, followed by a bellow of 'Report!' Trained to that sound, all three jumped to their feet.

'That's not Magmell or Shreddie,' said Tiago, scooping Bob up from the ground.

Standing just inside the garden doors to the living room was Sergeant Rotgut, a green-grey ogre with two tusks sprouting from his lower jaw, shoulders the width of a human doorframe and legs as thick as tree stumps. He could not step outside in case one of the neighbours spotted him so was waving at them to come to him.

'Quick!' Rick sprinted back to the house. Their weapons instructor made no bones about punishing laggards. The three changelings lined up on the soft blue carpet in front of the sergeant and saluted. Rotgut was just wrong in a human house—too big, too rough, too much of an ogre.

'Sir?'

'At ease, soldier.' Rotgut nodded at Rick's clothes. 'You pass.' He sniffed at Roxy and Tiago. 'You two are a disgrace! Give me ten.'

There was no point arguing that they were not under Dark Lore rules here. Rick had to watch as Roxy and Tiago did ten press-ups each.

Rotgut crushed the thick pile of the rug under his boots. 'Commander Morgan has sent me to check up on your progress. What news?'

Rick answered, giving the others time to regain their breath.

'We have been ordered to proceed with minimal magic, sir . . . '

Rotgut held up a stubby forefinger. 'Why no magic? How can anyone do anything without it?'

Magmell, who was leaning on the back of the sofa with his arms folded, answered that one. 'Obviously, sergeant, the commander doesn't want the people behind this attack sensing our presence and making a run for it. If they did, they could set up at another ring elsewhere in the world and that would put the investigation back at square one. A little bit of private magic is not banned, but nothing to attract attention.'

The ogre glared at the Fey's disrespectful tone but let it go. 'Carry on, Elfric.'

Rick fell into the familiar pattern of reporting to a superior officer. 'We have taken the following steps: one, we have infiltrated the recruiting ground of the suspected Round Table. Two, we have launched a search mission on the site of the power ring to find the Table itself.'

The floorboards creaked as Rotgut turned to pace towards the kitchen. 'And how, soldier, are you going to get into the places you need to search?'

'Under control, sir.'

Roxy's and Tiago's eyes widened. This was the first they'd heard of this, but then again, Rick was improvising so it was the first he'd thought of it. 'I have a contact at school whose parents work in the university. They will get us in.'

Rotgut chewed his tusks for a moment. 'That sounds . . . satisfactory. Military intelligence has put together information that will help you, Elfric. You are advised to spread the net beyond the young cannon fodder at school and look for the leaders. Note this: the leaders may not all be human; some Fey renegades may be involved. You are ordered to follow up all new societies or people training in warfare in the Oxford area.'

'Sir, I'll make a start on that tonight as I'm best with human technology,' offered Tiago.

'Humph.' Sergeant Rotgut didn't like Tiago but he couldn't find anything to object to in this suggestion. 'I suppose that will do.'

A bell rang. It took Rick a second to realize it was the front door. First to react, Shreddie dashed to the window to see who was on the step.

'Human!' she hissed. 'About six foot. Male. Armed with some kind of device!'

Rotgut immediately took command. 'Our perimeter has been breached! Elfric, you take the stairs. Tiago, the back door in case they come that way. Magmell, these windows. I'll take the kitchen. Pixie, stand by the doorway out of sight. Set your elfshot to stun in the first instance.'

'What am I to do?' asked Roxy in bewilderment. The bell rang again.

'You answer the door. Don't worry, soldier: we're right behind you.' Rotgut gave her a little shove into the hallway.

Heart beating fast, Rick took his position up the stairs just out of sight of the front door. He heard Roxy put on the chain, then open the door a crack.

'Ye-es?' Her voice was a little quivery.

'Come to read the meter, love. Is your mum or dad in?'

'What meter?'

'Electricity.' He lifted his device. Roxy flinched but he made no hostile move. 'Says here it's under the stairs. Is your mum in? I thought I saw her at the window.'

Rumbled. Shreddie came out into the passageway and joined Roxy by the crack in the door. 'What do you want?'

'There you go: here're my credentials.' He shoved a little plastic card through the gap. 'Can't be too careful, can you?'

There was a whispered conference by the front door and Roxy slid the chain off.

'You can go as far as the cupboard but no further,' warned Shreddie, holding up a rolling pin.

The man gave the diminutive Shreddie a startled look. 'It's all right, love. I'm not planning any funny business.' He pulled the cupboard open and shone his torch into the darkness. Rick could see the shadow of Rotgut's club falling across the man's back, just waiting for him to make the wrong move. 'There: all done.' He slammed the cupboard shut. 'Have a nice evening.' The man hurried out.

Roxy closed the front door and leant against it with a sigh of relief.

Rotgut bumped his head as he checked that nothing had been planted in the cupboard. 'Stand down, people. False alarm.' He cracked his knuckles. 'Good practice. Remember, you are in hostile territory: never let your guard drop; suspect everyone you meet.'

Rick forked lemon mousse carefully into his mouth. He was starving after having not eaten at lunch but it tasted really odd with the garlic mushrooms Shreddie had prepared and worse with the side dish of lentil curry. He was not surprised to find that she cooked vegetarian—that kind of went with the whole pixie worldview—but he was disconcerted by his first experience of a modern human dinner. Food at Dark Lore had been plain and predictable: bread, meat, cheese, fruit and vegetables. The menu had been set to what humans ate at the time the training camp was founded and not changed much afterwards.

'They really eat this?' he muttered to Tiago.

Tiago shrugged. 'I suppose they do. She got it out of a recipe book with this chubby faced blond guy on the front. Must be the real deal.'

Roxy was shifting her food around with a perplexed look on her face. 'You know, in all those programmes they showed us, you rarely see people eat anything. I've no idea if Shreddie got it right or not,' she whispered.

Magmell didn't seem bothered—he'd eaten his portion without complaint and was now stuffing a pipe with some tobacco. He looked happier now Sergeant Rotgut had left them to report to headquarters on their progress.

Shreddie came back in from the kitchen with a plate of fried seaweed covered in thick yellow custard for dessert. She slapped the back of Magmell's hand with her wooden spoon, her dangly toadstool earrings dancing. 'You shouldn't smoke—it's bad for humans.'

Magmell raised a mocking brow. 'I wasn't going to smoke it, Pixie. I just like the smell. Reminds me of the forests of my home.'

Shreddie took her seat and pushed her plate aside without actually tasting any of her own cooking—not a good sign, Rick decided. 'Here you are—eat up. Humans need at least three nutritious meals a day the book says.'

Thinking she must have got the food wrong in some way, Rick dared not say anything and forced down a couple of mouthfuls. Shreddie had a nasty temper.

'So, let us plan tonight's work.' Magmell pulled two paperbacks out of his dressing gown pocket. *The Adventures of Sherlock Holmes* followed by *Casino Royale*. The first explained the pipe and gown then. 'I too have been doing my own research into this detective and spying business—quite fascinating. I've been ordered to call the commander at midnight.' The Fey took out a seashell from his other pocket—a communication spell hovered in the deep pink hollow, a tiny glow-worm spark of magic. 'I hope you will have made more progress by then. Today's pickings were unimpressive and I'm sure the sergeant agreed.'

Rick glanced at the other two. 'Tonight? Tiago, will you have something for us to go on by then?'

Tiago nodded. 'I'll do my best.'

'I suppose this is all we can expect of the changelings,' Magmell said to Shreddie as if the three of them weren't there, 'they are only human, after all.'

'And remember, barely a quarter of an hour has passed since we left Avalon—even our commander will not be worried yet. Time here passes a hundred times faster.'

Magmell tapped his pipe. 'The sergeant said that the king's secret police are working on a list of known troublemakers, human and Fey, in this region and have promised to send it to us by the morning, our time. In the meantime, you'd better do what you can with the information you can gather here.'

Shreddie passed Rick a huge serving of seaweed in custard. 'Eat up—the Japanese love it, they say.'

With a fixed smile, Rick obliged by taking a spoonful of the stuff. If she had cooked this right, he had not been born with Japanese taste buds, he decided.

# Chapter 4

Linette hadn't been entirely straight with Rick: her parents were far more than ordinary academics. Her French-born mother was currently holding the position of Oxford Professor of Nanomaterials and her Hong Kong Chinese father, a Nobel Prize-winning economist, was Rector of Exeter College—in other words, he was the one who decided how the ancient college ran its affairs. This meant Linette's family got to live in the heart of the university in a house within the college that had a privileged position backing on to the Bodleian library. Their windows looked out on an enclave of ancient honey-coloured buildings, decked with pinnacles and life-size statues of Greek goddesses celebrating the arts and sciences with a flourish of trumpets and lyres. Not far from them, on his own rooftop over Broad Street, a modern sculpture of a man contemplated Oxford, treating the Greek muses to a superior view of his rear.

She kept the details of her home life quiet at school: how many other girls had homes guarded by uniformed porters who called you 'Miss' and a house that looked like a cross between a museum and a film set? It was bad enough being foreign and a wheelchair user, without adding genius parents to the mix. Before Oxford, Linette had lived in Paris, then the Far East as her parents held prestigious positions in a series of universities. After the colourful confusion of their last home in Hong Kong, the tiny apartment and hectic extended family life with cousins dropping by at all hours, a serene, highbrow Oxford college was not the kind of place she felt comfortable inviting anyone back to visit.

Her parents were still at work so Linette grabbed a book and her iPhone and went out into the Fellows' Garden to enjoy the sunshine. She adored this patch of earth crammed between the buildings with its stately trees and spring invasion of spear-like crocuses in purple and orange. Higher than the city streets below, the garden was surrounded by a stone wall shaped like the squared prow of a ship pushing its way into the cobbled sea of the quad containing the Radcliffe Camera. She sometimes imagined the round building an iceberg and the college garden the *Titanic* steaming full speed ahead. And like an iceberg, there was far more underground in the Camera than above, stacks of books rarely disturbed except by the most intrepid scholars nosing about the past. Subterranean corridors linked the different library buildings—there was even said to be a secret entrance in the cellars of Exeter—yet all were unseen by the tourists waddling around like penguins on the surface.

No one else was in the garden just at that moment. Linette positioned herself in the corner facing the library, channelling a brief *Titanic* movie moment as she flung her arms wide. Yes, Oxford was amazing—so old and beautiful, it made her head hurt to think of all the generations who had stood where she was, gazing across at the same view. She felt she would never solve all its mysteries.

'Linette, is that you?'

Oops. Linette peeked over the wall to find elderly Professor Marmaduke looking up at her. He was an Exeter don, a poet of some note and very keen on Shakespeare. He'd helped her with her *A Midsummer Night's Dream* essay only last week. He'd been in the college so long, no one could even remember when he joined the teaching staff and he'd outlived all his contemporaries.

She waved back. '*Bonsoir*, professor!'

'You mustn't lean over the wall like that—what if you topple over?'

Linette bet that he would have been tempted to do the same himself at her age, but his childhood had to be a very dusty memory. Winston Churchill had probably been in Downing Street and steam engines on the railways. 'I'll be careful. Don't worry!'

He wandered off down the lane, his walking stick tapping on the stones in a persistent rhythm—one, *tap*, two, *tap*, three, *tap*. As she watched him go, Linette did feel suddenly light-headed, as if she might just tumble over the edge as he warned. She pushed away from the stone ledge. Once the lane was out of sight, she felt immediately better. Then she glanced up at the Radcliffe Camera again and rubbed her eyes, wondering if the dizzy spell had struck again: the building seemed to be rippling like a giant concertina being squeezed up and down. A flock of pigeons flew off in alarm. Impossible. Was it an optical illusion—some kind of heat haze getting in the way and disturbing her perspective? Before she could decide, the strange moment passed and the building returned to normal. No one ran screaming from the double doors at the entrance so she guessed all was OK inside, but she also noticed that the pigeons did not return.

Her mother was cooking supper when Linette arrived home. With great style, she managed to stir a wok with one hand while reading emails on her BlackBerry with the other.

'Where's Dad?' Linette asked, taking over the chef's duties so her mother had both hands free.

'Dining in hall—he has visitors from America, *ma petite*.' Veronique Kwan thumbed a few final buttons then chucked the device in her handbag. Tall and slender, Linette's mother always looked so Parisian even in her clothes worn for the laboratory. 'How was school?'

'Fine. Except for this strange new boy. I felt so bad for him—says he's an orphan and he acts like a wooden soldier, stiff and over-polite.'

Veronique smiled. 'Nothing wrong with nice manners.'

'Ah, tell that to the rest of my class, *maman*.'

'I hope you didn't tease him. You should know how hard it is being new to a place.'

Linette bristled. 'Of course, I did not! You know I'm not like that. In fact, I decided to give him a few hints tomorrow—help him blend.'

'Blending is not always good—in fact, it can be very boring.'

'Not when you are a teenager: blending is very, very good.'

Veronique sighed. 'Be kind to him. Why not invite him here? I could make Peking duck with pancakes—most British guests enjoy those. And they're your dad's favourites.'

Linette cringed. '*Maman,* this isn't infant school. You don't invite boys back for tea—that is so lame.'

'How else are you going to get to know him better?'

'I don't want to get to know him better. Look, I think this is ready.'

Veronique passed two plates and they both dropped the subject of Rick as they talked merrily over supper. Linette's father called them his sparrows as they chattered brightly in rapid French like, he said, birds at a feeder. Thanks to her parents, Linette had developed the ability to switch between languages seamlessly: French with her mother, English or Cantonese with her father.

'Homework?' Veronique asked as they cleared up.

'A little.'

'You take one side of the table, and I'll take the other—I have work to do too.'

'What kind? Not that I'll understand any of it but I try.' Linette grinned at her mother, marvelling that her brain contained so much information.

'To be frank, I'm in the dark at the moment.' Veronique ran her hand over the top of Linette's head affectionately. 'I've been studying atoms with an electron microscope for a couple of weeks and in the last few days we've had some really strange readings. My graduate students are frantic, trying to locate the problem.'

'Without problems there are no advances in science.' Linette quoted one of her mother's favourite sayings back at her.

Veronique laughed. 'I do say that a lot, don't I?'

'*Oui,* whenever I lose my way in my physics or chemistry homework.'

'Doesn't feel so good now I'm on your side of the fence—I have no idea where to start looking.' Veronique got out a pile of printouts and started scanning the data. 'I simply can't seem to think straight.'

'Don't worry, *maman,* you'll figure it out. You always do.' Linette took out her Maths sheet and set to work.

Rick and Roxy were waiting for Tiago to complete his search of Round Table suspects. As Magmell occupied the entire sofa sprawled in front of a quiz programme about becoming rich, they had retreated to the stairs. His laughter erupted every so often as he shouted abuse at the humans who got their answers wrong.

'They wouldn't last five minutes in Avalon,' Magmell chuckled, sucking on the stem of his pipe. 'Feed them to the dragons, that's what I'd do.'

Roxy rolled her eyes and whispered to Rick. 'Yeah, I can see that really catching on: "Who Wants to be Dragon Bait?"'

This was the first quiet moment they had had to themselves since the rush of preparation to come to Earth and then establishing themselves at school. Rick felt his mind struggling with so many conflicting impressions. He wondered if he was alone in his confusion. 'So what do you think of the humans, Roxy, now you've met some?'

Roxy leant against the banister and twirled a lock of hair thoughtfully. 'I just don't understand. They aren't what I was expecting at all. I keep waiting for them to show their claws but if they are vicious, they're hiding it well.'

'The Fey were right about one thing: they're definitely ignorant. They don't even get simple Maths. Our lessons at Dark Lore covered all that stuff in the first year. Fey Mythmatics is much more complicated.'

'The Dark Folk are way more advanced in their knowledge. They've had centuries to get ahead, having existed long before humans arrived on Earth,' said Tiago fairly. He was sitting at the top of the stairs working on a little laptop Shreddie had acquired from a shop for him. 'I don't know about the people but I like the chips humans make.'

'What?' Rick thought back to his ICT lesson. 'You mean microchips? The computers do suggest some intelligence somewhere in the species, I suppose, but they're still fixed on using materials when there's magic that could do the job better.'

Tiago and Roxy exchanged an exasperated look.

'No, Elfric, not microchips; he means the sort you have with salt and vinegar. They were lush.' Roxy licked her lips. 'Worth taking on this quest just for them.'

'With or without chips, humans are still the enemy, don't forget,' Rick argued, though with less certainty than he would have done before coming into their world.

'I s'pose. We know that one set of them is definitely out to get us—the ones attacking the power supply,' conceded Roxy. 'But why set up a new Round Table and choke off life in Avalon? What do they hope to gain by it?'

Rick thought he knew that at least. 'Easy: they want Fey power? Oberon calls humans "magicless apes". They're jealous.'

'Yes, but I can't help thinking that we all know Oberon to be a heartless Fey—so maybe he's not such a great judge of character,' muttered Roxy.

Rick glanced into the sitting room but Magmell gave no sign he had heard. 'Roxy, be careful. The minders might report on us if we say that kind of thing.' Rick didn't like the king but he did owe him his allegiance. Military discipline demanded that you did not insult your commander.

'It's true, Rick. I don't trust humans, but now that I'm here and it doesn't add up to what we were told to expect, I'm not sure I trust the Fey either.'

Her little crack of doubt spread to splinter his certainty; he hated the sensation that he didn't know everything.

Tiago grinned. 'So who do you trust, Roxy? Me? Rick?'

She frowned, not wanting to answer. 'I trust myself. So, what've you got for us, Tiago?'

'I've got three possibles for us to check out tonight. Rick, you're going to love your one—it sounds spot on; Roxy, this is yours—the meeting starts at seven; I'm taking this last one. It's an outsider but there are enough hits on the name to suggest it could be of interest.'

Rick scribbled down the details of his mission. The Round Table, 8 p.m., Oxford Town Hall.

'Wow, Tiago—are they really so bold as to advertise out in the open like that?'

'I dunno but they might.'

'I can't wait. Meet back here for debrief at eleven?' Rick suggested, eager to be gone. 'No one take on knights on their own, agreed?'

'I'm not stupid.' Roxy tucked her assignment in her pocket.

'I am.' Tiago grinned, jigging with Bob on the spot. 'But I won't. C'mon my faithful hound: let's rock and roll.'

The trip to the Town Hall turned out to be a revelation—but not in the way Rick had expected. He hurried back to report his news to his teammates. Roxy was already home. Magmell and Shreddie were nowhere in sight.

'Tiago?' he asked.

'Not back yet.'

A yip by the front door announced Bob at least had returned. Tiago followed on his heels.

'So, what's the news?' Tiago asked. 'Any leads?'

Roxy switched off the programme she had been watching. Rick sat down in an armchair.

'Who's going first?' Rick looked at Roxy.

'OK, I will. Army cadets. Yes, they supposedly train for warfare; but no, they aren't our guys. Not a sword or Round Table in sight. I saw a couple of people from our school but that's about it. In fact, I'm not convinced the army here really knows about producing young warriors. I mean, we spent the whole session doing First Aid on each other and chatting. They wouldn't get far in a weapons practice at Dark Lore, I can tell you. What about you, Rick?'

'The Round Table. Sounded a good contender but it's way off target. First you have to be a middle-aged businessman or woman to get in so I wasn't let through the door. I sneaked in round the back to listen and they spent the whole meeting talking about raising funds for a minibus to send disadvantaged kids to the seaside. They are not going to be taking over Avalon in a hurry. Cross them off the list.'

Roxy hugged her knees. 'They sound nice. I thought humans didn't look after each other.'

'It seems that isn't true of all of them. We might have to rethink what we've been taught. Tiago?'

Tiago was already giggling. 'My evening was even more amazing than yours. I went to the Knit Circle, thinking it might be a misspelling of "knight", but nope, it was knitting as advertised. The ladies were lovely. They gave Bob lots of biscuits and were very encouraging to a new enthusiast for the craft. They told me I was a natural at picking up stitches. Here, Roxy, I made this for you.' He passed her a dark blue bundle.

She shook it out to reveal a scarf with robins on the end. 'Oh, Tiago, this is fabulous!'

'I did some of it at the meeting and finished the rest by magic on the way back. Do you like it?'

'It's really great.' She blew him a kiss. 'Thanks, *amigo*.'

'But I take it you think that they are no threat to Avalon?' asked Rick.

'Not unless Oberon corners the world supply of wool and they go for him with their knitting needles, no, I'd say we were safe from them.'

Rick rubbed his hands over his head, annoyed they had no more to show for their night's work. 'OK, that was a failure. I suppose it would be disappointing to find our foes were so easily tracked down. We'd better hope the list Magmell mentioned comes up with some stronger leads. Once we've seen that at breakfast, shall we try to persuade the girl in my class to get us on site?'

'Yes, that seems the next step,' said Roxy. 'Why don't you ask her here tomorrow so we can persuade her to ask us back?'

'I wish we could skip the socializing and start making real progress. It's been a day already.' Rick noted down their findings for Magmell's report, preferring to be in bed when the Fey read it.

'Just a day,' countered Roxy. 'As far as Avalon is concerned that is no time at all. And I've been thinking, perhaps we should be setting ourselves a quest of our own while we work on Oberon's.'

'What sort of quest?' asked Tiago.

'Explore this thing about humans not being like we were told. I came braced for a horrid time, like jumping into a freezing lake in winter, but it doesn't seem, well, as *cold* in the water as I expected. Why did the Fey lie to us about that?'

That had been nagging at Rick too. 'Maybe these humans are special? We've only seen one school in one city.'

'Perhaps. But from my conversations in class today I got the impression that they thought they were pretty average for humans. Something just doesn't add up.'

'Questioning our commanders, warrior?' asked Rick in a mock-severe tone, only half-joking.

Roxy hugged her arms tightly to her waist and shivered. 'Yes. Scary, isn't it?'

The list compiled by Oberon's secret police was waiting on the breakfast table when Rick came down. Shreddie was singing by the stove, frying eggs and ladling porridge and syrup over bacon.

'May I?' Rick asked, picking up the envelope.

'Go ahead.' Shreddie flipped some sliced bread into the toaster. She appeared to be enjoying the novel experience of human cooking.

Rick cracked open the seal and scanned the contents. A pixie renegade in Witney thought to own a car dealership; a quarter troll on the Swindon rugby team; a half-Fey working for the Ashmolean museum; a teacher at Isis with an eighth ogre blood but ignorant of his inheritance; no known humans who were aware of the existence of Dark Folk. Last intelligence on Merlin placed him in America and nowhere near Oxford so he was ruled out for the moment.

'Anything?' asked Roxy, entering the kitchen with a robin on her shoulder.

'Nothing that jumps out at me. I think the pixie is unlikely—it just isn't in them to create such a scheme.'

Shreddie was now spinning plates on her head and index fingers. She was a fair representative of her species: interested in games and fun, not power.

Roxy grinned. 'Yeah, you're right.'

Rick tapped the paper with a spoon. 'The half-Fey. She might be worth following up. Works at the big museum in the city.' He passed Roxy the list. 'I think the secret police must have let their surveillance of humans lapse over the years because they've nothing about any groups aware of the Fey.'

Roxy took a bite of the porridge-covered bacon and gagged.

The plates stopped twirling. 'Is your breakfast all right?' asked Shreddie shrewdly.

'Yes, lovely,' lied Roxy.

'Good. I really think I'm getting the hang of this cooking malarkey.'

'Er, yes, you're uniquely talented.'

Rick choked on his fried egg.

'Shame we haven't time to do it justice. Must dash.' Roxy pushed away from the table and called for Tiago to hurry.

'But I haven't had breakfast!' Tiago complained, trailing down the stairs, his toothbrush in hand.

'Trust me—you'll want to get to the bus early today,' Rick warned.

'Oh.' Tiago glanced over at the table. 'Oh, yeah. Must read the list and do . . . um . . . lots of stuff on the bus. Let's go.'

Izzie sat down next to Linette during registration, wafting a poison cloud of her latest perfume in her direction. 'Hey, Linette, I found out more about Weirdo from my brother.'

Recalling her decision of the day before to be kind to the new boy, Linette scowled. 'He's called Rick.'

'Whatever. But you knew who I meant, didn't you?' Izzie failed to notice Linette's frown, absorbed in switching off her phone before going into classes. 'Tomislav has the girl in their class. He says she's nice—instant success. And he played football at break with the other one, Tiago Dulac—he's really fast, make the team no problem if he wants. Seems to me we got the odd one out.'

'What do you mean?'

'You know, the head-case.'

As if on cue, Rick walked into the class. 'Good morning, Miss Milton.' He bowed slightly to the form tutor who looked up from her register in amazement at his old-fashioned greeting.

'Er, good morning, Rick.'

Rick scanned the students until his eyes alighted on Linette.

Oh no.

He approached her and took the empty seat to her left-hand side. 'Good morning, Linette.'

'Hi, Rick.' Linette could feel herself blushing. She dug her biro into her pencil case, puncturing the picture of Homer Simpson. Everyone was watching them—she could feel their eyes on her, just ready to tease her when they got out of Miss Milton's presence.

'Did you have a pleasant evening?' Rick continued undaunted.

'Yes, it was OK.'

'Are you free this evening?'

Izzie swallowed a giggle. Linette hoped she was choking on her own perfume.

'Are you all right, Elzbieta?' Rick asked with concern. 'Shall I fetch you some water?'

'No, no, I'm fine,' Izzie rasped. She was red-faced now.

It was kind of cute how caring Rick was—a real English gentleman, Linette's mother would say—but it was also very wrong for Isis School.

'If you're sure.' Rick had half-risen in his chair to charge to the rescue.

'Yes. Very,' Izzie managed. She nudged Linette, delighted to have a chance to stir things up. 'So what about it—are you free tonight or not?'

'My foster parents are looking forward to meeting you,' Rick continued seriously.

'Engaged already, Linette?' muttered Izzie. 'Why didn't you say something?'

Linette elbowed her. 'I . . . ' *Think up a good excuse, something that wouldn't hurt his feelings.*

'My sister, Roxy, wants to meet you too. And Tiago, of course.'

This was painful.

'My foster mother,' he said the word carefully, as if treading across slippery stepping stones, 'has promised to make a special supper.'

Linette had an image of her own mother planning the same thing—she knew how that was. Maybe that was why she found herself saying:

'OK, I suppose I could come. But not for long—I have to be home at six.'

Rick flashed an engaging smile, showing his even white teeth. He really was unfeasibly handsome. 'Thank you. I'll let her know.' He tapped his fingers on a cowry shell dangling from a key ring.

'Fine. So, OK, see you later then.'

The class dispersed to battle their way to their first lesson. Rick latched on to Izzie.

'So, Elzbieta, what do you do in your spare time? Have you joined any new societies recently?' he asked.

'What? No, of course not.' Izzie rolled her eyes at Linette.

'I was wondering: have you ever . . . er . . . felt any calling to be a . . . a knight?'

'You what?'

Linette didn't hear any more of this bizarre conversation as she stayed behind for a moment to bang her head on her desk in frustration. How had she let herself get into this position? She simply couldn't be mean enough to say 'no' and now the whole class knew about her 'date' with Rick's family.

Miss Milton approached before Linette noticed and laid a comforting hand on her shoulder. 'That was very nice of you.'

Linette pushed her long black hair off her face. 'You heard?'

Miss Milton smiled. 'I think everyone heard. Rick doesn't exactly have a quiet voice.'

True: he spoke as if he was addressing an army rather than someone sitting next to him.

'I shouldn't say this,' Miss Milton continued. 'But it's amazing that he's so open to making friends when you think about the kind of background he's come from—moving around between children's homes and the rest. That has to be tough. So thank you.'

Miss Milton left, leaving Linette to trail after her. She now felt even more of a worm: she'd been thinking about her own embarrassment when really she should've been imagining the courage it took Rick to make the first overture in a friendship.

If only he wasn't so peculiar.

Rick waited for Linette with his brother and sister outside the school gates.

'Be nice to her,' he warned them. 'She's a bit shy—I think that's why she avoids me in class.' At least he hoped that was why. All day he had felt uncomfortable in lessons; he sensed he was doing something wrong, but couldn't work out what. 'I don't want you two to put her off. It is vital we get the invitation back.'

He was just beginning to worry that Linette had forgotten their arrangement when he spotted her coming slowly towards them. She must have been held up in class for she was almost the last to leave; no one else was hanging about in the car park to see them meet up. Rick moved swiftly to put her at her ease.

'Good afternoon, Linette. Did you enjoy your day?'

She gave him a strange look. 'It was OK.'

Roxy pushed between them. 'Hi, Linette. I'm Roxy. So I see my brother's lured you over to our house. Have to warn you—we're all crazy.'

Rick almost intervened to stop Roxy talking—the truth would be revealed all too soon when they got home—but then he saw that Linette was now grinning. She shot a sideways look at Rick. 'I guessed.'

Tiago gave her a wave. 'Hi, I'm Tiago. Don't worry: none of us bite—not even Bob.' He stuck two fingers in his mouth and whistled. His dog trotted into view from under the hedge by the rugby field. Tiago knelt to scratch Bob's neck. 'How was your day, mutt?'

Bob yipped.

'That good? Excellent.' Tiago stood up. 'Any new discoveries?'

Bob shook his head.

'Come on then—we'll miss the bus.'

Linette was looking between the boy and dog. 'He's yours?'

'We hang out together,' Tiago admitted.

'And they let you bring him to school?'

'Oh no. He just does his thing then comes to pick me up.'

Worried that Linette would find the evidence of this strange pet disconcerting, Rick hurried them away. Tiago and Bob had a very intuitive relationship—Rick knew this now because he shared a bedroom with both of them and had witnessed their conversations at close quarters. Rick had considered that he was attuned to Aethel but that was nothing to the intelligence of the little crossbreed terrier.

They headed for the stop and found a bus had already picked up most of the students, leaving only a few stragglers like them to get the next service. Roxy took over the conversation with Linette, finding out more about her background in France and Hong Kong than Rick had with a day's worth of polite enquiries. They were soon exchanging views on various actors that Rick hadn't heard of—unlike Roxy with her passion for television, his interest in culture stopped with the Anglo-Saxon epic, *Beowulf,* which he knew by heart in the original Old English. Everything else he'd read or seen that had been written afterwards had gone downhill from the heroes and monsters of his era so he had only studied other things if set for homework. Finding people so different from what he expected, he was only just now realizing how narrow his view of humanity had been.

The bus arrived and they took up the front seats around Linette's chair for the ten-minute journey north. Bob now sat on Tiago's lap, barking at the car drivers passing the bus, growling at a Lycra-clad cyclist. Tiago had to have put a dampening shield around them too because none of the other passengers complained about the noise. Rick made a mental note to find out just how skilled Tiago was; his spells, though not powerful, were very subtle and very effective. Rick had always struggled with the more delicate aspects of spellcraft, his own power being more of a bludgeon to Tiago's scalpel approach.

'Our foster parents aren't your regular people,' Rick overheard Roxy explaining. 'But they're OK.'

'How long have you been with them?' Linette asked.

Roxy shrugged. 'It's a new arrangement. We were all in a home before moving here.'

Linette knotted her fingers together in her lap. 'So this is better, is it? Than the home, I mean?'

'It's different. Maybe better.'

'That is good. I hope it is a success.'

'I do have to put up with these two, but it's OK.' Roxy laughed at Rick's and Tiago's indignant expressions. 'But I'm glad Rick invited you back. It's nice to have another girl to talk to—the boys don't know how to chat about stuff.'

'But your foster mother: is she not good to talk to?'

'She's . . . well, you'll see.' Roxy shook her head, wisely giving up on explaining why a pixie might not be the best person with whom to discuss human girl interests.

Rick's anxiety about the reception waiting at home spiked on the approach to their house. Magmell was out in the front garden leaning on a bright orange lawn mower. He had got rid of the satin dressing gown and was dressed in corduroy trousers, string round the knees, green wellies, and a checked shirt. The Old MacDonald look clashed horribly with his poster-boy face. When the Fey spotted them coming, he fired up the machine and beheaded the dandelions and daisies that had previously been growing undisturbed in the patch of weeds that answered for a front garden.

'Hi, um, Dad,' Rick called cautiously.

With an unconvincing start of surprise, Magmell switched off the engine and gave them a hearty wave.

'Good afternoon, boys and girls! How was school?'

'Fine,' Rick said rapidly, wanting to cut this embarrassing scene as short as possible.

'And this young lady must be Linette.' Magmell held out a lilywhite hand that gave away the fact that the owner had never done any gardening in his life.

Linette shook it shyly. 'Hello, Mr Magmell.'

'Just getting on top of the chores,' the Fey explained unnecessarily. 'I love DIY.'

Fey-bells, this was dire. Shreddie had obviously been tutoring Magmell in how to be a typical dad; the result was ugly. Rick wished he'd stuck with Sherlock Holmes.

Magmell tucked his thumbs in his belt, taking a wide-legged stance that did not suit his lean frame. 'Have you met Her Indoors yet?'

Linette shook her head, looking a little shell-shocked by the Fey. Her brain was still trying to reconcile his beauty with his wellington boots.

'She's probably bustling about the house somewhere—dusting knick-knacks or rustling up something yummy for tea.' Magmell glanced at the back of his left hand, reading the next cue on his cuff. 'Do you like cake and ginger beer?'

Linette nodded slowly.

'Excellent! We have lashings of the stuff.'

Roxy tugged Linette's arm. 'Come on. We might as well get this over with.'

Roxy turned the chair round to bump it over the high step. She guided Linette into the big living-come-dining room where the table had been set with a white cloth; a cake-stand waited in the centre, piled high with fairy cakes, and sandwiches. Shreddie danced in from the kitchen, a white frilly apron around her waist. The pockets were loaded down by a feather duster and *Five Go To Treasure Island*. The juxtaposition between punk green hair and old-fashioned mother was even more glaring than the father routine Magmell was attempting in the garden. Rick feared she was mixing up her time periods in a way that Linette would notice.

'Hello, darlings!' Shreddie fluttered around them like a little black, green, and white butterfly, pausing only to air-kiss each of them on the cheek. 'It's lovely to see you've brought a chum home, Rick. Welcome to our humble abode.'

*Enough already*, as Roxy would say.

'Linette, would you like to see our garden?' Rick asked quickly. 'We can get out of Mum's way.'

'Actually, Rick, I think I'll take Linette to my bedroom.' Roxy was already halfway to the stairs. 'We can chat up there.'

Linette practically zoomed from the room, relief at the promise of normality written all over her face.

'Magmell, can you give Linette a piggyback?' Roxy called out of the front door.

Shreddie giggled, clasping her hands to her chest. 'Oh, what fun! I think she really likes us.'

Rick looked at Tiago. 'Garden?'

'Yeah.'

The two boys sloped out to give their familiars some fresh air, leaving Shreddie singing 'Zippidy Doo Dah' in the kitchen.

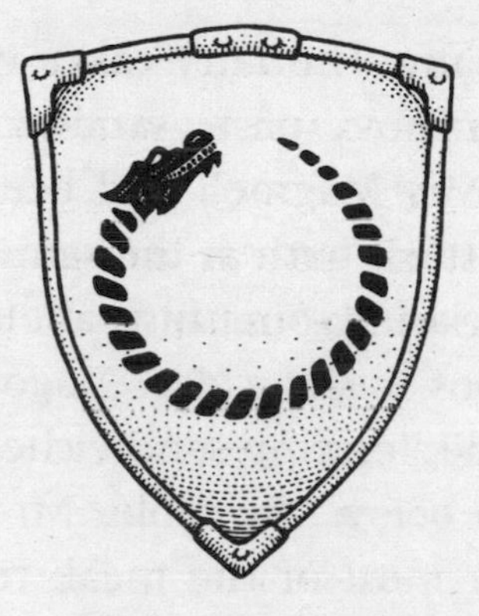

# Chapter 5

Bizarre. Astonishing. Curious. *Drôle*.

Linette ran through all the words that summed up Rick's family as she journeyed back into town. The only island of normality had been Roxy—though that was an odd type of normal as she seemed very grown up for eleven. After the embarrassment of being carried upstairs by Roxy's foster dad (who appeared not to know what a piggyback was until Roxy explained), the two girls had hidden in her bedroom—decorated in an overly pink Disney princess style which Roxy had excused as being chosen by their foster mother.

Tea had revealed the utter strangeness of the foster parents—making Rick almost unremarkable in their company. The fairy cakes were works of art but the anchovy paste sandwiches absolutely revolting. Mrs Magmell had been determined that their guest eat both at the same time in large quantities, declaring something about the need for three nutritious meals a day. Tiago had come to Linette's rescue, ferrying sandwiches off her plate and into Bob below the table. Mr Magmell had kept quiet for most of the meal, reading from a James Bond novel propped up on a teapot in front of him. He had changed from his garden clothes into an extraordinary green robe—a smoking jacket, Linette thought it might be called if her memory of Sherlock Holmes films was accurate. It had suited him better, but that was all she could say in its favour. Mrs Magmell—'call me "Shreddie"'—had maintained most of the conversation, interrogating Linette about her home life, finding the oddest things interesting, like the fact that she helped out by doing the ironing and that her dad hated gardening.

'So not all fathers have a potting shed?' Shreddie asked seriously.

'Er . . . no.' Linette gulped back her laughter. What planet was Mrs Magmell from?

'And your mother works out of the house?'

'Yes.' Linette felt an urge to boast in the face of this hopelessly old-fashioned view of gender roles.

'She's the head of her department—Professor of Nanomaterials.' Shreddie looked puzzled. 'In Oxford University.'

'Ah-ha!' Coming to a decision, Shreddie chucked *Five Go To Treasure Island* on to the pile of discarded books on the coffee table and untied her apron. 'Excellent. I can't tell you how tired I am of cooking now I've mastered it. I think I'll see about getting a . . . what is it called? Yes, a job. Tomorrow. Magmell, you can be one of those men who stay at home. What did you say they were called?' She looked to Linette.

'Um . . . house-husband?' Linette offered.

'Yes, you can be one of those.' Shreddie twirled a fork in her fingers, making it appear and disappear in a most disconcerting manner.

'As you like, Pixie,' Magmell said languidly.

A hush fell over the table. The fork clattered on to a plate. Linette could sense he'd said something that had shocked the others, but she couldn't work out what. The conversation had not been any odder than before.

'Er . . . Pixie, his term of affection for our foster mother,' Rick explained hurriedly.

Yes, of course—what else could it mean?

'You see she's a bit short,' Roxy continued.

'It's fine. I understand,' Linette assured them.

The tension around the table relaxed. Bizarre.

Relieved to have escaped the Magmells, Linette got off the bus by the rocket-shaped Martyrs' Memorial and headed down Broad Street to Exeter College. It was only when she reached for her keys that she realized that her charm bracelet, a present from her French grandmother, was missing. She patted her clothing and the chair cushion in the desperate hope it had got caught up somewhere, but there was no sign. The loss of the bracelet was a blow—it was her most valued item of jewellery, not because it was expensive but because her friends and family had added to the charms over the years until it was loaded with special memories. Linette retraced her path to the bus stop but could not find it. It was possible that she'd dropped it when she took off her jacket at Rick's house. She'd have to wait to ask him to search for it because the Magmells did not have anything as ordinary as a phone in their house, not even a mobile.

The next morning, Rick came downstairs, braced for the breakfast experience. He was surprised to find an empty kitchen with no signs of food preparation. Relieved, he took a box of cereal out of the cupboard and helped himself to milk—he'd seen this on adverts and thought it looked appropriate for the first meal of the day.

The pixie came in from the garden, a bird's nest in her hair. Some blackbirds would have to rebuild if they were planning to raise a family this spring.

'Good morning, Shreddie,' Rick said politely. 'I hope you don't mind—I served myself breakfast.' He gestured to the popping bowl of tiny yellow grain things.

'No, that's fine,' she said airily. 'I'm not doing the cooking any more. I'm going to be a professional mother, like Linette's. You all have to do the ironing and cleaning from now on. I'm going to the University this morning to get a job to make our cover more convincing.'

Rick suspected it wouldn't work out quite as smoothly as she anticipated. 'Well . . . um . . . good luck with that. You might want to lose the bird's nest before you apply.'

Shreddie checked her reflection in the round mirror over the electric fire. 'Doesn't it suit me?'

'It . . . er . . . looks great, but not very human,' Rick explained diplomatically. He then noticed a new bracelet clanking on her thin wrist—one he'd seen at school on the desk beside him. 'Hey! That's Linette's!'

The pixie jingled the charms. 'Lovely, isn't it?'

Rick thrust his fingers into his hair and tugged in frustration—it was either that or yell. Years of living with pixies had taught him that property rights were very fluid for them. 'Yes, but you can't steal from our guests.'

'But I like it.' Shreddie's expression hardened, her eyes glinted with stubborn determination. Separating a pixie from their haul was like tooth extraction—*dragon* tooth extraction.

Roxy came into the kitchen at that point, her hair as tangled as the bird's nest in Shreddie's. She pushed it back and yawned. 'Morning.' The awkward silence alerted even her sleepy head to the stand-off between Rick and Shreddie. 'What's up?'

'Shreddie stole a bracelet off Linette.' Rick gestured to the pixie who now had her hand clasped defensively over her other wrist.

'Yeah, I noticed her do it. Don't worry.' Roxy slumped in to a chair and poured some strawberry and banana smoothie into a glass. Rick didn't fancy it: it reminded him of the slime left behind by the feyslugs that lived in Dark Lore moat.

'But the bracelet is Linette's!' protested Rick.

Roxy caught his eye. 'Don't worry about it,' she repeated, with the hint of a wink.

Not sure what she meant by that, Rick gave up the argument and finished off his bowl of cereal. At least he would be going to school without feeling sick today.

Tiago entered from the garden, his bare feet glistening with dew. He looked a mess: jeans smeared with mud at the bottom and his T-shirt ripped at the shoulder from where it had got caught on a twig. '*Hola!*' he said cheerfully.

'Morning.' Rick frowned. He couldn't understand how Tiago got away with looking so scruffy at school. Rick always made sure his shirt was buttoned up to the neck and his shoes polished; Tiago by contrast appeared to have tumbled out of bed into a pile of tatty clothes. But now Rick came to think of it, most boys at the Isis didn't take the time to tidy themselves up. They'd never pass inspection if they were in his army.

'So what's our aim for the day?' Tiago snagged a chair and sat on it back to front. 'Get an invitation back to Linette's and find out more about recruitment for a Round Table?'

'That's about it. We've got to do an onsite inspection in the next day or two or Morgan will be wondering what's holding us up. I don't know about you, but I'd prefer not to have the sergeant back.' Rick had a second bowl of cereal.

'You work on Linette then and we'll ask around at school about recruitment,' suggested Roxy.

'I can do that too. I already made a start yesterday.'

Roxy fiddled with her bowl. 'Yeah . . . um . . . about that. I'm not sure you're asking in the right way.'

'What?'

'You're being too direct. You need to make friends with the people in your class first before you grill them about their desire to be a knight.'

Rick folded his arms. 'I can make friends. I'm not completely useless.'

'Rick, this isn't Dark Lore. You're not the oldest, not the leader. You need to . . . ' She ran out of steam and looked helplessly at Tiago.

'You need to relax, *amigo*. No one says anything to someone who looks like they are about to bark orders at them and give them six punishment laps of the sports field. They've got PE teachers for that.' Tiago turned to Roxy. 'Did you see on the list that Mr Gaddon is part ogre? How cool is that?'

'I know.' Roxy smiled. 'He has hair on his palms to prove it. Makes you wonder how many other mixed bloods there are out there, doesn't it? I don't believe we have a complete list, what with the long history of travel between the two realms.'

Rick was left feeling a bit bruised by their dismissal of his people skills. Breakfast over, he grabbed his bag and followed them to the door.

'You must get an invitation back to Linette's house,' Shreddie said sternly. 'Commander Morgan is waiting for our next progress report. There is no point going to this school place if you are not making strides to find answers for the king.'

'We'll see what we can do,' Rick promised. After what the others had said about his tactics, he had no confidence in the success of last night's tea party: Linette had been very quiet when she left.

'Bye, Mum,' Roxy threw her arms wide with a sudden outpouring of daughterly affection. She leaned in to give the pixie a peck on the cheek. 'Neighbours!' she whispered in explanation as Shreddie reared back from the show of human love.

'Oh. All right then.' Shreddie tugged her clothes straight as they separated, flustered by the close encounter. 'Study hard, darling, so you can be as successful and well qualified as me!' she called loudly as they headed to the bus stop.

Rick raised an eyebrow at Roxy once they were out of earshot. 'Were the neighbours watching?'

Roxy smiled and jingled something in her fist. 'Course not. Only way to get something off a pixie is to steal it back.'

In a departure from her normal behaviour, Linette did not avoid Rick at registration. As he made his way to a seat on his own at the back of the class, she moved from hers to intercept him.

'Hello, Rick, I was wondering . . . '

He put her out of her misery. 'Looking for something?' He held up the charm bracelet.

'Oh, you found it!' Her face blossomed into a delighted smile.

'Roxy retrieved it for you.'

'Did I drop it in her room? Yes, I probably did. We were fooling around chucking pillows.' Not waiting for a reply, she took it from him and tried to fasten it back on her wrist, fumbling with the catch.

'Here, let me.' Rick deftly connected the loop through the little metal clasp.

Linette jiggled the charms back in their proper place. 'Thanks.'

Rick cleared his throat. 'I guess you must live near all the old university buildings?'

She laughed. 'I live *in* them actually.'

'I'd like to see them sometime.' There, that should be hint enough.

'Hmm, ah, yes, perhaps, when the students aren't there. You can see most of the sights anytime—from the outside.' With a vague smile, she returned to her place just as Miss Milton began the roll call.

What had just happened? He had been hoping for an invitation from Linette in return for theirs, but she had obviously not wanted him anywhere near her home. Morgan was going to kill him. Rick sat straight-backed, feeling desperate. He managed to rouse himself to answer his name with his usual clipped acknowledgement, reining back on his desire to stand and salute. Years of training for Dark Lore head counts were hard to suppress. Still, for some reason his smart reply provoked a wave of sniggers. He wondered why Miss Milton let them get away with this show of insubordination. The commander would never have stood for it. A troll guard would have been cracking heads together by now.

He glanced round the room, noting the relaxed positions of the students, some lounging back on their chairs, others slumped over the desks.

*I'm missing something here. Why aren't they scared of the instructors?* He couldn't afford to get this wrong. He hated the slippery feeling of failure.

That thought reinforced Rick's intention that morning to excel at the only aspect of his quest in the human world he seemed able to control: his academic achievement. He aced the physics test and even managed to correct a slight error in the teacher's explanation of thermodynamics—all very basic stuff for a student of Feysyks. He couldn't understand why the teacher was not more pleased with him. On the contrary, Mr Bowra seemed positively annoyed by Rick's ability to spot the mistake, giving his gratitude a sarcastic edge.

'Thank you, Einstein. Perhaps you want to take over my job, eh?' He held out the whiteboard marker.

Rick stood up. 'No thank you, sir. I'm sure you are doing a creditable enough job for a human.' He noticed out of the corner of his eye that Linette had buried her head in her hands. 'I mean, for a man.'

Mr Bowra flushed with temper. 'As opposed to what? A Vulcan like you, Spock?'

Rick frowned, trying to remember what a 'Vulcan' was. 'My name is Rick, sir, not Spock or Einstein.'

'Exactly. So sit down and shut up!'

Rick obeyed the man's order, still puzzled by what had caused this flash of anger. Part of him was relieved to find that humans were as horrid as he had been brought up to expect. It had been a weird feeling to question the basic training he had been given at Dark Lore; this was much more familiar territory.

No one came near him at the beginning of break, hurrying away in different directions when he approached. Rick decided reluctantly he had to report his failure with Linette to the others. Roxy might have more luck with her. He spotted Tiago in the middle of a group of Year Seven boys; they were dividing themselves up into warring factions: one side tying jumpers across their chests like slings for a scabbard. He hurried over to check everything was OK. It had taken a day but humans were beginning to show their true colours. He wouldn't put it past them to hurt Tiago.

'Hey, Tiago, you all right?'

Tiago nodded. 'Yep. Fine. Just blending—making friends like we agreed.' His eyes were already on the other players. 'Centre forward?'

The captain of his team nodded and slapped him on the back. 'Can't do without you, Tiago. Run 'em into the ground like yesterday.'

Rick was impressed at how quickly Tiago had been assimilated into his peer group. Perhaps team sports were the key? He'd played football at Dark Lore so knew the basics, though he preferred the Tudor rather than the modern rules. 'Can I play?'

Tiago shuffled, toeing the ground. 'Um . . . it's for Year Sevens only, Rick. I want to get them to trust me so I can . . . you know.'

So he could ask them about rumours of young people training for a new Round Table. Rick tried not to take it as a rejection. 'Oh, OK, have fun then.' He'd save his confession until later; Tiago was enjoying more success with his part of the mission. He refused to feel jealous.

'Yeah, thanks.'

Rick walked away, conscious that half the team were watching him leave—it felt like an itch in the back where he could not reach to scratch. He was slowly dying inside of embarrassment.

'Who was that?' he heard the captain ask Tiago.

'Just someone I live with, Tom,' Tiago replied in his usual off-hand manner. 'My foster brother.'

'Oh yeah. My sister told me about him. Is he that weird all the time?'

Rick increased his pace to get out of hearing. What was he doing wrong? Tiago had told him to relax, not act as if he was in command. OK, so he had a vital mission to complete; he had to find out what was really going on in this school; he needed to be accepted. The ones who showed leadership qualities were surely the most likely to be recruited? If he infiltrated one of those groups in his own year, he would likely find the answers.

He knew exactly who he should try first. So far Rick hadn't had anything to do with this boy because Linette had steered him away. Rounding a corner at the back of the kitchens, he came across the one from his class who led the pack: Tyler Walsh. Surrounded by his mates, Tyler was playing his own version of football with a red can, kicking it against the wall hiding the wheelie bins. Rick took a deep breath, steeling himself for another attempt. He jogged up to Tyler.

'Hey, that looks fun. Can I join in?'

Rick immediately sensed that his question had fallen flat. Tyler was the first to break the silence.

'Rick wants to play.' He took a step closer. 'You 'avin' a laugh?' The other boys chuckled at this question—quite why, Rick didn't know. It didn't seem a particularly amusing remark to him.

'No, I was being serious. I . . . just wanted to, you know, be on your team.'

'On my team? Oh yeah, I'd love to have you on my team.'

Rick wasn't sure if Tyler really meant it. 'You would? I'd be a good follower if you were, you know, planning any quests or stuff like that.'

'Quests! What planet are you from again? Planet of the Insane?'

'Forget it.' Rick began to back away. 'I guess I'll just go.'

Tyler grabbed the front of Rick's shirt, tugging him towards him. 'Don't go. Yeah, we'd love you to play with us.' Tyler picked up the can they'd been kicking about. 'Here, want a drink?' He moved right up to Rick's face and bent the tab on the can. Rick leant closer to take a look at the strange fastener, unprepared for the drink that spurted all over him.

'Hobspit!' he gasped wiping the stuff from his eyes.

The boys howled with laughter.

'Hob-what? You're crazy!' jeered Tyler. 'Better finish it now you've started.'

'No, I . . . I don't want any more.' He just wanted to get out of there. But two boys caught Rick's flailing hands and held him still while Tyler emptied the rest of the drink over his head. 'Not so squeaky clean now, are you?' He rubbed the Coke into Rick's scalp then wiped his hands on Rick's shirt.

Son of a troll! Scalding rage boiled up inside Rick. The Fey had been absolutely right: humans were vile! He kicked sideways in a vicious move he'd learnt from Sergeant Rotgut. Tyler went down with a grunt, clutching his stomach. But instead of earning Rick's release, this appeared to be a signal for the others to bundle on top of him, breaking all rules of honourable combat. Rick was buried under squirming bodies, his cheek grinding into the grit of the asphalt. Alarmed for Rick, Aethel wriggled free and bit a hand pushing his face into the dirt. Someone yelled then booted him in the head—accident or not, he couldn't tell in the melee. The crush of boys was so heavy, he couldn't breathe; desperate, he reached for his powers even if it got him expelled back to Avalon. His fingers began to tingle as he drew energy to himself, ready to throw them all off.

'Boys! What is going on here?' Mr Bowra arrived on the scene. He hauled the topmost pupil off the pile. The rest quickly slithered away, leaving only

Rick and Tyler on the ground. Aethel slid under Rick before anyone noticed her.

'He started it!' one boy said swiftly, jabbing a finger at Rick. 'He kicked Tyler.'

Rick pulled himself to his knees, drawing desperate breaths into his oxygen-starved lungs.

'Yeah, he went mental, Mr Bowra!' protested another.

With two injured boys on his hands, ineffectual Mr Bowra dithered. 'Tyler, are . . . are you hurt?'

A mate pulled Tyler to his feet but he was still huddled protectively over his stomach. 'I don't know, sir,' he rasped pitifully. 'Think he broke something.'

'Medical room. Rick, what about you? Do you need to see the nurse?'

Warriors did not run crying to nurses for minor injuries. Rick wiped the blood from his nose. 'No, sir.'

'Right, you go to the pupil referral room and wait for me there. I'll see to Tyler then get your head of year to deal with you. Outrageous behaviour—I'm appalled at you and I'll make certain she knows that!'

Mr Bowra led the other boys away, the coward Tyler cradled in their midst. Rick knew his attacker had not been badly bruised as he'd pulled the kick but it must suit Tyler to look the injured party. He remained on the ground, arms looped around his knees, conscious of the sticky coating of drink over his face and chest. An order to report to the referral room—he had no idea what that was or where it was. Rick thought he'd just sit here for a moment, out of sight by the bins, before facing anyone. Besides, his head was buzzing—he wasn't sure he could stand up yet.

Aethel wound round his wrist; she throbbed with distress, hissing and spitting in the direction Mr Bowra had taken.

'OK, Legless?'

She ventured up to his neck and nestled against his chest, giving and taking comfort.

He'd been fooled yesterday. He had begun to think the humans were not like he had been taught, that maybe they had something special that he had never known—a kindness and caring in relationships that was lacking in Avalon. He had been stupid. The majority of humans in his class were turning out to be every bit as cruel as Morgan had claimed.

'Have you seen Rick?' He could hear Linette nearby.

'No, why?' That was Roxy.

'I am so worried. He's been in a fight.'

'What, Rick? No, I don't believe it!'

At least they cared. He almost called out to them, but couldn't find the energy. He didn't want them to see him in this state.

'It's true. I saw Tyler Walsh being carried out of here. The others said Rick's been sent to the head of year.'

Still dizzy from being on the bottom of the boy-mountain, Rick leaned his head back and closed his eyes.

Roxy muttered a curse. 'I knew it! Rick can be so arrogant sometimes—he was bound to get us into a fix. He should never've been chosen.'

Oh, Roxy. That hurt.

'What do you mean?' Linette sounded puzzled.

'He can be a pain in the neck—inflexible like a steel rod. You must have noticed?'

She was talking about him. Rick's heart squeezed as if a metal band had tightened round his chest.

'He certainly stands out—that's true.'

'He can be so embarrassing.' Roxy sighed. 'He's got his good sides though. Should we go check on him?'

'Yes. Don't worry: they won't expel him. Maybe exclude him for a week or make him stay in the referral unit—it depends how much damage he did.'

The girls' voices died away, leaving Rick alone. A wet snout pushed into his palm.

'Hey, Bob. You think I'm an embarrassment too?' Rick whispered, trying not to let his voice break.

The dog licked his fingers.

He began to feel angry—really angry, not just at Tyler, but the school and even his so-called friends. He would prove to Roxy that he was worth his place on the team.

He was going to track down the ringleader of the plot against Avalon, not mess around with the cannon fodder, as Sergeant Rotgut had called the students.

'Tell them I'm not coming back today, OK?'

Bob whined.

'I'll be fine. Just need to . . . need to get away from here for a bit.'

Pulling the tattered remains of his shirt around him—the buttons were scattered all over the ground—Rick stumbled to the back gate and headed into the city centre.

# Chapter 6

The strongest contender on the list provided by the secret police had been the half-Fey at the museum, Rick recalled, as he walked into Oxford. He was tired; his ribs hurt, his nose ached and he had a headache from where his temple had struck the ground.

A warrior doesn't complain about minor injuries, he reminded himself, gritting his teeth. He had a job to do.

At what had once been the medieval entrance to Oxford, the road broadened out as it joined with another, together wide enough to be a parade ground for a battalion. Tall plane trees stood on guard down the western and eastern sides, bark flaking off in jigsaw pieces. Surrounded by colleges and churches, the street looked as if it was rimmed by castle ramparts. One building stood out as the exception—a white temple structure that resembled the shape Dark Lore House had assumed when the commander had put them through a crash course on the Greeks. Rick risked his neck crossing the road, dodging the stream of taxis and tour buses, to arrive outside the columned entrance and read the sign. *Ashmolean Museum*. Excellent: he'd found what he was looking for.

He then noticed the list of galleries under the opening hours, his eyes drawn to Anglo-Saxon England. His time—his people. That was where, Rick decided, he would cast his bait for the half-Fey employee.

At the revolving door, a short-statured guard with bleached hair curling from under her cap stepped in his path. 'I'm sorry but you can't come into the museum like that. You look as if you need to go to the doctor.'

Following the door in a complete revolution, Rick cast a Fey glamour over his blood-stained shirt and filthy clothes. With a subtle weave of magic he was able to emerge in the same crisp uniform as the school party that had just entered the building.

'Sorry, what did you say, ma'am?' he asked politely.

The guard rubbed her eyes. 'Oh, er, nothing. Please, enjoy your visit.' She moved out of his way.

'Thank you.'

They had been trained at Dark Lore to use what tactics were necessary to win. He decided to ignore the ban on magic for the two very good reasons: it didn't take much power to maintain the glamour to fool the humans and it would lure the half-Fey out to discover what was going on. Many Fey were sensitive to magical outbursts like some humans could sense the approach of a thunderstorm through a change in air pressure.

Rick walked through a cool hallway lined with beautiful Greek statues, giants compared to the tourists staring up at them. Following the signs, he went further into the museum, out of the lofty Greek-inspired hall, through sliding glass doors and into a modern atrium. Perplexed at this sudden shift of architectural styles, he spun round to check the hall of Greek statues. Nothing had changed there. So it wasn't some magic trick then, shifting the museum through different time periods. Someone had sliced off the back of the old museum and slotted on a completely different style of building.

Humans were strange.

Climbing the stairs to the second floor of the atrium, he made his way into the darker galleries, kept at this level of lighting to protect the fragile exhibits. He was tempted to stop by some Samurai armour—he had always admired their discipline—but the desire to reach home ground spurred him onwards. Finally, he reached the Anglo-Saxon gallery. A guard slumbered in a chair in the archway leading to the Early Medieval period. Whispering under his breath, Rick deepened the man's sleep so he would not be disturbed. He then turned his attention to the artefacts on display.

Broken pots, jewellery, remnants of horse tack, weapons—this was all that was left of his civilization?

Deflated, he sat down in front of a case of rusted blades. It was hard to imagine them in their original splendour as they were so eaten away and blackened.

Rick bit his cheek against a welling of emotion, reminding himself he was on a mission. His glamour lure had not yet worked: he'd need to cast a stronger magical enticement. Rick whispered a little restoration spell. It had the power to recall things to their original state, a bit like the glamour but with the difference that they really became what they had been for as long as the charm lasted. That was better: he was now looking at a case of the finest blades in Anglo-Saxon England. They reminded him of his own sword which he had brought with him on the mission but so far kept under his bed.

'Impressive.' A woman stepped into the gallery, tall and thin with long brown hair. She moved with regal assurance. Her features were strong: dark brows, eyes rimmed with kohl, strikingly beautiful for a human.

Rick quickly reclaimed his spell, blades turning back to rust. Was it her—the half-Fey? She looked the type.

'Oh!' The woman touched her throat. 'I could have sworn they'd put up some replicas in this case.' She rubbed at the glass with the end of a bright silk scarf knotted around her neck. 'Did you see that?'

Shrugging, Rick checked his own glamour spell was intact. 'See what? I was miles away, Miss.'

She folded her arms. 'So you didn't see the beautiful swords hanging a foot from your nose?'

He stood up and peered intently at the exhibit. 'Yes, I see them. Bit battered, aren't they?'

'Hmm.' She inspected him with intelligent, assessing eyes. 'I could've sworn . . . ' She shifted, revealing a label on her jacket: Natalia Ventikos, Curator of Ancient World Galleries. He got his desired result—the half-Fey on the list had indeed sensed his magic. 'Still, there is more than one way of seeing, isn't there?' She was now studying him with a knowing expression. 'Especially if the one doing the looking is particularly *charming*.'

So the curator understood magic. That made her a good suspect. He wondered if he could get her to recruit him; that would be all the proof he needed. 'If you say so, Miss. Maybe you know more about that stuff than me? Strange things happen around me all the time, but I don't know what it means.'

The lady looked intrigued. 'I see. What sort of things?'

'Well, it kind of feels sometimes like magic could almost be real.'

'Natalia! How delightful to see you today. I thought you rarely stepped a foot away from your ancient Greeks and Egyptians.' An elderly man approached, his cane tapping on the floor with every other step. Rick was annoyed by the interruption. He had felt sure the lady had been about to snap up his magic hint.

'Professor Marmaduke, here again? Why am I not surprised?' The curator did not seem too pleased to see the newest arrival, greeting him with a mocking bow.

'Of course, I imagine we both felt it.' Marmaduke turned to the case. 'Ah, the Abingdon sword. Were you just showing it to the boy?' He nodded affably to Rick.

'No, Lucien.' The curator gave no more explanation. 'I wanted a word with him.'

'The same word I wanted?' Marmaduke scraped the floor tiles with the polished end of his stick, sketching out some sign which, if he'd not appeared to be human, Rick might have thought a warding spell.

The lady glared at the ground. 'No doubt.' She retreated a step as if shoved in the chest. 'Warn him about careless charms, won't you? I'll leave you to it.'

'Hmm, yes, you do that, my dear.' Marmaduke waved a jaunty goodbye. 'If he has anything interesting to say, I might tell you over a cup of tea later.'

'I won't hold my breath.' The curator spun on her heel and walked out with staccato footsteps ringing on the tiles.

Marmaduke breathed a sigh of relief. 'That's better. Can't have another Fey-blood poking her nose into our business can we?' He sat down on the bench and beckoned Rick to join him. 'Now, what was all that: casting spells in public? It won't do, you know. Had my alarms ringing the moment you did so; I had to rush to get to you before Natalia sank in her claws. And if you don't mind me saying, you already look like you've come out worse in a battle with Grendel.'

Rick tried not to let his jaw drop. Evidently, Marmaduke could see right through his magic.

'That's what she senses, you see—a burst of Fey power in the middle of her museum. It's no wonder she came running. What's your name?'

'Rick Halfdane.' Who was this man who knew about the Dark Folk? He didn't fit the profile of any of the names on the secret police list. Rick searched his face for clues: lined skin unlike any Fey he'd ever met, a shock of white hair, but silver-grey eyes that belonged to Avalon not the Earth. He thought he could see through any illusion cast by a Fey-blood but for once he could not tell if the professor was disguised or not; that meant very strong magic was involved.

'Excuse me, sir, this may seem an odd question but you're not part Fey, are you by any chance?'

'No, not part.' Marmaduke folded his hands over the top of his stick, enjoying watching Rick reason his way through the puzzle.

'Pixie?' He didn't look like the car salesman, but you never knew.

Marmaduke narrowed his eyes in disgust. 'Please!'

'Then what are you exactly?'

'Ah-ah, not so easy. That is for you to find out.' Marmaduke turned his attention back to the case, examining a gold ring of interlaced serpents. 'Such a shame the other poems did not survive. There was an excellent epic about a hero called Wulfric—he wore something exactly like that—but the manuscript ended up as kindling in the eleventh century thanks to one careless monk.' He began chanting the opening stanzas—in the original Old English as Rick had learned it.

'You remember Wulfric's story being destroyed? No, you can't.' Rick tugged the hem of his ragged shirt in frustration, knowing the answer was fluttering just out of sight if only he could net it. He'd thought the last remaining copy of that poem had been preserved in Avalon in the Dark Lore library.

Marmaduke shrugged. 'I saved what I could—but too much would have been suspicious and they burned people for witchcraft in those days, so you had to be careful.'

Rick realized the solution to the clues the old man was giving him. No human could live so long; it was a stretch even for the extended life of a part Fey. 'You're a full-blooded Fey. Somehow you've been missed off the lists.'

Marmaduke spluttered indignantly. 'Not just any old Fey, please! One of the Mage Fey—and proud of it.'

'But . . . but you're so old!' He meant the professor *looked* old—the Dark Folk were ancient but rarely showed their age, remaining hale and hearty for millennia.

'Of course, I am. I'm two thousand years old, give or take a few hundred—half of that lived in Avalon and the rest in this world. I'm getting on by anyone's calculation; I left them all behind long ago when I made the switch to HT.'

'HT?'

'Human time.'

Rick had so many questions they were queuing up like fighters at a siege, ready to go through a breach as soon as there was an opening. He settled for the simplest. 'Why are you here, sir?'

'Why live in this world?'

Rick nodded. 'Surely no Dark Folk would want to live with humans?'

Marmaduke rubbed his left palm over the back of his knobbly right hand. 'I'm in exile. I thought you would guess that. I was sent here as punishment and I am not allowed back on pain of death.'

'I see.'

'I don't think you do. Don't tell me you don't understand what you really are?'

'Sorry?'

'I heard your name right? Elfric Halfdane? You are a human changeling, aren't you?' Closing his eyes, he sniffed. 'Yes, I can feel that you are.'

Rick nodded, not sure what he was agreeing to.

'The clue is in the word "changeling". You were *exchanged* for a Fey to keep the balance between the worlds. There is a rule of "one in, one out" to keep nature chugging along smoothly in both realms. The Fey snatched you from your parents and put one of us in your place.'

'No.' Rick shook his head, though from the horrible squirmy feeling in his chest his body had begun to recognize truth before his brain did. 'No, the Fey rescued us—we were thrown away by the humans. We were told they changed our life for the better, that's why they gave us the name.'

'That is a lie told to keep you quiet. You were *exchanged*, not saved. No, I'm afraid you are just an unfortunate by-product of the changeling programme Oberon started to deal with his rivals. He sometimes sent the children of his opponents as hostages, but he also used it as a means of disposing of his, shall we say, more challenging subjects—the ones that were too powerful to kill. He never appreciated the Mage Fey, so many of us were banished to this world. I was one of the first.'

Rick felt sick. Could this be true? If it was then everything—absolutely everything he had believed was wrong. He had been betrayed in the deepest way possible by Fey who claimed to be his only friends.

'Oh, my dear boy, I'm so sorry.'

Rick brushed his sleeve over his face, embarrassed that he was showing so much emotion. 'Not your fault.'

A wrinkled old hand patted his arm. 'Oh, but it is in a way. You see, dear boy, I am *your* changeling.'

'What?' Rick crumpled forward, hugging his arms to his side. Each revelation felt like a stab wound.

'I had your place on Earth—your family, your life. Of course, I've lived many more human lifetimes since, but you never forget your first assignment.'

'I don't know what to say. Fey-bells, I feel so . . . so . . . ' He shook his head, remembering all he had learned from the fragments he had found in the library. Mercia had been one of the leading English nations in the eighth century. His parents had been recorded as a happy partnership and his father a good ruler. Mercia had fallen apart in the battles between the members of the next generation, pointless squabbles that let in the Vikings and other enemies. 'What were they like—my parents?' Rick was proud that his voice held firm when he wanted to howl.

Marmaduke smiled sadly. 'Ah, that is a long story—not a subject for a hasty conversation in a public place. You must come to tea in my rooms and I'll tell you all about them.'

'Please, can't you tell me something, any little thing you can remember?' Rick couldn't leave without a hint; he was desperate to have a small piece to take away with him. He had to know why they'd swapped him for one of the Mage Fey of all things.

Marmaduke nodded, understanding the plea. 'Our mother had the sweetest smile and quietly ruled the household even though our father was something of a blusterer—all sound and fury—and thought he was in charge. They were excellent parents despite the fact they suspected I wasn't quite what I seemed. Your mother tried to find you, you know. She was not fooled by the switch.' Marmaduke tapped his brow. 'Silver eyes—not your baby blue, you see. They make most humans look twice.'

'But she gave me up.' At least, that was what he had been told.

'Bite your tongue, young man! She would never have given you up. Neither your mother nor your father ever knew what happened except that one day you were there, the next there was a Fey changeling. Like all parents in their situation, they sensed the baby in the cradle wasn't their own, but what could they do? They had to give shelter to the cuckoo in the nest. I was enough like you to make their suspicions seem foolish to others.'

'How did you do it?'

'Part of my sentence was that I had to sustain the illusion of being a child for a few years until I could drop my glamour and take my place as their oldest son. That was a humiliation I never wish to repeat; I'm sure Oberon was cackling with glee to think of me back in the schoolroom. Still, I was weakened by a recent defeat at the time and had to knuckle down. Your parents were too kind to be cruel to me. So I hope you see that you changelings are swaps. The humans don't give you up; the Fey take you to keep the balance when they leave one of us.'

'Godfled and Elfstan.' Rick muttered their names like a charm. 'My parents. They'd wanted me. Me.'

'That's right. How did you learn their names?'

'I read everything I could find out about them at school.' He researched, thinking to track down his relatives and punish them when he got the chance.

'They were good people, Elfric. They were happy and had long lives for people of their time—I made sure of it.'

Rick cleared his throat. 'Thank you for that.' His hands were shaking. Everything he had thought was wrong. He couldn't get his head around that.

'I was King of Mercia for a bit, you know. Elfric the Able. Made quite a good impression in your name.'

Rick nodded, unable to speak. He happened to know that the counterfeit Elfric's reign had been short. He had never realized that it had been a Fey, not another human, who had held his throne. He had assumed one of his brothers had taken his name.

'Not the best job I've ever had, I must say—all those bickering warriors and your brothers and sisters were the worst. I think they must have picked up on the changeling rumour early on and never let me forget I wasn't quite one of them.'

Rick felt like pummelling something, crying, shouting: his brothers and sisters had stuck up for the rights of their stolen brother. He had cursed them for years, which made him feel terrible now that he knew they had stayed loyal to him.

'Still, all water under the bridge now.' Marmaduke fumbled in his top pocket and produced a card. 'My contact details. Let's have a good long conversation about the past very soon.' He got to his feet with the aid of his cane. 'Do call on me.'

The water hadn't passed under any bridge for Rick yet. He was still coming to grips with finding everything he believed was a lie. He needed desperately to be alone to take it all in. He slipped the card in his pocket. 'I will.'

'And you'd best visit the Gents on your way out. Your face is covered in blood and you look a bit peaky, if you don't mind me saying. Drop the glamour and you'll frighten the humans.'

Rick stared at the Abingdon sword for a long time after Marmaduke had left, ignoring the tingle coming from his cowry shell that meant Roxy or Tiago were trying to reach him. He'd not been given away; he'd been stolen. Why had he not questioned the Fey more closely, tested what he had been told?

He had been brainwashed, that was why. He'd been a sad little child looking to put his faith in something and he had chosen to believe the ones who surrounded him with lies. The terrible truth was that too much time had passed for him to do anything about it. Like the rusted weapon in the case before him, he was beaten and useless, perhaps once fit for purpose but now out of his time. Marmaduke had lived Rick's life. There was no going back and Rick had trouble imagining what his future could be. It was too late for him in every sense of the word.

It would have been better never to have been born. Rick felt so angry that, right now, if someone came and invited him to sit at the Round Table and destroy Avalon, he'd be very tempted just to spite Morgan and Oberon.

But what about the others? Not just Roxy and Tiago—the other changelings he left behind had to be protected, had to be told.

Finally, when he had been sitting so long he knew he was becoming conspicuous, he made the effort to move. He took the sleep spell off the guard and headed to the Gents as Marmaduke had recommended. A rank of mirrors confronted him. He looked grim—cheekbone rubbed raw, angry from the bits of grit he had not bothered to clean out, a nasty bump on his forehead. He washed his face, sucking his teeth to stop the hiss of pain as the soap cleansed the wounds. Nothing could be done about his shirt. He wrapped the ends around his waist and tucked what he could into his jeans.

'Rick, you are an idiot,' he told his reflection. 'You've believed a lie all your stupid life.'

The Rick in the mirror looked back glumly.

How could he go on working for the very people that had ruined everything? But if he didn't, he'd be executed—Oberon did not mess around when it came to treason. Now he knew what the Fey were really like, their brutality towards the changelings made perfect sense. It wasn't military discipline as he had thought, but more like a herder choosing when to cull a flock that had lost its value.

What should he do? He dried his face on a hand towel, trying to get a grip on the situation. OK, number one: the attack on the power source was real; someone had to do something about that or his fellow changelings stuck in Avalon might not escape another meltdown.

So who was behind it? What of the two Fey people he had met—one on the list, one off? They must be involved surely? The curator had clearly been on the watch for magic users: what did she have to hide? The professor had also come running, though he said he did so to protect Rick. Marmaduke seemed nice, sympathetic that the changelings had not known the truth about themselves—apologetic that he had lived Rick's life. Rick didn't want to think of him as a villain but it had to be a possibility.

Gazing at his reflection, the world in reverse, it suddenly struck Rick that maybe he was looking at it all wrong. Maybe setting up a Round Table was the act of a hero—a challenge to Oberon? It was only the Fey in Avalon who called it an attack. What if the magic could be siphoned off and used for empowering an army to stand against Oberon without doing harm to either world, as Merlin had once done? Perhaps Rick should be applying to join a new Round Table, not attempting to find it so that Oberon's feygents could kill the rebels? He had so much more he had to ask Marmaduke.

He leant over the sink, breathing hard. Too many shocks—too much to take in.

Sensing his distress, Aethel transformed into her living form and curled around his neck affectionately, offering serpentine comfort.

'What should I do?' Rick whispered, stroking the smooth diamond-patterned skin.

The snake unfurled and stuck her head into his pocket, withdrawing with Professor Marmaduke's card in her jaws.

'Yeah, don't lose that. I'm going to go and see him as soon as I can.'

Aethel waved the card insistently.

'What?' Glancing down, Rick read it. The address on Professor Marmaduke's card was Exeter College, Linette's home, next door to the Radcliffe Camera.

'Aethel, you are a genius! The clever old Mage Fey is sitting right on top of the trouble spot. I think this has just bumped the professor up to the top of our suspect list.' Gloom began to lift. 'You see what this means? If he's not behind the new Round Table, it gives us an ally who will understand what's at stake and he can help find it. If he is, then maybe I should just transfer to his side. What do you think?'

His snake wriggled with something that was suspiciously like serpentine glee.

Rick's battered confidence rebounded. 'OK. OK. I can do this. I can't give up now. I'm going back to school and I'm turning the tables on that troll boy, Tyler Walsh. I'm not letting my fight with him turn into a reason for sending me back to Dark Lore in disgrace. Then I'm fetching Roxy and Tiago and tracking down the professor and finding out what's going on at the Fey Ring.' Rick chucked the crumpled towel into the bin—score!

It was not his fault that he'd been stolen as a baby, neither was the fight with Tyler, so why should he carry the blame? If there was any justice it should be that useless teacher, Mr Bowra, and Tyler and his mates who got into trouble. And it wouldn't even take magic—just the absence of it—to achieve this.

Jogging back to school, Rick dropped the glamour once in sight of the gates. He let every rip and wound show. Ignoring the shocked gaze of the receptionist, he walked along the corridor until he found a door marked 'Pupil Referral Room'. It wasn't long before his head of year, Mrs Proudie, rushed in.

'Rick! Where have you been? You've been missing for hours. I was about to inform the police. Good gracious, what happened to you?'

Rick weaved with what he hoped was convincing confusion as he got up. 'I . . . um . . . I got lost. I don't feel so good.' This was true—now he came to think about it, his wounds were throbbing and he felt light-headed.

'Mr Bowra said you weren't hurt! Did you hit your head? Yes, yes, you have—I can see the bump on the side of your forehead! You'd better lie down in the medical room—I'll phone your parents. We'd better take you to hospital to get you checked out.'

Mrs Proudie helped him to a little room near reception where Tyler Walsh was stretched out, flicking through a football magazine.

'Tyler, what are you still doing here? I told you to go back to your class.'

'Still don't feel well, miss,' moaned Tyler, his gaze hooking on Rick with spiteful glee. 'He hurt me really bad.'

'But you're well enough to read a magazine, I see.' At least, Mrs Proudie wasn't as easily fooled as Mr Bowra. 'I'll sort you out after I've phoned Rick's parents.'

'We don't have a phone, miss.' Rick heaved himself on to the couch as if his legs were carrying concrete boots.

'I see. Look, I'll get your brother for you and we'll go in my car.' She asked the receptionist to keep an eye on them while she hurried off to make the arrangements.

Rick lay on his side, facing the wall, grinning at Aethel now back on his wrist. Time for some fun.

Aethel winked and slid off his arm.

It didn't take Tyler long to start on the sneers. 'You're a nutter, you know that, Halfdane. Stupid name. Who's called Halfdane anyway? Sounds like a mongrel dog.'

Rick smiled at the wall. Not long now.

'Ran off, did you? Scared I was going to get you back? You wait, when we're out of school, I'll . . . Jeez! Help! There's a snake in here! Mrs Proudie, Mrs Proudie!'

Rick turned over lazily to see Tyler backed up against the wall, knees hugged to his chest, Aethel menacing him by swaying dangerously close to his ankles, jaws snapping. 'Snake? Oh yeah, Tyler, meet my pet.'

'You brought a snake to school! You really are crazy!'

'I'm never without her. You might like to remember that. Aethel, come home.'

Point made, Aethel slid back to Rick's wrist.

Miraculously healed, Tyler leapt up and ran into the corridor, bumping into Mrs Proudie and Tiago coming the other way. 'Mrs Proudie, that boy . . . that boy has a snake!'

'Now don't be ridiculous, Tyler.' Mrs Proudie came into the room, Tiago following. Tiago glanced down to check that Rick's familiar was back in place then grinned.

'Yeah, my brother likes snakes,' Tiago said blithely.

'See, he knows!' spluttered Tyler.

'It's on his arm. Show Mrs Proudie, Rick.'

Rick slid back the cuff of his shirt.

Mrs Proudie looked shocked. 'Is that gold?'

'No,' Rick was able to answer quite honestly. It had once been but now it was transformed into one hundred per cent magic snake that just looked like gold.

'Well, we prefer pupils not to wear jewellery—health and safety—but I hardly think, Tyler, that you need make such a fuss about it.'

'But miss, it was alive. It hissed—and moved. It threatened me!' Tyler waved the rolled up football magazine at Rick's wrist, trying to swat the bracelet.

Mrs Proudie put her hands on her hips. 'Tyler, I think you've caused enough trouble for Rick today; don't make it worse by spinning such fairy tales. Go back to your class.' She tugged the magazine out of his hand. 'I'll be writing to your parents about the incident earlier, understood?'

Too shocked to argue, Tyler backed off, his eyes flicking nervously between Rick, Tiago, and Aethel. With a vigorous gesture, Rick shook his cuff back down; Tyler ran.

# Chapter 7

The news about Rick returning injured spread through the school. Linette was eaten up with guilt. While she and the rest of her class had been blaming him for the incident that morning break, he had been suffering from concussion. Everyone had assumed he'd cut school when he didn't show up in the pupil referral room. She was the closest thing he had to a friend in her year so she at least should've considered the other side of the story—after all, she had several months of experience to know that Tyler Walsh was more likely to be guilty than a well-behaved loner like Rick.

At the end of the day, she searched the crowds leaving the building hoping to find Roxy. She located her in the middle of a group from her year, Roxy's hair catching the sunlight like a beacon.

'Roxy, how's Rick? Have you heard?'

Roxy quickly said goodbye to the girls from her class to join Linette. 'He's OK. Still at the hospital, but Tiago says he's doing fine. They'll probably let him go home if they can get our parents to fetch him.'

'What's the problem there?'

Roxy shrugged. 'No phone, no car.'

Oh yes, Dysfunctional Central didn't run to such normal things. 'I feel so annoyed with myself that I didn't look harder for him when we couldn't find him.' Linette twisted her jacket ties in angry knots. 'I should've checked. When they came to ask where he was, I jumped to the conclusion he'd bunked off. And Tyler Walsh was acting the injured martyr all afternoon—I could scream!'

Roxy smiled pityingly, wrinkling her freckled nose. 'Not for you to feel bad, Linette. Rick'll be OK. He's survived much worse, believe me. And Tiago says he's in a good mood in hospital—a bit hyper if anything.'

Linette moved to a bench by the school field so Roxy could sit. The three foster kids were very tough, but then perhaps they'd had to be. 'We've got to do something for Rick or I'm going to die of guilt.'

Roxy hopped up beside her and balanced on the back, feet on the seat. A robin flew out of a near-by bush and landed a few inches from her untied shoelace, cheeping and fluttering as if it suspected it of being a new type of worm.

'I think he likes you.' Linette watched as the bird pecked Roxy's toecap.

Roxy looked a little embarrassed. 'Yeah, robins have a thing for me. What did you mean about doing something for Rick?'

'He's good-looking, no? Under all that bizarre formality of his.' All three of the newcomers were super-attractive, as if they came airbrushed from a glossy magazine. Tiago had the most amazing eyes, like looking into liquid mercury. She'd wondered if he wore special contacts but Roxy had said no.

Roxy sniffed. 'Don't ask a sister to judge a brother. I've spent too much time with him—know all his bad habits.'

'Believe me, he has the potential to be really fit—that was what we all thought on the first day.'

Roxy didn't appear convinced. 'If you say so.'

'I do. So we can help him.'

'How?' Roxy's tone was doubtful.

'Do a Cinderella—transform him from ultra-dork into Mr Cool. It would simply take some different clothes and an attitude adjustment.'

Roxy rubbed her upper arms. 'So, we're what? Fairy godmothers?'

'Yes.'

Roxy laughed at a joke Linette couldn't quite see. 'OK. Let's do it.'

'Will you tell him? Persuade him it's a good idea?'

'Yeah. Let's go back to yours after school tomorrow, take him shopping and start his lessons in un-dorkishness.'

Shy of allowing people into her home, Linette almost refused but her need to make amends won out. 'OK. I'll tell my parents to expect us. They'll probably go a little mad when they hear I'm bringing guests home—they're like that.'

Roxy jumped down. The robin fluttered, circled, then landed on her shoulder. 'You don't have to worry, Linette—nothing your parents can do comes anywhere near to what ours are capable of.'

That was true. Linette suddenly felt much better about the plan. No need to be embarrassed with that as the standard by which she was being judged.

Rick couldn't quite believe the vehicle Magmell had brought to collect him from hospital. An open-topped Rolls Royce from 1930 in bright yellow: if there was ever a car that shouted 'look at me!', this was it. For once, Magmell's satin jacket did not seem out of place, especially since he'd accessorized the outfit with cap and goggles. The nurse who had accompanied Rick to the exit didn't know quite what to say as he held out the release forms for Magmell to sign.

'Yours?' he croaked with an envious look at the tan leather upholstery, shining headlamps and spotless paintwork.

Magmell scrawled his signature carelessly. 'It is now.'

'Where did you get it, if you don't mind me asking?'

'Gaydon. My wife picked it out for me.'

'There's a brilliant motor museum there.' The nurse took back the clipboard. 'In fact, they have a Rolls just like this one.'

Rick exchanged a look with Tiago.

'I think you'll find they don't any more.' Magmell dismissed the human, turning his back on him. 'Come on, boys.'

Rick was about to get into the front when Bob jumped in beside the driver.

'Humans in the back.' Magmell fumbled in the glove pocket and pulled out a little pair of goggles and fitted them over Bob's eyes with a flash of adaptive magic.

Resigned, Tiago and Rick climbed into the rear seat. Magmell fired up the engine and gave the boys his first ever enthusiastic smile. 'Ah, the beauty of a well-tuned combustion engine—nothing like it in all Avalon! So primitive.'

He drove with great panache, taking the long way home so he could show off the car's abilities. As a former engineer on the Dew Track, he was skilled at anything mechanical. Rick half expected to hear the sound of police sirens in pursuit, but there was nothing but admiration for their vehicle from onlookers as they rode home in the twilight. Whatever means Shreddie had used to liberate the car from the museum, she must have managed it without triggering the alarms. There was something unexpectedly normal about a dad—even a pretend one—taking his boys for a spin in the car that Rick decided to enjoy the ride rather than spoil it for Tiago by revealing that the changelings had been living a lie. He hadn't yet decided how he was going to break the news to the others. How would Roxy react to the information that they were taken by force from their families, not chucked out as they had believed? And Tiago, as a half-Mage Fey, wouldn't it put him in a tricky position with loyalties even more split than they already were? Their quest had become nastily twisted. There was the real prospect of execution if Oberon or Morgan found out that they knew the truth. They wouldn't want them to spread the news to the other changelings and foment rebellion at the training centre.

The car splashed through a puddle, wetting a woman in a cream coat walking her Labrador. Shrieking with outrage, she shook her fist at Magmell but the Fey just laughed.

Now didn't that just sum up the Fey attitude to humans? Once Rick would have found it funny, only part of what mankind deserved, but now it struck him as callous. Humans were no angels, but the Feys were much worse as they really didn't care. He just couldn't go on living with them, under their control.

So what to do? In the days of the humans' Cold War, Rick remembered learning, citizens from enemy powers used to be able to defect to the other country, seeking asylum. But how could he tell the humans that he wanted out of Avalon? That just sounded plain mad. And if there was a balance to maintain—one in, one out—who would go in his place? In fact, how could they be here now without upsetting it? He would have to ask Tiago.

But not now. He would save his questions and tell Tiago and Roxy about Professor Marmaduke when he was certain that they could not be overheard. He doubted their Dark Folk minders would look kindly on someone the Fey king had effectively exiled by bundling him off in the changeling exchange programme. Safer for everyone if Marmaduke's presence in Oxford was kept on a 'need to know' basis.

Closing his eyes, Rick tried to imagine a good outcome from this situation. He supposed his best hope would be that Marmaduke was gathering a circle of brave warriors to take on Oberon. He imagined them all seated around a new Round Table; humans drawing on magic to be unbeatable super knights; Rick taking his place among them . . .

Yeah, like that was going to happen.

Tiago flicked his ear. Rick's eyes shot open. 'Wake up. That nurse guy said you were to stay alert as long as possible in case you did your brains in when you bumped your head.'

Dreams blown away like his medical notes from the front seat of the car—Magmell hadn't considered them worth reading—Rick dragged himself back to the present.

'Thanks.'

Tiago wasn't meeting his eyes. 'Feeling OK?'

'Yeah, fine.'

'I . . . um . . . wanted to say sorry for not letting you join in with the football.' His bronze cheeks flushed. Tiago hated making personal comments to anyone, particularly apologies which involved all sorts of messy feelings.

'It's fine. You were on the quest for answers.'

'No, it's not fine. I mean, we have to stick together, don't we?' He jerked his head at their driver. 'The Fey aren't gonna be on our side, so we have to be our own back up.'

'Well, thanks.' Rick felt uncomfortable too with this heart-to-heart stuff. He searched for a lighter topic. 'Magmell's unbelievable, isn't he? Drives like a maniac but Bob seems to like him.' The little dog had his front paws up on the dashboard, snout raised in excitement, tail wagging furiously.

'In his way. Bob accepts the Fey for what they are so isn't let down when they do bad things to us. You don't expect a wild tiger to play nice, do you?'

No, Rick thought, it was about time he stopped expecting 'nice' and started working out how to cope with nasty.

Roxy was waiting on the wall of the front garden for their return, her concern for him plain in the miserable hunch of her shoulders; it only disappeared when she saw him alive and well.

'Rick! You're OK!'

He grinned. 'So I keep telling everyone.'

Magmell disappeared into the house, leaving the three of them to pull the protective cover over the car.

'Tyler Walsh is such a goblin brain. I'm gonna get him,' Roxy vowed with relish as she considered her magical options for revenge. 'What you reckon? Warts? Hair loss?'

Rick laughed. 'Really, no need. I can fight my own fights.'

Roxy raised an eyebrow. 'Yeah, like that went so well for you today.'

'I was rather outnumbered.'

'That's because you haven't made any friends.'

'Thanks, break it to me gently, why don't you?' Rick tried to make light of his failure.

'Apart from us,' chipped in Tiago.

'Thanks, Tiago.'

'Aethel scared him good but do you want Bob to bite Walsh's butt for you?'

The dog cocked his head, ear lifted attentively.

Rick shook his head. 'No. That wouldn't be fair—on Bob, I mean. He might catch something nasty.' Bob whined with disappointment. 'But you could do your business against his school bag if you get a chance.' The little dog cheered up at that prospect.

Tiago laughed. 'Walsh will steer clear for a bit, I guess. He'll be wondering how he hallucinated that snake.'

'You risked magic?' Roxy rubbed Bob's neck.

Rick shrugged. 'Only a very tiny bit. No one will believe him so it's OK.'

'Look, Rick, we need to do something about you at school.'

Rick folded his arms. 'You're not going to tell our handlers that I'm not blending in, are you?'

Roxy scowled. 'Do you want me to?'

'No! The last thing I want is to be sent back—not now.'

'If you don't want them to find out,' she nodded to the house, 'then you need to get more in tune with us, I mean *other* teenagers.'

'I see.' And he did. Today had made plain that he needed new tactics.

'Linette and I, well, we came up with a plan to sort that out. Now don't go all troll on me when I say.'

'Uh-oh.' Tiago sat down on the running board of the Rolls and gathered Bob on to his lap.

'We want to take you shopping—get you a new image.'

'What's wrong with my clothes?' Rick asked stiffly. They'd each chosen their wardrobes while in Avalon from a catalogue. He'd gone for the smartest ones he could find in his size: decent shirts, fine knit jumpers, smart jeans—none of that ripped and frayed rubbish.

'They're just not . . . ' She twirled her hand, suggesting all sorts of fashion sins.

'They're good quality, sensible garments. They cover me and keep me warm and dry. That's enough.'

'No, it's not.' Roxy steeled herself to tell him the truth. 'You look a dork.'

'A what?'

'Sore thumb—you stick out like one. Like a shaven monk among hairy Vikings.'

'I still don't understand. Why must I be judged on what I wear, particularly when I like it?'

'I know, I know, it is very narrow-minded of every teenager to think like that—but we do and you aren't going to be here long enough to change the way we think. I'm right, aren't I, Tiago?'

'Don't drag me into this.'

'I am. You aren't doing that keeping-yourself-separate thing you do in Dark Lore.'

Tiago held up his hands in surrender. 'OK, OK, your idea is not completely rubbish. Rick'll have an easier time at school if he gets a new image.' Tiago hugged Bob. 'Think of it like camouflage, *amigo*.'

'Yes!' Roxy seized the concept and ran with it. 'You're a soldier, Rick, a warrior—you know the value of dressing for your environment. Looking at you now, I'd say you were in your dress uniform; you need to get out the everyday stuff—you know, teen combat gear.'

Rick realized he didn't have much choice; he would have to wear the stupid clothes other kids did if he wanted to stay and see this through.

'OK, I'll do it. Take me shopping.'

Bob howled. At least he understood the pain and humiliation involved.

'Grand. You were easier to persuade than I thought.'

'That's because I've got some news.' He checked that Magmell and Shreddie weren't in earshot. 'Things are hotting up and I don't want to do anything to risk the quest. I didn't just walk out of school; I found two suspects.'

Roxy grabbed his sleeve. 'You did? Who?'

'I went to the museum and did a little bit of magic . . . '

'Rick! They'll send you back for sure if they find out about that.'

'It's OK. It was on purpose—like bait.'

Tiago laughed. 'Sergeant Rotgut's favourite disobeying orders? I like it!'

Rick smiled. 'Yeah, well, I just thought that Morgan was wrong about magic making the Round Table go into hiding; it did the opposite: I drew two Feys to me—the museum lady on the list—she was the one I was expecting, but also—you're going to love this—I also found someone else the secret police have entirely missed. They both need further investigation; I'd actually lay money on Professor Marmaduke being involved.'

'Wow, well done!' exclaimed Roxy. 'I was

beginning to think we'd never get a lead. So what do we do? Tell Morgan?'

'I don't trust them to handle it properly, do you? Oberon is likely to send in a hit squad even if they are innocent.'

Roxy rubbed her arms. 'True.'

'And I want Tiago to have a chance to meet Marmaduke first. He's a Mage Fey, Tiago. Full blood. Lives in the same college as Linette.'

'No! This I have to see!' Tiago looked ready to set off there and then.

'Let's go tomorrow,' suggested Roxy. 'Keep to the plan I set up with Linette—get you your new clothes and then go back to hers. You and Tiago can go see the Prof while I find out what I can from the Kwans about him.'

'Good idea. Thanks for thinking of the new image thing, Roxy.'

'Linette's idea, actually, but you're welcome. I don't want to see you sent back to Avalon, but neither do I want to live through another day when you are set upon by the idiots at school for being different. We're . . . well, Tiago and I, we're your family now, and a family looks out for each other. Don't we, Tiago?'

Tiago looked embarrassed. 'I suppose so.'

'Thanks, Roxy.' Rick felt a strange flutter in his stomach: he had never had a family before.

Roxy jumped up on to the running board beside Tiago so she could reach to give Rick a kiss on the cheek. 'You'll see: it'll be fun. Linette thinks you could look fit.' She leapt down and danced off into the house.

Fit? Rick already knew he was healthy, having been disciplined about taking enough exercise to keep up his warrior skills. Clothes couldn't make him more fit. Bemused, he touched his face where she had planted her kiss. He'd never had one of those before either. It felt odd, as if she had burst through an invisible shield wall he'd constructed around himself.

Tiago inspected Bob's ears for dirt, not looking at Rick. 'She's doing it because she worries about you, not because she wants to change you.'

Rick leaned against the car. 'Really?'

'Yeah. Roxy's got a strong protective streak—probably her pixie upbringing. They're good at family stuff, unlike the rest of the Dark Folk. I think Tyler Walsh is going to find his life very uncomfortable for the next few days until she feels she's avenged you.'

Rick's first instinct was to object to someone taking over his battle, but then he decided he liked the idea of Roxy defending him. It was how proper families behaved, wasn't it? He looked up as Roxy opened her bedroom window to let the robins in for a visit. 'I always thought Roxy had it in for me but she's OK, isn't she?'

'Yeah, she's OK. So are you—most of the time.'

Rick hid his smile. 'I like Bob.'

'Good.'

'His master is a bit of a pain but he's growing on me.'

'Good to know. Let's go find out if Shreddie has been made Chancellor of the University yet.'

# Chapter 8

A pixie in a rage is not a pretty sight. Singed patches on the living room carpet showed where Shreddie had taken out her anger with a few well-placed fireballs.

'And they didn't even interview me!' she shrieked, thumping the table so that the meal Magmell had produced piping hot in little plastic boxes leapt up into the air and dropped back down.

Rick quickly shovelled the delicious rice and sauce combination into his mouth as fast as he could just in case Shreddie decided to set the table on fire.

Roxy cracked flat bread into pieces for her robin. Shreddie glowered at her, considering it a betrayal that Roxy could give her attention to something other than the pixie's traumatic day.

'Oops, sorry. I am listening, Shreddie,' Roxy said quickly. 'I'm really sorry that they didn't realize just how perfect you would be for Professor of Economics.'

Shreddie sniffed. 'And I lost my bracelet.'

*Linette's* bracelet.

'What a shame,' Roxy commiserated.

'But at least I put a curse on the man who wouldn't give me the job.' Shreddie cheered up at this thought and helped herself to some rice.

'You did?' Rick asked cautiously, wondering if he could sneak out and undo it later.

'I did. He'll have hiccups for a week. Serves him right.'

Rick let it go. He couldn't undo every piece of Dark Folk malice and as curses went this was a mild one.

'But enough of the stupid university!' Shreddie leant forward to confide her next big plan. 'I've decided my talents lie elsewhere. I went into the Museum of Modern Art while I was in Oxford and realized I'd prefer the cover of becoming an artist. It doesn't look half as difficult as being a professor. So, boys, I'm turning your bedroom into my studio. You'll have to make do with tents in the garden.'

Tiago and Rick looked at each other in confusion. They were being relegated to the lawn?

'You do know it's forecast to rain all weekend?' said Tiago. Fey bloods—even half ones—knew in their bones exactly what the weather was going to be for days in advance.

Shreddie frowned, unable to imagine how that was relevant to her plans to conquer the art world. 'So?'

Magmell looked up from the secret police list. He had spent the day investigating the pixie car dealer and announced that he was an unlikely candidate for running a Round Table as his only interest appeared to be selling old bangers to unsuspecting humans. The pixie charmed the cars so they didn't fall apart until they had been driven off his forecourt.

'I'll spell the tents to make them properly waterproof,' Magmell offered. The Fey taking any kind of action that did not benefit himself was worthy of note; but, then again, perhaps he was just afraid they would demand to share his bedroom. 'And you can put your beds inside—I'll make sure there's plenty of space.'

Tiago shook his head in disgust, but Rick just shrugged. With the Dark Folk, you just had to roll with the punches. Compared to child stealing, this was small fry.

'OK, that sounds fine. When do we move in—I mean, out?' Rick asked.

'Now.' Shreddie took off her business suit jacket. 'I've an idea for my first project. But I'll need one of your beds.'

'And where are we supposed to sleep?' fumed Tiago.

'Don't worry—I'll manage with a hammock.' Rick got up, concluding it best to retrieve their belongings from their ex-bedroom before Shreddie decided she needed more things for her art. The pixie was getting far too involved in her cover story but at least it meant she wasn't prying too closely into their activities.

Magmell was less easy to fool. 'Wait, you haven't told us about your progress.'

Rick exchanged a quick glance with the others. He was going to lie—the first time he had done so blatantly to the Fey—and he didn't want them to give him away. Roxy looked innocent; Tiago gave him a subtle nod. 'Nothing to report tonight, sir.'

'There had better be some developments tomorrow or the commander's patience will run out.'

'Understood. Let's go, Tiago.'

The class treated Rick with subdued respect when he turned up at school the next day. Word had got round that he'd taken on the entirety of Tyler's gang. No one was quite sure what to make of this: he was either very courageous or completely mental. Most chose to continue to steer well clear of him, despite Linette's best efforts to integrate him into the class. He hadn't helped by turning up in yet another ironed shirt and pressed jeans. Who had creases down the front of their trousers these days? Linette fretted. It wasn't right. She couldn't wait for his makeover session.

Rick accompanied her as she made her way to the changing rooms for PE, holding the doors so she didn't have to get caught up manoeuvring through.

'You feel OK today, Rick?' she asked.

He looked mildly surprised by her question. 'I'm fine. Thank you for asking.'

'But with the hospital and everything . . . ?'

'It was nothing. Really.' He gave her a conspiratorial grin. 'You should've seen the other guy.'

She laughed. 'I know; he complained all yesterday. Everyone thinks he's soft.'

That made Rick's smile widen, but he nobly avoided gloating by changing the subject. 'Your college is Exeter, isn't it? Do you know Professor Marmaduke?'

'*You* know Professor Marmaduke?' She swivelled round to look up at him.

Rick shrugged. 'Not well. I bumped into him in town the other day, and we got talking.'

'Oh. Me, I've only known him since we arrived in September. He's ancient—lived in the college since time began according to the porters. Nice though. He helps me with my literature essays. Why do you ask?'

Rick looked away. 'No reason. I just found him fascinating. Have you heard if he is interested in . . . um . . . Arthurian stories—certain ones in particular?'

'No. He likes Shakespeare and Chaucer, I think. Why: did he say he was?'

'Just wondering. I thought I might call by his rooms when I come over to yours this afternoon.'

Linette turned to enter the girls' changing room. 'He'd like that, if he's not teaching. But don't accept the offer of biscuits—I fear his packet of Hobnobs is almost as old as he is.'

Linette sat on the sidelines for much of the PE lesson, playing table tennis when one of the girls took a break from gymnastics. She adored her special riding and swimming training out of school but there was less she could do at Isis. Izzie came over to join her.

Linette picked up the ball. 'My serve?'

Izzie nodded, looking about as excited by the game as a cat at the prospect of a bath. It was a shame because Linette loved a really competitive round of table tennis and Izzie was a dud with a bat.

She launched the ball in an easy serve, her thoughts circling back to her new friends. All was not as it should be. Roxy was the only one who seemed normal, though even she had a strange perspective on the world and a totally freaky relationship with robins if the way they flocked to her was any proof. Tiago seemed sweet but distant. And as for the parents, what foster agency would allow such people to look after goldfish, let alone three teenagers? It was as if they were aliens landed on a new planet trying to fit in.

Smashing the ping-pong ball past her opponent, Linette quickly dismissed extra-terrestrials as a working hypothesis. Way too Hollywood.

'Sorry, Izzie!' she called, having forgotten she was supposed to be conducting an easy rally. Izzie huffed and scooped up the ball to put it back into play.

Linette returned it with a flick. OK, so there had to be something else going on. The fostering system had let down Roxy, Tiago, and Rick, placing them with a couple who were not all present and correct in the brain department. But what could she do about it? Not that it was really her business. What made her heart ache was the way none of the three expected anything better. She felt very thankful for her own family.

The ball whistled past her ear.

'Wow, Linette, I got one by you!' Izzie marvelled.

'So you did. Well done you.' She'd better pay attention if she wasn't going to end up losing to Izzie of all people. Nevertheless, that wouldn't stop her taking note of what the foster kids did in case something more sinister was going on with the Magmells than English eccentricity.

'OK, so where do you want to start?' Roxy asked Rick as they got off the bus at the Martyrs' Memorial.

Rick's mind went blank. Shopping—oh, the horror. 'I don't know. This was your brilliant idea, not mine.'

Linette passed them by, a determined look on her face. She at least seemed to have a plan. 'Let's go to The Zone in the covered market. It's got some fantastic clothes.'

Rick fell in with Tiago behind the girls. 'Should I be worried?'

Tiago snorted. 'Oh yeah, Rick. You've handed yourself over to Roxy: remember her, the rebel pixie foundling? You'll be lucky if you don't end up shaved, pierced and tattooed by the end of the afternoon.'

Rick dug his hands further into his pockets, vowing that no one was coming near him with a needle or hair clippers while he still had strength to fight. 'You're enjoying this, aren't you?'

'Yep. But really I'm here for the professor. Oh and the pancakes as well. We've been promised pancakes back at Linette's if we cooperate.'

'Cooperate?'

'Yes. You have to buy a new outfit to stop you being sent back and I have to refrain from snide comments—those last are Linette's words, not mine. She's growing on me. Another girl that should've been born a Mage Fey.'

'Who's the other one?'

'Roxy, of course.'

Rick smiled to himself, looking forward to introducing Tiago to Professor Marmaduke. Tiago hadn't had much opportunity to mix with the real thing, the Mage Fey not being allowed near Dark Lore for fear of their rebellious ways. It had once been their kingdom's capital so Oberon made sure it was occupied by his most loyal commander.

The Zone was located down one of the narrow alleyways of the covered market, sandwiched between a delicatessen and a hat shop, a dark passage that smelt of old cabbage thanks to the greengrocer's by the entrance. Rick was not encouraged by the outside—all the advertising was scrawled in graffiti style writing and the clothes on the window display could do with a good deal of patching and mending.

'I like it!' enthused Roxy, gazing happily at the rumpled T-shirt and cut-offs on the mannequin.

'That's really not me,' said Rick.

'Exactly! That's why it is so good!' She pushed the narrow shop door, holding it open for Linette. The girls went inside and started pulling clothes off the hangers like people about to be evacuated with only a minute to pack their suitcase.

Tiago paused. 'You want me to get lost or come with you?'

'Come with me. Definitely. You wouldn't be so cruel as to leave me with them, would you?'

Tiago began singing some lyrics about the female of the species being more deadly than the male. Rick recognized it because Mr Gaddon, the PE teacher on the list for his Dark Folk blood, had it as his ringtone. Rick wondered what it was about girls that made even a part-ogre scared. He feared he was about to find out.

When the two boys entered the shop, Roxy bundled some clothes into Rick's arms.

'Start with these.' She pushed him towards the changing rooms.

Resigned to his fate, Rick hurriedly tried on the lurid garments she had picked out for him. Chains, rips, skulls: so not him. He presented himself for the girls' verdict. They gazed at him for a moment,

Linette chewing on her bottom lip, Roxy giggling, then they turned to consult each other.

'No. Not right,' Linette announced.

Phew.

'Well, I thought I'd start him on the extreme stuff to soften him up for something halfway decent,' explained Roxy.

The girls were manipulating him—and Rick didn't like it. It was bad enough agreeing to do this without them taking advantage. No matter: he knew how to turn the tables.

He turned in the mirror, standing straight to see the whole outfit. 'Oh, I don't know. Maybe this is exactly what I was looking for. The scorpion belt is a nice touch.'

He was pleased to see Roxy go pale. 'I'm not sure, Rick. Try something else before you decide.'

'No, no, you picked it out. I trust your judgement, Roxy. Let's go with this. You say it will go down well at school?'

Linette coughed. 'Well, it would undoubtedly be a real game changer. No one would look at you in the same way again.'

'Tiago?'

Tiago glanced up from the row of T-shirts he'd been checking out. 'Vile, Rick. Go for it.'

Rick turned back to the girls and gave them a beatific smile. 'That's settled then.'

Their horrified looks made up for the humiliation they were putting him through.

'Rick . . . ' Roxy squeezed her hands together. 'Please . . . '

He gave a bark of laughter. 'Joking! It's vile as Tiago says. I'm sacking you as my fashion adviser and employing him.' He grabbed the next set of clothes from Linette's lap. 'What he says goes, OK?'

Cowed by this near miss, the girls nodded their agreement. Linette's choice proved to be a much more acceptable collection of jeans, T-shirt, and jacket. Rick felt he could live with this. He had not spent much time in front of a mirror before but he could see that it did make him appear less formal and younger—thirteen rather than thirteen hundred. He stepped out from behind the curtain.

'Tiago?'

'They're OK,' he replied in an off-hand way.

'Then I'll get these.'

Roxy passed him a couple more shirts and another pair of the same style trousers. 'That should do for now.'

Loaded down with his new purchases, Rick walked beside Linette as they made the short journey to Exeter College.

'Satisfied?' he asked.

Linette pushed the chair up a kerb. 'Almost. Did Roxy explain there's also an attitude adjustment to go with the clothes?'

'You mean I have to slouch, swear and be rude to everyone?'

'I hope you won't go that far. Try toning down your natural politeness.'

'I'll see what I can do.' Being a teenager was way harder than he had thought it would be.

Linette's parents met them at the door to the Rector's House in the heart of Exeter College.

'Welcome, welcome!' Mrs Kwan, a slim, neat woman with shoulder-length dark hair, bubbled over with embarrassing enthusiasm just as Linette had predicted. 'I've got a table set on the lawn as it's such beautiful weather today.'

'It'll rain on Saturday,' muttered Tiago, scanning the sky.

Linette's dad, a middle-aged man with high forehead rimmed with brush-cut black hair, wasn't saying anything and his smile was a little strained. Then his shoulders jerked—and again.

'Sorry,' Mr Kwan said. 'Can't get rid of these hiccups.' He took a deep breath and held it.

Roxy frowned. 'You didn't by any chance meet a rather odd lady yesterday?'

Mr Kwan nodded, still holding his breath.

The three changelings quickly traded looks. Rick

was the most powerful, Tiago the most subtle, but Roxy knew the most about pixie curses. Silently, they gave her the task. Rick moved into distraction mode.

'Pleased to meet you, sir,' he said, extending a hand to Mr Kwan. 'I understand you are originally from the Far East?'

Mr and Mrs Kwan were instantly charmed by his manner. Mrs Kwan moved to her husband's side.

'That's right—I'll answer for him. Hong Kong. Do you know it?'

While Rick kept them talking about their old home, Roxy moved behind Mr Kwan and fished something out of her pocket. Quickly, she dropped it down the back of his neck.

Mr Kwan leapt as if she had just stuffed an ice cube down his collar. 'What the . . . !'

Linette was staring at Roxy aghast. 'You just put a *worm* down my dad's back!'

Mr Kwan pulled his shirt loose and shook out the wriggling creature. Roxy swiftly pocketed it.

'Old Irish remedy,' she lied. 'Guaranteed to get rid of hiccups. Has it worked?'

Rick recognized a bit of pixie magic attached to the worm—an undoing spell that had to make contact with skin. Unorthodox carrier though. He bit back a grin.

Protests dying on the tip of his tongue, Mr Kwan paused, waiting for a renewed spasm. When it didn't come, his shock turned to delight. 'Yes, yes, it worked.'

'Normally I use a key,' said Mrs Kwan, not entirely convinced.

'Really?' Roxy fidgeted, wondering how to change the subject. 'I'll have to remember that one.'

'What was that about tea on the lawn?' Tiago prompted, as if nothing weird had just happened. He gave a whistle and Bob trotted across the neatly mown quad towards them.

'Where did he come from?' asked Linette. 'He wasn't on the bus.'

'He had business in town,' Tiago replied as if this was perfectly reasonable. 'Can he stay for tea?'

Mrs Kwan rubbed her forehead. First worms, now dogs. She turned to Rick who so far had appeared the most normal of the bunch for once. 'Yes, tea. Let us go through to the garden.'

Rick fell in step with her. 'Thanks, Mrs Kwan, or should I call you professor?'

'Veronique, please. What do you usually like for your tea, Rick?'

Rick held the door open for her. 'I'm not so keen on crispy seaweed and custard, but otherwise I'm not fussy.'

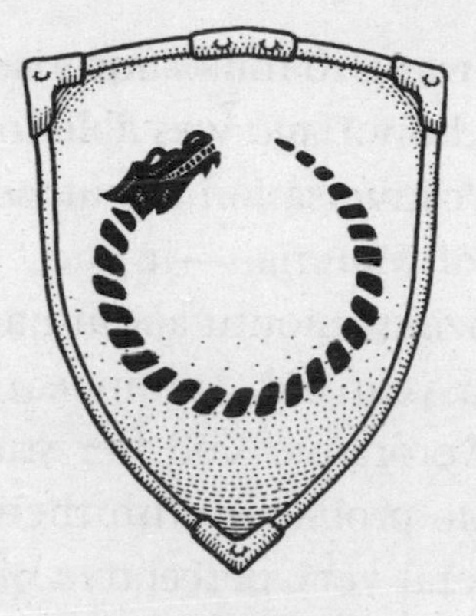

# Chapter 9

After the bumpy patch of the introductions, Linette's parents warmed to her three eccentric visitors and tea turned out to be an enjoyable affair. The Peking duck pancakes were greeted with rapturous praise. Rick in particular helped himself to as many as he could, wolfing them down as if he hadn't had a decent meal in weeks. Linette tried not to stare as Tiago fed Bob carefully assembled pancake rolls, complete with spring onions and Hoisin sauce, which the dog ate with surprising delicacy, enjoying every scrap. The more she watched Bob, the odder he seemed; his eyes were so expressive she was getting close to thinking he would one day open his mouth and talk.

His master was also full of surprises. Linette was astonished at how Tiago was able to keep up with her mother's conversation about her work in the Department of Materials—in fact, he seemed to know an amazing amount about nano technology for an eleven year old. He appeared very interested when Veronique said her students had recently run into problems with their experiments; he asked several very perceptive questions about what she thought had caused the fluctuations.

'I really don't know,' Veronique admitted. 'We had another problem last night when we were using the electron microscope. Normally you can see every atom—but yesterday, nothing! There's a doctorate waiting to be written to figure it out.' She smiled at Tiago. 'And when you're older, perhaps you'll be the one to do it. I've never met such a bright boy of your age. Indeed, you put the rest of us to shame: we've been so short of good ideas the last week or so.'

'If you show me your data, I could do that this evening if you like,' Tiago offered.

Veronique laughed lightly, treating this as a good jest, but Linette had a suspicion that Tiago had not been joking.

Rick got up from the table, stopping that particular conversation in its tracks. 'Would you mind very much if I excused Tiago and myself for a brief time? I would like to call on Professor Marmaduke and I want Tiago to meet him too.'

Linette's dad showed them to the door. 'Extraordinary the number of people the professor knows—who would have guessed you'd be a friend of his?'

'We just met recently. We won't be long.'

The departure of the boys was the signal for clearing the table. When the plates had been ferried into the kitchen, Linette took Roxy into her bedroom. It had a ramp leading from the French windows into the little patch of garden out the back where they had eaten.

'This is nice,' Roxy said with approval, gesturing to the Wedgwood blue walls and white trim. All Linette's posters were framed like proper paintings and hung from a picture rail—her parents had insisted as they were only lodgers in this historic house and she wasn't allowed to spoil it. She had won the battle replacing the posh brocade drapes with bright curtains to match her duvet. The only aspect they had not argued about were the shelves—there were many of them and Linette took great pleasure in filling them with her favourite books, French, Chinese, and English.

'Sit anywhere you like.' Linette manoeuvred the chair to the window. Roxy followed her and sat on the floor, leaning against the double doors. 'I'll park here.'

'Did it take you long to get used to a wheelchair?' asked Roxy.

'Certainly.' Linette grinned at Roxy's embarrassment when she realized what she had just asked. Linette wasn't the least bit offended by the question, far better than people tip-toeing around the issue. 'It is not my first choice of transport obviously. I can use crutches but I find them very fatiguing. I couldn't last a full day at school like that.'

Roxy ran her fingers through the long tassels of an Indian rug in reds and blues. 'How long have you been using it?'

'Since the accident. I was eight. We were in Hong Kong and someone jumped on me in the swimming pool. Stupid.'

'That . . . that's terrible.'

'Life is like that, no? You're fine one moment and then you're not.'

Roxy stared wistfully out of the window. 'I know.'

And Linette realized that, as an orphan, Roxy did understand. 'There are more of us with bad things happening in our lives than you would first think when you look at other kids at school. At least my problem is obvious for everyone to see. I get so angry about it at times I just have to scream—but it does no good. I can't change the past.' She paused, wondering if, by her answer, she'd earned the right to ask. 'So, how did you get to be in foster care?'

Roxy grimaced. 'Bad luck. I was abandoned by my parents when I was little.'

'Do you know if they are still alive?'

Roxy shook her head. 'No, long gone. I lived with some travellers for a bit then ended up at school with Rick and Tiago. This is our first experience of living in the community. How're we doing?'

'Ah. OK, I think.'

'That bad, hey? And we've been trying so hard.' Roxy found this very amusing, her humour feeding itself so she was soon helpless with giggles.

'You know, I don't understand you sometimes.'

Roxy wiped her eyes. 'It would be more remarkable if you did. We've had a strange life so far.'

'Have you other friends at your old school?'

'Some. But mainly you sort of survive there.'

'Wow, that's harsh.'

'Yeah.'

'You must feel lonely then.'

Roxy's smile faded and she hugged her knees. 'All the time,' she admitted hoarsely. 'You don't know how lucky you are—your family, friends. I feel so . . . so totally on my own. The boys do too, I expect.'

Linette reached out to touch her lightly on the shoulder. 'I know a little about that. Even with my family. I have friends in other countries but not in England. Not real friends. I have many people I chat to, but no one who'd really care if I turned up to school or not.'

Roxy rocked forwards and back. 'We'd care—the boys and I. We may be odd but we care—in our own way.'

'Thank you.'

'Just don't get too attached to us, will you, Linette? We probably won't be here long.'

'Why not?'

'Oh you know, things change when you're in the foster system.' Roxy knotted her hands together. 'Actually, Linette, I wanted to ask you something . . . about Professor Marmaduke. This might sound odd but have you heard if he's involved in any new groups being formed in the college? A place for special kind of friends, comrades-in-arms really? Knights?'

'What, here?'

Roxy nodded.

'You mean some kind of Dungeons and Dragons society? People who dress up at the weekend to play at being magical heroes?'

'Exactly!' Roxy had become very alert.

'I don't know—it seems to me unlikely. He's so old and, well, too feeble to go round waving a sword.'

'Still, I'd be interested, just to know.'

'I'll ask my father, but why do you want to find out?'

Roxy frowned. 'I suppose because I need to know what kind of man he is. Rick was really impressed by him.'

Linette could understand that Roxy might want to protect her foster brother but that didn't explain the weirdness of her question. 'Roxy, you're not making much sense, you know.'

'But you'll ask for me?'

Linette sighed. 'Naturally. That's what friends are for.'

Rick felt light-headed with anticipation as he steered Tiago and Bob to Professor Marmaduke's rooms. Tiago was about to meet one of the Mage Fey, a full blood.

He knocked on the heavy door just inside the stairwell.

Tiago slouched against the wall, hands dug into his pockets. 'How are we going to find out if he is involved, Rick?'

'We'll have to be careful. Let's take it one step at a time—see if he knows anything about a new Round Table. I'm backing my hunch he might be behind it.'

The door opened and Professor Marmaduke stood in the opening, a sheaf of papers in hand. Beyond him, two undergraduates sat either side of a little table.

'Elfric, my dear boy, you came!' The professor's eyes turned to Tiago. 'And you brought a friend—a *most* interesting friend.'

Rick realized they were interrupting a tutorial. 'Shall we come back later?'

'No, no, come in, come in. We were just sweeping up the crumbs of knowledge and trying to stuff them into our empty skulls, weren't we, ladies?'

The two girls looked rather offended but began gathering up their books and bags.

'Same time next week and do read the whole of *The Canterbury Tales* before you write your essay.' Marmaduke deftly ushered the students out of the door and brought in his guests. 'Ah, relief—they're gone! Neither of them are the slightest bit interested in anything before 1500—I quite despair.'

Tiago held out his hand. 'Santiago Dulac, sir.'

'Really? Well, well, who would have thought? I am pleased to meet any friend of Elfric, particularly a Mage.'

Bob trotted in and jumped up, demanding recognition.

'Ah! Your familiar! A very clever hound, I can tell that at one glance.' Marmaduke gave Bob a

Hobnob which the dog gulped down enthusiastically. 'Make yourself at home.' The professor bustled about the room to find something for them to drink. He returned with cherryade that must have gone flat in 1980. 'Here you are, boys.' Marmaduke handed over the glasses and gestured to them to take the seats vacated by the students. 'Lovely, lovely.'

Rick risked a sip of the cherryade then put it to one side. Tiago was still staring at the professor, taking in his first meeting with a full blood Mage Fey.

Bob hopped up on to the professor's lap, circled, then sat down for a snooze. There was a growl and a scratch at the door that led further into the apartment.

'Oh dear, Gordon is jealous,' remarked Marmaduke.

'Gordon?'

'My dog. Very possessive. Must be able to see through doors—or at least he smells when his territory has been invaded. Shut up, Gordon!'

With a yelp and a final assault on the door, the noise of the dog faded.

'I expect he will take his anger out on my slippers again.' His silver eyes twinkled with amusement.

'Rick told me that you're a Mage Fey,' said Tiago.

'Full blood and proud of it.' Marmaduke nodded, enjoying the boy's admiration. 'And I see you must be half blood—mother's or father's side?'

'Father.'

'That was my guess.' Marmaduke held his hand out, palm upwards, and let a spell gather in the hollow. A little chocolate coin appeared. 'Go on, take it. My little reward for you, my first Mage visitor in centuries.'

Tiago cautiously took the present, unwrapped it and bit down. 'It's real! How did you do that?'

The professor shrugged as if it were of no account. 'A little summoning magic; I had them in the larder. I save the old biscuits for the humans.'

'Can you teach me? I can't bring things unless I can see them.'

'I can teach you that and much more. From what Elfric here told me, you've been kept back by your instructors at Dark Lore. It sounds to me as if Oberon is scared of your abilities. He probably sees you changelings as potential rebels.'

'I thought he saw us as tools for him to use,' said Rick. 'But I haven't had a chance to tell Tiago what you told me yet—about the changeling programme.'

'Tell me what?' Tiago crumpled up the gold paper and lobbed it in the bin.

'I'll explain later—with Roxy. If that's OK, sir?'

'Of course, we've far more interesting things to discuss than Oberon.' Marmaduke wrinkled his nose as if he smelt a bad odour when he mentioned the king's name. 'You never said, Elfric, why exactly are you here? I must admit that has been on my mind since we met yesterday. Why is Oberon risking the balance by sending you into the world when your changeling is still here?'

'Risking the balance?'

'Yes, of course. I am your swap. You and I shouldn't even be in the same room—the universe could start shaking itself apart.' The professor's lips curved in a wry smile.

'I was going to ask Tiago about that—about the balance.'

'You were exchanged for Rick, sir?' asked Tiago.

'That's right.'

'Amazing, but I suppose it explains how you met.'

'Quite so.' The professor nodded his appreciation of Tiago's intelligence.

Rick didn't get it. 'What do you mean?'

'When two objects are exchanged across the divide, they are linked magically.' Tiago illustrated with his fists. 'You are drawn to each other like magnets even if you aren't aware of it.'

'I felt you come over,' the professor admitted. 'I was looking for you.'

'Why? To warn me to go back?'

'He's pulling your leg, Rick, about the shaking universe thing,' Tiago said quickly. 'The two of you could upset the balance in theory, but it's not very likely. The universe can put up with a few anomalies for a while—like our team being here on our mission; but you shouldn't, you know, move in or anything. That would be asking for trouble.'

That was all right then—not.

'What about you? Don't you have the same effect?' Rick asked Tiago.

'Nope. Half-Fey bloods like me can live in both worlds, just as long as we don't all choose to live in one or the other. That would be like the passengers all rushing to one side of a life raft—not a good idea.'

'Who keeps count?'

'The king and queen, I guess.'

The professor snorted. 'You are crediting them with far more intelligence than they possess. I doubt Fey bureaucracy runs to keeping accurate records on you Fey mixed bloods, not like under the old Mage king when he ran Avalon. You only get reported to them when someone stumbles over you or when they sell you out for their own reasons. They try and track us full bloods as a condition of our parole in this world, but to be frank, it's child's play to get lost.'

That explained how Marmaduke had been missed off the list.

'There's a reward posted for this kind of information,' continued the professor,'—or at least there was when I was last in Avalon. Since then, I've met many living in the human world undercover. I'd guess the balance has shifted to Earth as it is far easier to live freely here than under Oberon's thumb.'

'So would you welcome a change in . . . er . . . leadership in Avalon then?' Rick asked carefully.

'Of course! Can't wait to see that rogue tipped off his throne. But it's impossible to imagine anyone succeeding. After all, I got sent here for making an attempt centuries ago; I learnt my lesson and intend to keep a very low profile.'

'And you've not heard of anyone setting up a plot—here in Oxford?'

'What's this? Do tell.' Marmaduke leant forward with a mischievous twinkle in his eyes.

'We don't know exactly how it is being done, but it might be connected to the technology of the Round Table.'

'Good lord. I thought we'd heard the last of that in the fifth century!'

'So you've not heard any rumours?'

'Not a whisper. Whoever they are, they must be fiendishly clever to keep it a secret from me.'

'What about the lady from the museum?'

'Dr Ventikos?' Marmaduke started laughing. 'She only knows her pots. Still, I'll ask her if she is aware of anything going on. She keeps up with more exiles from Avalon than I do. I've rather let myself fall out of all the networks, preferring to fly under the radar as far as Oberon's informers are concerned. Why do you want to know about this plot? I hope you've more sense than to work for Oberon to defeat it?'

That was a bit complicated, thanks to the re-adjustment Rick was making to his new knowledge. 'We just don't want Avalon or Earth to be damaged in any power struggle. I'd like to talk to the people involved, point out the dangers. If humans are behind it, it's possible they might not know.'

'Humans? Pah! Only Merlin ever managed to steal the power for the Table, and he was half-Fey. If you've been sent to look for a human plot, someone is wasting your time.'

'Thanks. That's helpful. We were thinking that maybe a Fey might be at the centre but with humans involved—like the knights of the Round Table were human.'

'I suppose it is possible. But, no offence, I wouldn't want to work with humans if I were the guilty party—far too fragile. What do you think of the humans, Santiago?'

'They're OK. Most of the time.'

'There. Damned with faint praise. Poor Santiago: you're wasted at Dark Lore.'

Rick didn't like the turn the conversation had taken and felt he had pressed the professor as far as he reasonably could about the plot. His eyes were drawn to the wall in front of him, on which hung an ugly landscape of horse and hounds chasing some poor fox across a muddy field. The picture shimmered, hunting party vanishing into the mist and emerging again.

'So you spotted my glamour spell, have you?' The professor waved his hand and the painting and the rest of the room disappeared, being replaced by an Aladdin's cave of curiosities. 'You can cast them over objects as well as yourself, did you know that?'

'Yes, I did.' Rick was barely thinking of what he was saying, so caught up was he in the amazing transformation that had come over the room. Gone was the boring study of a fusty old professor, in its place was a magician's workroom: shelves of heavy books, piles of parchment, and curiosities lodged on every surface like a flock of exotic birds come down to rest. Weapons from all over the world hung on one wall: Crusader broadsword, Tartar bow, Samurai sword, Italian duelling pistols, Lee Enfield rifle and many more that Rick had not yet met in his training.

'That's quite a collection,' said Rick.

The professor spun the chamber in a Colt revolver, cocked and fired at the window. The gun clicked but there was no explosion. 'Unloaded, of course. I do like my little trophies. History in the making—that's what they are. I try to pop in on all empires at their rise and fall—so terribly fascinating. I haven't spent all my time sitting in this study, you know.'

Tiago picked up an hourglass on the table beside him and shook it.

'I wouldn't do that, if I were you—oh dear, too late!' The professor smiled as a simulacrum of him, slightly faded, entered the room and began the tutorial again with the two girls.

'Is there any way of stopping it?' Rick asked as he leapt up to prevent the shadow-student sitting in his lap.

'Not easily. You can't mess around too much with time without causing far worse problems.' The three evacuated to the far side of the room while the tutorial carried on unaware of their presence. 'Shame it was not one of my best—neither girl had anything interesting to say.' The voices burbled on as they read extracts of their essays at the shadow-professor's request. 'I think we have about a half hour's worth, I'm afraid. Bit like being forced to sit through someone else's holiday snaps, eh?'

Rick had learned his lesson and did not touch anything, but he couldn't stop himself from looking. The objects were beautifully made from expensive materials—gold, silver, and other metals he could not identify at a glance. It was Fey technology at its very best, refined and improved by contact with Earth ideas. One particularly striking curio appeared to be fashioned out of marble, carved in a spiral like the inside of a nautilus shell.

Marmaduke stroked the marble with no bad effects. 'You like this one?'

Rick nodded and tentatively reached out to touch the white surface. It was cold, a little damp as if dew had collected on it. He couldn't sense any magic.

'Organized on the Golden Ratio. Can you tell me what that is?'

Rick dredged up his last number theory class. 'A special formula that works out to produce very harmonious patterns, like this shell, as each segment gets bigger in proportion to what went before.'

'As in flower petals, arrangement of leaves, Oberon's castle, Leonardo da Vinci's paintings (he was part Mage, you know). It is the secret sequence behind everything, the basic code used in many of our spells.'

Tiago had wandered into the middle of the tutorial, ignored by the three shadows who were now earnestly discussing *The Anglo-Saxon Chronicle*. 'What's this?' He pointed to a brass face stuck on the wall where the painting had been. It was shaped like an old man with a long beard, eyes shut in repose. Rick thought it could do with a good polish.

'Ah, another favourite: my talking head.' Marmaduke clapped his hands and the eyes sprang open, revealing black stone pupils with no irises.

'What do you want, Mage?' snarled the head.

'Now, now, play nicely,' chided the professor, not at all put out by the rude tone of his wall hanging. 'I have some friends visiting and they asked after you.'

'Tell them to get lost.'

'What's wrong with him?' Rick whispered to Tiago.

'He's probably fed up with hanging there. Can't be very exciting if he has to sit through all those tutorials year after year.' Tiago turned to the head. 'Hey, Mr Bronze Face, what do you do?'

It clamped its lips together.

'Remember your founding spell,' warned the professor. 'You have to answer when asked.'

The eyes glared. 'What do you mean, *what do I do*?' sneered the face. 'I speak wisdom but you are an imbecile so wouldn't like to hear it.'

'OK, pretend I'm not an imbecile for a moment. Will you tell me something I need to know to solve our quest?' bargained Tiago, warming to the challenge.

The face closed his eyes again with an aggrieved expression. 'Not telling. You've used your question.'

'As a favour to me,' said Professor Marmaduke. 'He's half Mage—and we've never had one of those here before.'

'All right, all right.' The face furrowed its brow, searching for something to say. 'Beware red socks. They are unlucky for you.'

Tiago grinned. 'Cool. Almost completely useless and there I was thinking you'd help us. Thanks. You ask him something, Rick.' He elbowed Rick in the ribs. Rick wasn't sure he wanted to play this game; the face wasn't exactly a friend. He didn't find its attitude as amusing as Tiago did.

'OK, what should I know?'

The face hooted. 'How long have you got, changeling? We could be here until the end of the century if I had to answer that. And you, the only one who can change the fate of Avalon—bah!'

Marmaduke whistled, eyes resting on Rick with renewed interest. 'Is he indeed?'

'Not saying no more, not to you. Mage Feys are always defeated by their arrogant belief in the intelligence of their own species, as I've told you. You've had your question long ago and wasted it.

The human warrior here will do the same, just you wait and see.'

Rick scowled, not amused by the taunt. 'Fine.' He tried to think of a clever question that would not allow the face to duck giving him a useful answer. 'Will you tell me one *essential* thing to help our quest with the Round Table—not rubbish about socks?'

The black eyes bored into him, expression solemn. 'Beware: one of you changelings will meet with disaster if you enter the Fey power ring.'

'Thanks, that's cheery. Does he make a habit of spreading such words of comfort, professor?'

Marmaduke didn't seem that bothered by the pronouncement. 'Oh, always. It is how he gets his revenge on us all. He's told me I'm going to die many times, so I wouldn't put much store by it. Note he didn't say if you'd change Avalon for the better—he could mean you are its destroyer. Ah well, such is the mystery of foretelling. You can go back to sleep now, Brazen Face.'

The shadow tutorial had ended and Rick was alarmed to see himself enter with Tiago in tow. Perhaps now would be a good time to simplify things by really leaving.

'Thanks for showing us your stuff, professor.'

'My pleasure, dear boy, my pleasure. Now you know where I am, do come back any time. I don't go far these days even if I'm not in my rooms; the porters should know where to find me. I'll keep my ear to the ground about you know what.'

Pleased to have secured this commitment, Rick shook the professor's hand. 'We'll be back very soon then—tomorrow if that's OK?'

'Come on, Bob.' Tiago whistled to the dog who had eerily managed to curl up in his shadow self on the same chair where the shadow professor sat.

'See you soon then.' The professor waved, restoring the glamour so that the study returned to its staid Oxford image.

As Rick closed the door, he heard the professor's dog explode in another tirade of barking from deep within the apartment.

# Chapter 10

When the three of them left Linette's, Rick knew it was time to tell Roxy and Tiago the truth about the changeling programme. With no Dark Folk or humans to overhear, there was no excuse to delay.

'Let's not head back immediately,' he suggested. 'Let's stay in town. I've got something I want to tell you both.'

'What's this? Righteous Rick thinking of not reporting in on time?' laughed Roxy. 'That attitude adjustment already started?'

'You bet,' he replied with a smile. She didn't know the half of it. 'I can't see either Magmell or Shreddie caring what time we come in, can you?'

'True. I want to hear what your professor had to say. So where shall we go?' Roxy zipped up her jacket. 'It's getting dark.'

Rick decided that a big open space was necessary for this revelation in case either of them lost it and let off some magical fireworks. 'How about the University Parks? I think they're down that street.'

Tiago whistled to Bob. 'Sweet. He'll show us the way.'

Bob trotted on ahead, stubby tail erect like a tour guide's umbrella; checking they were keeping up, he paused at the traffic lights before herding them across the road when the green man shone. He led them past the tower of the Natural History Museum and shiny windowed science labs to the gates leading into the park. Made of black wrought-iron furled like tendrils, the gates were firmly closed. Splendid lawns spread out behind them like a king's private gardens.

'It's well after dusk,' said Roxy peering at the sign on the noticeboard, 'they've locked up for the night.'

'So?' Tiago picked Bob up and dropped him over the fence.

'Um, Tiago, should you be doing that?' Rick asked.

'Nope.' Tiago hopped over and did a cartwheel on the grass.

It went against the grain to disobey a regulation but Rick forced himself to follow Tiago over the railings.

Once on the ground, he turned back to the street. 'Need a hand, Roxy?'

'Are you joking?' She vaulted the five-foot fence with ease.

'Let's head for that building.' Rick pointed to the large cricket pavilion in the middle of the playing fields.

'Won't someone be living in it?' Roxy asked, wiping her hands on her leggings.

'No. According to the park guide,' Rick waved a leaflet he'd picked up at the entrance, 'it's only used when they play cricket. I don't suppose they show that sport on TV at Dark Lore, do they?'

'I know what cricket is—white clothes, bats, ball—yeah, it's like very, very slow baseball.' She headed across the lawns for the immaculate pitch. 'So what's the house thing for?'

'Tea.'

'What?'

He jogged to catch up with her. 'That is why cricket is so much better than baseball. Mr Gaddon told me in PE today that it is the only sport that stops for tea—how civilized is that? Humans have got something right.'

Bob yipped an agreement.

'Nutters,' muttered Roxy.

'My kind of nutters,' added Rick. 'Imaginative ones who make up excellent games where no one gets hurt and they serve cake—unlike Troll wrestling or dragon baiting.'

'That's the first really positive thing I've ever heard you say about human customs, Rick. What about "humans are the enemy"?' She obviously hadn't noticed his change in attitude; that might be a good thing because it probably meant their Fey handlers were ignorant of his altered loyalties too. 'I kind of like it here, don't you?' mused Roxy. 'It's way better than I was led to believe at Dark Lore. I feel . . . I feel at home.'

'I know.' That was the problem, wasn't it? They had been trained to forget they were humans, despise everything about them, and now they were remembering their roots. Avalon was incredibly beautiful, full of wonders and beings with amazing powers, but what was that worth if they had not the first idea about loyalty, love, and laughter? Rick was coming to believe that Fey spells were just tricks compared to the amazing magic of human relationships. He'd swap every scintilla of power he had to have his parents back.

The four of them sat on the steps up to the pavilion veranda. It was quiet here. Traffic rumbled away in the distance; leaves rustled; the stars stretched overhead, faint pinpricks of light in the orange-tinged sky. Shadows darkened under the trees, stretching out to meet the night. Rick knew he had no more excuses for delay.

'OK, guys, I've got something I want to say. I . . . look, it's all a bit complicated.'

Roxy smiled. 'Just spit it out, why don't you?'

'The professor was really helpful about the Round Table plot,' Tiago chipped in, assuming this was what Rick was about to say. 'I don't think he is involved in any of it, but he says he'll find out if any of the Fey he knows are scheming.'

'Yeah, he's dropped down the suspect list but, actually, Tiago, it's not about him—it's about what he told me the first time we met.' Rick scrubbed his hands through his hair. 'Look, there's only one way to say this. Roxy, Tiago, we weren't given away, we were stolen. The Fey lied to us.'

'What!' Roxy leapt to her feet. 'No, no, that's not true—my parents sold me. I was bought for a sack of gold.'

'No, you weren't. That's a fib to make you accept what happened more easily. Oberon has this exile programme running for the Dark Folk that he wants out of Avalon. The deal is they get to live here—instead of execution I suppose. The point is—our families were not volunteers—they were ignorant victims.'

'But that's . . . that's outrageous!' Roxy sank onto the step and hugged her knees. 'How? And why, for hob's sake?'

'Yeah, it totally stinks. It was never about us being rescued but always about Oberon and his twisted ways of dealing with opposition. As for why, the exchange is for maintaining the balance between matter in both worlds—we are like ballast to keep the ship steady, taken over to Avalon to make up for the exile who is sent here. It's OK to take a few over but if lots of people start moving across, you have to compensate by taking back. Tiago says it makes a link between the changelings—that was why I met up with the professor. You could find yours if you put your mind to it.'

'I . . . I . . . ' Roxy shook her head, her eyes filled with a lost expression.

'I know, Roxy. I've changed my mind about a lot of things since yesterday. If anyone is our enemy, it's Oberon and his people, not the humans. It casts our mission in a whole new light.'

'You can say that again!'

'It opens up the possibility we might want to support the plot, not expose it. Tiago, I don't know what this means for you as you're not strictly a changeling, but I thought you should know.'

The half-Fey boy shredded a blade of grass. 'But I've always known. Didn't you notice we were in a prison? Call it a training camp if you like, but it had bars around it.'

Shocked, Rick turned to look at him. Tiago had known and never said anything! How could he live with the human changelings and not mention this crucial fact about their lives? But then Tiago had known about the connection; Rick should have realized Tiago was aware of the truth when he wasn't surprised that the professor was Rick's swap.

'Why didn't you tell us?' Roxy asked fiercely. She got to her feet, bristling with fury. 'Troll snot, the number of times I've cursed my parents for selling me and . . . and they were innocent.' Her voice cracked. 'I . . . I want to kick something.' Sparks were shooting from her fingers, her eyes glowing with an intense green light as the magic boiled inside her. 'When I get my hands on Oberon, I'll . . . I'll . . . '

Tiago shrugged. 'You'll what? Say "you're a very bad king"? There's nothing any of you could do so I didn't see the point of rubbing it in. We're like animals in a zoo to the Dark Folk. No point howling about the cage if you can ignore it.'

'There is if you can break out.' Rick put an arm around Roxy's shoulders and pulled her to sit beside him. 'Easy now. You don't want to let that magic out without channelling it properly.'

She was shaking but tried hard to clamp down on her temper. An angry magic wielder was a danger to herself and everyone around her. 'I'm OK. Really. Or I will be. Do you think they know—Shreddie and Magmell?'

'If Tiago knew, then I guess they do.'

She rounded on Tiago again. 'I still can't believe you've lived with us all these years and never said anything!'

'Yeah, well, I didn't, so what?' Tiago edged away, picking up Bob for an unnecessary paw inspection.

'I'm not sure I can forgive you for that.' Roxy's tone was serious now, which made it worse as it wasn't temper speaking any longer. 'You robbed me of years of loving my parents. I've hated them for so long—been all twisted up inside—I felt completely worthless.' Tears shone in her eyes. 'You understand, don't you, Rick?'

He understood all too well. 'Yes, but it's not Tiago's fault, Roxy.'

'But by not telling us, he chose their side.'

Tiago got up and walked away, shoulders hunched, hands dug into pockets. Bob whined and followed.

'I'm not sure that he did.' Rick felt a tightening at the back of his own throat but he refused to cry. He never cried. Warriors didn't. 'He's trapped too—neither one thing nor another. At least we know we're fully human. Perhaps he thought we'd turn on him if he told us what the Dark Folk had done—turn on him for the part of him that's from them.'

Roxy rubbed the heel of her hand over her cheeks. 'That's dumb.'

'Is it? Didn't you just tell him he had to have sided with them? He might've had another explanation, but you leapt to that conclusion because you know he's part-Mage.'

'Dragon dung, I hate it when you're right.' She took a deep breath and then called, 'Hey, Tiago! Come back!' He stopped walking but didn't turn. 'I'm sorry for jumping down your throat like that. Bad moment for me, OK? Just give me a little time to process all this, please? Rick's had longer so he's the reasonable one just now. You can at least talk to him.'

Tiago slowly faced them, the gleam returning to his silver eyes. 'You think *Rick's* reasonable?' He pretended to search the sky. The moon had risen; it was already midnight. 'Bob, can you see any pigs up there?'

But for once Bob was not listening. He gave a yelp and took a leap into Tiago's arms, knocking him backwards.

'What the nix!' exclaimed Tiago.

Roxy shrieked as robins zoomed from their roosts and mobbed her—not attacking, Rick realized, but seeking shelter.

The ground rumbled and then seemed to wave as if a giant worm was working its way under the cricket pitch. The trees shook, petals from the blossom on the hawthorns falling in drifts like icing sugar. The grass split like bread crust, torn apart by the forces underneath.

'Quick! Get away from the building!' shouted Rick, dragging Roxy off the steps.

A stronger quake hit. The roof of the pavilion snapped in the centre, the rafters collapsing inwards. Glass shattered. They threw themselves clear, ending up in the middle of the pitch.

Then it stopped. The earth quieted, the trees stopped trembling, and stillness returned to the park.

'What was that?' Rick rubbed grit from his eyes.

Tiago hugged Bob then put him down. 'An earthquake.'

'Caused by the ring?'

'I guess so. But it seems to have passed.'

Roxy coaxed the robins out of her hair where they had huddled, sending them back to their night roosts. 'That was really, really scary. Like the attack on Dark Lore but on this side.'

Rick's head shot up as he looked back towards the Radcliffe Camera. 'They must be attacking the

Fey ring again. Hurry—we might catch them red-handed.'

When the earth tremor struck Linette had just fallen asleep—that was until she found herself sprawled on the floor. She narrowly missed being knocked out by a framed poster that fell on to the very spot where she had been lying but a second before. The house was creaking and groaning; ornaments leaping off shelves like lemmings and cutlery rattling in drawers in crazy sleigh bells cacophony. Cracks ate up the wall and across the ceiling. Plaster collapsed in one corner, releasing a cloud of choking dust. The bookshelf by her bed swayed then toppled forward on a path to crush her. She pulled herself half under the bed. The shelf fell on the mattress trapping her in the little crawling space on the floor.

Linette screamed for help.

No one came.

A stronger earthquake arrived instead.

The house split apart easily like an orange being segmented. Buried under her bed, Linette couldn't see; she could only hear the crash of masonry and her own screams. It seemed to go on for ever, but then, it stopped.

*'Maman,* Dad! Where are you? Say something!' Her head was hurting—the earthquake might be over but it felt as if all her thoughts and ideas were being sucked out of her, like water going down a plughole.

*OK, Linette, think,* she told herself. *They could be hurt. You have to get to them.* The problem was she couldn't work out a way of extricating herself from under the bed. Not that it was impossible, but her brain had stopped working, like a computer when it freezes and no amount of thumping the escape key will start it again.

Ten minutes of terror must have passed when she heard scuffling near her.

'Under here! I'm under here!'

A wet snout pushed itself into her hand. Bob.

'Just a second, Linette. We'll get you out.' There was a muttering and a flash of strange green light. The bricks and fragments of glass were shifting—how she could not see. Weight lifted off her shoulders and then there was Rick heaving the bookshelf out of the way. He reached down and touched her forehead.

'Are you OK? Any injuries?'

She had little lower body sensation at the best of times but now she could not bear to look. 'I don't know.' Rick pushed aside a scattering of books and bedclothes. 'Are . . . are my legs still there?'

He gave her a sympathetic glance. 'Yes, all present and correct.' He ran his hands over her spine and arms, a quick check for any problems. 'You seem fine. I'll lift you out of there.' Without waiting, he scooped her up. She knew she was no heavyweight, but still she was impressed that he could pick her up with no sign of effort.

Then she saw her room—what was left of it. It looked like London in the Blitz. 'Oh my.' She swallowed. No point crying. What mattered was whether anyone was hurt. 'My parents?'

'They're OK. Bob located them. Tiago and Roxy are just getting them out now.' He took her into the garden, which was oddly unchanged while around it familiar parts of old Oxford had collapsed. He eased her down onto the bench under the pear tree. Roxy emerged from behind a heap of rubble that had been the dining room, leading her mum and dad. They looked as shocked as Linette felt, eyes wide and clueless.

Tiago popped his head round the door that had somehow hung on in the kitchen. 'Electricity is cut. Gas off too. We've water though as I've found a bottle that didn't smash. I'll get you all a drink to wash the dust away.'

Rick returned to the remains of her bedroom. Another flash of green light and he reappeared with her wheelchair. One wheel was wonky but he gave it a kick and it seemed to repair itself.

Roxy towed Linette's parents away from the wreckage. 'Come on, Mrs Kwan, Mr Kwan—the dust is so thick we can barely breathe in there.'

'I'm sorry, *ma petite,* I just can't . . . can't think . . . ' Linette's mum rubbed her temples. 'My head feels fuzzy.'

'Probably just the shock. Not every day you get caught up in a quake.' Rick heaved the chair over the debris. 'Your chariot, my lady.'

'Thanks, er . . . ' Linette gawped, unable to string two thoughts together. She noticed that Roxy and Rick were whispering.

'Um . . . Linette, just want to check on that shock thing,' Roxy said with an overly bright smile. 'Who gave us the theory of relativity?'

'No idea. Donald Duck.' Why ask stupid questions in the middle of an emergency?

'What's ten plus ten?'

Linette knew the answer should be obvious but at the moment she couldn't think her way out of a paper bag. 'Do we have to talk about this now?' She flicked the dirt off her lap.

'Mrs Kwan, do you know?' Roxy persisted.

'No idea.' Veronique buried her head against her husband's chest. 'Nathaniel, shouldn't you be doing something?'

Linette's dad looked ghostly as he too was covered in a layer of plaster, his normally tidy black hair gone white. 'Yes . . . yes . . . but what?'

'I think, sir, you might want to go and check on the students?' Rick prompted gently.

He snapped to attention. 'Yes, of course! How could I have forgotten? Stay here until I give the all clear.' He suddenly seemed charged with energy, his confusion lifting.

'Linette, what's ten plus ten,' asked Roxy in a low voice.

'Twenty of course!' Why was Roxy asking these foolish questions?

'Who gave us the theory of relativity?'

'Einstein. But what's that got to do with anything?'

Roxy sighed with relief. 'I think the ring is working properly again,' she told Rick.

'What ring?' Linette asked.

Roxy bit her lip. 'Um . . . '

'She meant your thoughts—you know, the brain connections. Shock messes with them.' Tiago appeared beside her with three glasses of water on a tray. Linette wondered where he had managed to find unbroken ones; probably the same place as the bottle of water but that seemed a miracle when she saw the state of the house. He handed her a drink. 'Have some. It'll clear your throat.'

Linette gulped the water. It did help but only a bath or shower would get rid of the plaster stuck in her hair. 'Why are you here and not at home?'

'Bob took us for a walk in the park.'

'Won't your foster parents worry?'

'No, not really,' Roxy replied. 'They know we're together. Mrs Kwan, is there a blanket we could fetch for you both? I think the back of your house got hit the worst, the front half is still standing.' She wrinkled her nose. 'Sort of.'

'In our bedroom but you're not going back in there!' Veronique said shrilly. 'It's a death trap.'

'Don't worry about me—I've no intention of entering. Bob, can you do it?' The dog barked once, scurried away. 'He can get places safely humans can't.'

Linette didn't know what to say. How could this have happened? Oxford was the most stable place in the universe: it did not have earthquakes!

Bob returned quickly dragging a quilt.

'Did you see that?' Veronique muttered.

Linette was learning not to be too surprised by anything Tiago's pet did. 'Yes. He is the best trained animal I've ever met.'

Roxy tucked the cover over Linette and her mother. 'Perhaps you'd better stay out here until you've got the all clear to go inside.'

'And we've got to get going. We should check on the professor,' added Rick. 'Bob, can you do that too?'

The dog bounded off immediately.

Linette was reluctant to see them leave. They'd seemed to be the only ones who had kept their heads during the initial panic. 'Thank you. I was fortunate you were close by or I'd still be trapped.'

Roxy gave her a hug. 'We were happy to help.'

Bob reported that, according to the robins who lived on that side of the quad, the professor had gone out to dine in another college and his rooms had not been badly hit. Taking advantage of the confusion, Rick, Roxy, and Tiago quickly searched the college, the Bodleian quad and the area around the Radcliffe Camera, hoping to find the entrance to the Fey ring and spot who it was interfering with the power but could see no sign of anyone obviously suspicious. There were too many students huddled in evacuation areas, coats over pyjamas; if the plotters had already emerged they could have mingled with the crowds.

'It's no good; we're too late,' admitted Rick. 'We spent too long at the Kwans.'

'We could hardly leave them buried under the rubble,' said Roxy.

'Course not but still, it's really frustrating. The plotters are here—right under our noses: why can't we find them?'

Giving up for the night, they decided to head back to Kidlington. It was a long walk home but there was no chance of catching a bus or taxi as all the drivers were busy helping with the crisis. After the initial paralysis that had frozen the emergency services and seen them driving round in circles, crews were back on track doing their job.

Roxy pointed at the fire engine parked outside the college; fire fighters were dealing with two students trapped on a window ledge. 'Thank goodness they've shaken off the mental blackout. It was so scary, wasn't it—Linette and her parents not being able to work out what to do? I suppose I hadn't really believed the link between human imagination and Fey power before but now I've seen it.'

Rick shuddered. 'I didn't think what happens this side if the power is cut to Avalon, but of course they suffer here too. If we don't carry on with our quest, they're basically stuffed along with us. Human civilization will stop—they'll be surrounded by books and machines they no longer understand.'

'But you've missed something.' Tiago kicked a stone off the pavement. 'Isn't it odd that you were fine? You could do those sums, yeah? Tag Einstein as the relativity guy? I know I could—but then I'm half-Mage.'

'And we're not.' Roxy finished the thought for him. 'Any clue why?'

'You're probably inoculated against the disruption because you've lived in Avalon. Changelings might end up as the only humans who can still think if the rings go down worldwide.'

'But why then would someone set up a new Round Table and risk all that?' asked Roxy.

'Bit extreme, isn't it?' agreed Rick. 'I don't think the old one under Merlin had that side-effect. He must have worked out a way to steal power from the Fey and keep the imagination flowing in as human progress didn't grind to a halt in the fifth century.'

'There were a few bumps along the way though—end of the Roman Empire, rise of the barbarians,' Tiago pointed out. 'Might have been him then and he is still unaccounted for.'

'But why risk it? He's been hiding for over a millennium.'

Tiago shrugged and leapfrogged a pillar-box that had pitched to one side. Huge parts of Oxford were nothing more than rubble, but fortunately it looked as if it was the shops rather than the residential areas that had been worst hit. Fires licked away at piles of paper, magazines, books and clothing heaped in Cornmarket. Roxy had sent a robin to check for anyone who might be trapped but so far there had been no distress calls and the emergency services were doing a good job reaching those who needed help.

'Surely it would be suicidal of humans to set one up if they choke off Fey power to this world.' Roxy buttoned her jacket up against a chill breeze and the swirling dust.

'But what if they don't understand what they're doing—dabbling in Round Table magic without having a clue of what they are tapping into?' Rick suggested.

'That sounds possible. Give someone a box of matches and they're gonna have a go even if they live in a paper house.'

'The professor didn't think humans had the intelligence to be behind it.' Tiago took a little run and vaulted a car, setting off the alarm. It joined the chorus of wailing sirens already splitting the night sky.

'Are you going to keep doing that?' grumbled Roxy. 'It's annoying.'

'Why walk in a straight line when you can take another path?'

'Duh. Because it's more normal, maybe?'

Tiago grinned. 'For a human. Not for one of the Mage Fey. We like the twisty-twisty stuff. Natural tricksters.'

Roxy threw her hands in the air. 'I give up. Rick, what are you doing?'

He'd been using their little bickering session to root through a skip on the side of the road. He pulled out a piece of tattered carpet patterned with faded space rockets. 'Thought we'd find a quicker way home.'

'You're not . . . ?' She began to smile.

'Yeah, I am.'

'That is cooler than cool.' Tiago did a cartwheel and walked on his hands. 'We get to fly.'

Rick muttered a hover spell. The carpet shivered and then rose three inches off the pavement. 'It was something I read about once. Climb aboard the magic carpet, folks. Next stop, home.'

'Won't someone see?' Roxy stepped on, swaying a little as she got her balance. They'd already used lifting spells to free the Kwans but this seemed more blatant somehow.

'I'll handle that,' volunteered Tiago, producing a clever little glamour that turned the carpet into a wisp of fog.

The carpet shot off into the dark, Bob woofing with excitement at the front.

'Barking fog,' laughed Roxy. 'I like it.'

# Chapter 11

When Linette woke, she had a brief moment wondering if it had all been some bizarre dream until she realized where she was. She didn't recognize the room; the last thing she remembered was falling asleep outside. Her dad must have carried her indoors and put her in the guest room of the college for the rest of the night. She swung her legs out of the bed and grabbed the chair that someone thoughtfully had put on hand.

'*Maman*, what's happening?' she called, making her way to the door.

A clock nearby struck nine—she was very late for school. Then again, perhaps school was closed?

With half of Oxford in ruins, surely normal life was suspended?

'*Maman!*' she called again.

Her mother hurried out of the room next door, tying her robe closed. 'Linette, we're here. You're safe.'

'How is everyone?'

Veronique ran her fingers through her hair, sweeping it off her face. 'A few casualties, unfortunately. The damage was along very specific fault lines, radiating out from the epicentre under the Radcliffe Camera. Our house took a hit as you know, as did the science labs, the University Parks—but as only a few people live there it was not so bad. Worse damage was to the west in the shopping district. They've not found any bodies in the rubble but there are hundreds of hospital cases. We've a couple of students with broken bones. There was a horrid moment when we thought Professor Marmaduke was missing but he turned up unharmed. I think he must have taken a little too much wine at dinner in All Souls. That terrible dog of his led him home. Wait a moment, *ma petite*, I'll fetch your father to carry you down.'

'What about school?'

'Isis was not hit but the radio says it is not opening till eleven.' She gave Linette a wry smile. 'At least the local builders will be happy, no? We'd like you to go as you'll be safer there than you will be here while we sort out the mess.'

Linette had a similar update and a reassuring hug from her dad as he carried her down the narrow staircase. He couldn't stay as the university was holding an emergency meeting to assess damage. The Radcliffe Camera, which was miraculously still standing, had been declared unsound. Structural engineers were debating if it was safe to go in and remove the books.

Mr Kwan kissed Linette on the top of her head.

'I've asked the porter to take you to the bus stop today as the pavements will not be clear yet. You don't mind, do you?'

Linette shook her head. 'Fine. Thanks for thinking of it.'

'The college maintenance team will come in and see what they can do to adapt your new bedroom.'

'My stuff?'

'Not good news, I'm afraid. The students have lent us some clothes when they heard what had happened—thank God, their accommodation was spared. Our house was the main casualty.'

Linette shook out the hoodie and jeans she had been given. Borrowed clothes were the least of their worries this morning. 'It's not a problem. I can manage.'

The porter came knocking on the door at ten-fifteen. Linette had dressed and washed off most of the dust from the quake, but she knew she must look a little bedraggled.

'Are you all right, Miss Kwan?' asked Mr Fry, the head porter, as he manoeuvred her around the broken paving stones of the quad. A short, stout man with the kind of shiny face that insults just slid off, he terrorized the students but was nothing but charming to her and her family. 'Your father said you were thrown clear out of bed, then buried under fallen masonry. It was lucky your friends were able to get you out as quickly as they did; I can't work out how they did it.'

'Their dog sniffed me out.'

'Handy animal that.'

'Yes, Bob definitely is.'

Mr Fry pushed her chair into Broad Street, bumping over the new cracks. A figure lay stretched out on the ground with a ring of people surrounding it. For a horrid moment, Linette thought someone must have fallen from a window, but then she realized the statue had plunged from its place on the roof of the building on the corner. Fortunately, no one had been standing below it at the time. She glanced over her shoulder and saw that the emperors' heads on top of the plinths outside the Sheldonian Theatre had also toppled as if some giant guillotine had been at work during the night. The trumpet-playing muses had managed to hold on to their spots on the roof of the Bodleian but one hung at a terrifying drunken angle. Police incident tape stopped people walking underneath. Most of the plate glass windows in the shops had shattered or cracked.

'I don't think I'm ever going to look at this place in the same way again. It all felt so permanent before, as if nothing would ever change.'

'Me too, Miss,' agreed Mr Fry. 'But I suspect we'll all be back to normal far quicker than we think. A little earthquake can't make much of a dent in a thousand years of history.'

Tapping awake the hovering glow-worm lantern, Rick got out of his bed and took a look outside. After their late night, day had already dawned; the lawn was soaked with dew and the birds were trying to out-sing each other. Cutting through all that was noise of the emergency services heading into the centre of Oxford—ambulances, fire engines, and a police helicopter rattling overhead, ferrying the last casualties to the hospital. Rick shut the flap. Thanks to Magmell's very accomplished spelling of the tent, it deadened all noise and cut out the light. The inside walls were a canvas version of the boys' bedroom, complete with babyish train wallpaper, pictures of Lego models on shelves and a tapestry of a window that had the old view of the garage rather than the garden outside. Just big enough to fit Tiago's single bed and his hammock, the tent was snug to say the least. All their belongings were bundled into suitcases under the bed, an arrangement which played havoc with the neat row of shirts and trousers Rick had before kept hanging in their wardrobe. Not that he'd need those this morning. Today was supposed to be the introduction of a new Rick—that's if the earthquake hadn't driven it out of everyone's minds. Perhaps he could sneak out with his favourite pressed jeans after all . . . ?

Tiago rolled out of bed. 'Morning.'

'Hi.' Rick reached a hand into his suitcase.

On cue, Roxy stuck her head into the tent. 'Don't even think about it! We're still on our quest even if we're not sure on whose side. Your clothes are in the bags.'

Rick sighed. Rumbled.

'Hurry. You've got to get up. Shreddie's had an emergency call from Dark Lore House.'

Pulling on their clothes, the boys followed Roxy across the dew-damp garden and into the kitchen. Shreddie and Magmell were standing in front of a wall mirror where the commander's face was reflected rather than their own.

'We're all here, sir,' Magmell reported.

The surface of the mirror rippled like water. Rick recognized a portal spell in the making. Morgan poured through the gap like a slow-motion waterfall, taking shape on the rug in front of the electric fire, purple robes, crimson fingernails, ice-white arms and neck, long oil-slick of hair curling down her back. She grew to her full seven feet, head brushing the lampshade. With a flick of her fingers, the three changelings were seized by loops of magic and flung against the walls. Power cords writhed across the carpet, ripping free of television, toaster and kettle, to bind their hands above their heads. They dangled, feet not touching the floor, hanging from invisible hooks.

'I am not pleased,' Morgan announced.

What a surprise. Rick's arms ached but he knew better than to say anything when the commander was in a mood. Not all his team-mates were so wise.

'But we didn't do anything, sir!' Tiago protested, pulling at his bonds.

Morgan flicked her hand; orange sparks scorched his cheek. 'Exactly. We sent you to find out the cause of the power failures and you've turned up precisely nothing!'

Tiago glared at her, eyes shining with tears. Rick prayed he would keep his mouth shut about the professor.

'We searched last night, sir, just after the attack,' Rick said in what he hoped sounded a respectful tone, 'but we couldn't find the Round Table. It is too well hidden.'

'That's no excuse for your failure. I've had to empty Dark Lore completely this time. The changelings are being relocated to the dungeons underneath. You've just run out of time!' Her gaze included the two Fey minders in the threat.

The pixie wailed and shivered.

Magmell took the news with greater calm, his cunning mind turning to bargaining. 'Don't worry, sir, I promise we will solve this case for you, never fear. If they don't, I will.'

Morgan snarled. She strode from wall to wall, fixing Rick, Roxy, and Tiago with her baleful glare. She was too big for the room; it felt like having a wolf in a dog kennel. 'It is not me who has to fear, Magmell. There are some nasty rumours in court that Fey rebels have joined a Round Table to undermine the king.'

'Rumours?' sniffed Shreddie.

'That the plot has spread to Avalon. You do not want anyone asking why it is taking you so long to produce an answer for us!' Morgan paused before Rick, pressing her talon against his jugular. He lifted his chin but hanging like this he couldn't avoid her. 'As for you three, your fellow inmates from

Dark Lore House will never see the light of day again if you fail. You changelings only have a welcome in Avalon as long as Oberon thinks you are worth something to him. So, do your job. I want results, not excuses. Expose the traitors. Find me that Round Table!'

She turned back to the mirror, raised her hands over her head like a diver taking position, then poured back through the portal. As soon as every scrap of her was back on the Other Side, the holding spell broke and the changelings fell to the carpet.

'Give me the pupil referral room any day,' muttered Rick, rubbing his wrists.

'Why does it have to be us?' Roxy hugged her knees. 'It's not fair.'

Magmell turned on her. Sparks shot from his fingers as he barely kept his magic in check. '*You* should be grateful you have this chance, human. I refuse to have my future spoiled by you three.'

Roxy shuffled backwards until her spine rested against the wall. 'We've hardly had any time—and you know it!'

Magmell shrugged that argument aside. 'You've had time to mess around—playing at being human.' He gestured to Rick's new clothes. 'I think you're forgetting where your loyalties lie.'

'What? Because we bought Rick some T-shirts?' fumed Roxy. 'That was so he could question his classmates about recruitment in Isis without standing out!'

'Nonsense: you are enjoying yourselves far too much. You have a quest. You will find the traitors or feel my displeasure before you have to face that of Morgan and Oberon. There'll not be much left of you if I get my hands on you first.'

'Don't you threaten her, Fey!' Rick got up to position himself between Magmell and Roxy. 'We've been trying our best.'

'But what have you to show for all the time we've put into your quest here?' scoffed Magmell, bearing down on Rick with an ugly expression marring his good looks. 'Nothing but a trip to the hospital!'

'We're making progress!' He wished he could throw what he knew in Magmell's face, but no way was he going to betray the professor or even the half-Fey, Dr Ventikos, to Oberon's feygent.

'Not. Enough.'

'Leave them alone, Magmell.' Shreddie pulled the Fey back. 'They're only human and this is not helping. We have our orders.'

With a snort, Magmell flung out of the house, disappearing through a portal he had hastily summoned in the garden. It closed behind him with a crack.

'He shouldn't have done that,' sighed Shreddie,

her green hair drooping over her eyes. 'What if the humans see?'

Roxy scrambled to her feet and moved closer to Rick; Tiago took a step to stand at her shoulder.

'I doubt anyone will notice Magmell—too much else going on,' said Tiago, rubbing his cheek. 'OK if we go get ready for school? We've got lots of stuff to do. We've still got leads to follow up there and in town.'

Shreddie nodded. 'Yes, off you go. But please remember, I do not want to spend the rest of my life in Oberon's dungeon either.' She appealed to Roxy, knowing she would understand. 'I'm a traveller and I have to be free—life on the open road, you know? If you care anything for pixies—and we've been the best friends to the changelings, you all must realize that—find the answers the king wants to hear.'

The three retired to the tent—Roxy not fancying being on her own in a house of angry Dark Folk. Tiago brewed some hot chocolate for breakfast on a little camping stove Bob had unearthed from the shed at the end of the garden. The smell was more comforting than words anyone could have offered.

'Do you think Magmell suspects,' asked Rick, 'that we know the truth about being changelings? I mean he mentioned us playing at being human, didn't he?'

Roxy flinched. 'I don't know. But we'd better be careful. The first hint to Morgan or Oberon that we're no longer ignorant mugs of the changeling programme, then we're dead.'

'And did you get the message? That they now think the attack might involve people on either side of the divide—a new Round Table that combines both?'

'Yes, look for traitors, Morgan said. Who has it in for Oberon?' Roxy pretended to think, finger to chin. 'Why, only everyone he's exiled or hunted down. That narrows our options—not.'

'So what are we going to do?' asked Tiago.

Rick wished the doing was as easy as the saying. 'We've got to solve the mystery of who is behind it here, not to hand them over but so we can work out what to do next.'

'Professor Marmaduke might know more after last night's meltdown,' suggested Tiago.

Roxy hadn't met him yet and wasn't so quick to put her faith in the Mage changeling. 'Why should we trust him to help us? You've said he'd dropped down your suspects list but you only have his word for that.'

Rick could understand why she was suspicious; he was not absolutely sure himself what the professor was up to. 'I know but I don't think he's ready to launch another attempt to overthrow Oberon. What did you think, Tiago?'

'Yeah, he didn't seem ready for that. But I suppose the professor is Mage Fey which means he knows everything there is to know about Fey technology—his kind came up with most of it, that's why they were exiled rather than killed. Oberon realizes he might need them, us, eventually.' Tiago poured the remainder of his hot chocolate in Bob's bowl. 'We can't rule him out just because we like him.'

'OK.' Rick grabbed his bag and checked he had all his kit. 'We ask him again—go there after school. You know, if he fooled us and is involved somehow, it may work out that he's the hero not the villain here—maybe he's got a way of setting up the Round Table without harming Avalon and Earth?'

'An earthquake hasn't convinced you there isn't a harmless option?' Roxy argued. 'Whatever is going on, the Round Table is out of control.'

Reluctant though Rick was to admit it, she was probably right.

# Chapter 12

'Wow—first an earthquake, now Rick rocks the school!' marvelled Izzie as the new boy entered the classroom.

Linette looked up from her planner and broke into a delighted smile. She had forgotten about the makeover they had given him, what with the earthquake and everything that followed. But Rick did look fantastic: not so different that it was unbelievable, but he no longer appeared uneasy in his clothes. Even his hair was mussed, something she had not thought to mention but it improved his image tenfold. He strode confidently through the ranks of gaping students to her table.

'You OK?' he asked.

'Yes, thank you. Our house has been condemned but the rest of the college is all right. Did you get home OK?'

He smiled. 'Yes—very smoothly.'

'Thanks for helping last night. It was incredible—the state my bedroom is in now I've seen it in daylight—you were brave to pull me out.'

He shrugged. 'Couldn't leave you there, now could we?'

'I suppose not.' She tugged at her borrowed hoodie. 'I lost all my belongings.'

'That . . . um . . . sucks.'

Linette gave him another point for using the right kind of language even if he did wince as he used the phrase.

He took the seat on her other side without asking—progress on the manners front too then. 'We're coming round later to check on Professor Marmaduke.'

'I've heard that he's OK. He was dining out when it happened.'

'I still want to see for myself. We'll come back with you on the bus.' He paused, his urge to be polite not quite killed off. 'If that's OK with you, I mean.'

'Of course. It would be nice.'

Tyler Walsh had been watching them from his seat on the far right of the classroom. The admiring looks of the other students were getting on his nerves.

'New clothes don't stop you being a headcase,' Tyler sneered.

Rick kicked back on his chair, rocking with great indifference to the fact that he was being picked on.

'You can try to pretend but you're still the same old Sick Rick.' Tyler chucked a ball of paper at him.

Rick's hand shot out and caught the missile mid flight. 'Rubbish shot.' He flicked it back and struck Tyler square on the nose. 'That's how it's done.'

A few of the boys sniggered disloyally.

Tyler flushed with rage. 'Shut your mouth, freak.'

Rick stretched his arms above his head so his snake bracelet became visible. 'Why? I'm not afraid of you. You're just a troll-brain who needs his friends to fight for him.'

Tyler got to his feet and pushed his chair roughly out of the way. Rick looked quite eager for the battle. Fortunately, before fists began to fly, Miss Milton walked in.

As the register was read, Tyler returned to his seat but did not take his eyes off Rick or his bracelet. Rick found his reaction mildly amusing—the boy was very small beer compared to Oberon,

Morgan and the threat to the world. He nodded at Tyler then turned his attention to Linette.

'So, how's that for blending in? Are you going to tell Roxy and Tiago that I'm improving?'

Linette shook her head. 'You really are mad, aren't you? You're doing well—too well. You've gone from class loser to leader in one confrontation. Tyler is going to be out to get you.'

Rick rubbed his hands together. 'Bring it on.'

Linette folded her head on her hands. 'Help: I've created a monster.'

Rick just laughed. He was enjoying himself. For all his magic, he had never felt more powerful. Being a normal boy, answering back, having friends behind you: they beat casting spells for the adrenaline rush.

The changelings' attempt to see Professor Marmaduke on his own was foiled when they found him with the half-Fey from the museum, Dr Ventikos. Marmaduke had kept to his word to find out more about rumours in the Fey exile community; unfortunately they had walked right into the middle of his fact-finding mission.

'Bit young for your tutorials, aren't they, Lucien?' Dr Ventikos said crisply when she saw them on his doorstep.

Professor Marmaduke chuckled. 'I expect they know more than most of my students, Natalia.' He stood back to let them enter, not bothering to activate the glamour for them so the room had its true wizard's workshop appearance. His chamber had not suffered in the quake, no cracks or smashed windows like the rest of the college; all his instruments were safe on their shelves.

He must have had a holding spell on the place, thought Rick, wondering what kind of charm that would be and if he could learn it.

Professor Marmaduke inspected Roxy with keen interest. 'And who is this lovely young lady?'

Roxy narrowed her eyes at his gallantry. 'Roxy Topley.'

He waved his hand over her, gathering information from her magical aura. 'Ah, another inmate of Dark Lore House, I see. Natalia, let me introduce you to our human changelings—Elfric here is mine, Tiago is a mixed blood, and Miss Topley—when exactly were you taken, my dear?'

'From Ireland in the early tenth century.'

'Not from Kerry by any chance?'

Roxy gave a guarded nod.

'Then perhaps Marilyn might know more about that. She came from there, didn't she, Natalia? Do you know where she is these days?' The professor's tone was conversational as if this was a completely normal discussion to be having.

'In Washington. On her fifty-first husband,' Dr Ventikos said. 'We skype from time to time.'

'You should be able to sense her direction, Miss Topley, if you are her swap. Your body will be tuned to her.'

'How exactly do I do that?' asked Roxy.

'Oh, just look within.' He left Roxy with a very perplexed expression on her face as she tried to work out how that felt. 'Santiago, no dog?' Marmaduke looked disappointed not to see Bob trotting along at Tiago's heels.

'No, not today.' Tiago drummed the fingers of his right hand on his thigh, uneasy without his best friend by his side.

'In that case, I'll allow Gordon in to see you.' Marmaduke pointed at the door. It flew open letting a huge hound into the room. Rough black coat and big brown eyes, he made a beeline for Rick and shoved his nose with unerring doggy aim where he shouldn't. The dog reached his waist and would be as tall as him if he stood on his hind legs. Quickly, Rick lifted Gordon's chin and stroked under his neck, finding the spot that made the back leg shiver in a reflexive scratch.

'What breed is he?' Rick asked, thinking the beast quite the most formidable dog he'd met.

'A Gabriel hound.' Marmaduke threw the dog a bone-shaped biscuit.

'Tell him the rest, Lucien,' drawled Dr Ventikos. Marmaduke smiled blandly so Dr Ventikos took up the task of explaining. 'Gordon is a corpse hound, Elfric, a harbinger of disaster. Only a mad Mage like your professor here would think to tame one. They normally travel in packs, visiting those under the shadow of death or calamity. If you hear them pass over the roof of your house, then someone is doomed.'

'What? They fly?' marvelled Tiago. 'Cool!' He moved closer to receive a lick on the face in greeting.

'But Gordon didn't like all that gloomy business, did you, Gordon?' Marmaduke crooned to the hound. When the professor sat down in a straight-backed armchair by the fireplace, the dog instantly removed his attention from Rick and Tiago to slump so that his head was cradled on the professor's lap. He stared up at his master with obvious devotion, hairs over his eyes twitching. The professor gestured the visitors to be seated. 'Now, what can I do for you today?'

Rick looked at the others but they seemed to expect him to take the lead. They took places on the chairs by the tutorial table, waiting for him to speak. Rick perched on the footstool next to

Marmaduke, face now on a level with the Gabriel hound. The dog's breath smelt of mushrooms, not unpleasant, just reminiscent of dark places and mould.

'We thought we'd come because we were worried about you—after last night,' Rick said, cautiously patting Gordon.

Marmaduke beamed. 'Isn't that thoughtful of them, Natalia? Just like you, they believe this old Mage couldn't take a shake or two.' He leaned forward. 'I was in San Francisco in 1906—now that was an earthquake!' He sat back, spreading his arms. 'As you can see, I am in tiptop condition for a two-thousand-year-old Fey-blood.'

Rick bit his thumbnail, wondering if he could risk broaching the subject of the Round Table with a stranger in the room. Roxy must have been pondering the same dilemma, but come to the conclusion it was best to confront the matter head on. 'If you don't mind me asking, Miss . . . er . . . ?'

'Dr Ventikos,' the lady said coolly, turning her dark eyes on Roxy.

'Dr Ventikos.' Roxy produced a charming smile. 'We're very interested in the Fey in this world. What kind are you exactly? Are you another changeling like the professor?'

Natalia patted her perfectly groomed hair, which was caught back in a French plait. She did have an unattainable air that reminded Rick of Morgan La Faye. 'A changeling? No. I am more like Tiago here—I am half-Fey: human father; my mother was one of Oberon's sisters.'

'So . . . so you're a princess? The king is your uncle?' Roxy darted Rick a worried look.

The lady gave a cynical smile. 'He is not very . . . how would you say? Familial. He does not recognize mixed blood relatives, so no, sorry, I am not a princess.'

'Have you always lived in this world?' Tiago asked, his interest sparked to find someone in a similar position to him.

'Indeed. I have lived here for nearly a hundred years.' She put her finger under her chin and playfully turned her head. 'Not bad for an old lady, am I?' Dr Ventikos grew serious once more. 'We half-Fey are not immortal but we do age more slowly than humans. I won't be old until I'm a thousand. That's perhaps the one thing I have to thank my mother for. And it has given me plenty of time to become an expert in my chosen field—the antiquities of Ancient Greece and Rome.'

'Oh, I see.' Roxy encouraged the lady to continue. 'How did you get interested in that?'

'The other half of my blood. My father was Greek—met my mother during the First World War. He thought she died in the confusion of the fighting but she really returned to Avalon. I was her parting gift to him.'

'Extraordinary—leaving you behind,' muttered Marmaduke in a disapproving tone.

Dr Ventikos gave an elegant shrug, a little rise and fall of her shoulders. 'I was too human for the Fey and would probably have ended up at Dark Lore despite her position in Oberon's court—she told me she thought it best.' She fingered her scarf which was decorated with a pattern of coronets. 'So why has my dearly beloved uncle sent you three here? I thought being incarcerated in Dark Lore was a life sentence.'

Rick took the decision to trust her—she might be half Dark Folk but her sympathies—what ones she had—appeared to lie with them. 'Do you know about the Fey ring under the Radcliffe Camera?'

'Of course. I assume some malfunction caused last night's debacle?'

'We don't know. But it's not the first problem we've had with the ring. Avalon has been getting interruptions to the green energy supply for a while now and last night the effects were definitely felt by the humans.' Rick did a quick calculation. 'It's been going on for at least one of your years, I would guess.'

'Could it be the system backfiring? Humans have drained away so much of the natural energy that once fed the system; it might now be causing a breakdown.' Dr Ventikos directed the observation to the professor. 'Pollution, mass extinctions, global warming—surely these must have an adverse effect on what is now an ancient technology?'

Marmaduke gave a rumbling laugh. 'Natalia, my dear, you had better stick to archaeology; anyone can tell that you do not understand Feysyks. The ring can withstand normal human activity. It is calibrated to adjust to declining flows. The flipside is that humans are getting in return less imagination and invention from Avalon. I fear we are entering very dull times with such things having to be rationed.'

'Oberon thinks that a new Round Table is behind it as the last time anyone managed to break the supply was under King Arthur,' said Rick.

Marmaduke shook his head. 'I admit that was a very clever piece of magic by Merlin, but I can't see any modern human coming anywhere close without destroying the balance and what Fey would want to imperil Avalon? I asked around but no one has heard a whisper of a new Round Table. I think the explanation is likely to be more prosaic. The system is due for a maintenance overhaul and that idiot Purl-E, who I left in charge of the blueprints, is trying to hide the fact from his masters by blaming others.'

Rick realized he was hugely disappointed that the Round Table might not exist. He had been thinking that joining it, making it safe, would be a way out for him, Roxy, and Tiago. 'Blueprints? You designed it?'

'It's one of many things I did.'

'So you know how to get down there?'

'Naturally.'

'Can you help us get down there to see it for ourselves?'

The professor shook his head. 'Preposterous! What do you think you would "see", Elfric? Do you know how to judge if a Feysyk particle reactor is on the blink?'

Rick flushed. 'No, but Tiago is pretty good at that stuff.'

'Is he?' Marmaduke caressed Gordon's ears, studying Tiago intently. 'I would have thought it might still be beyond the most advanced of Purl-E's disciples. The dim-witted pixie barely understands the system. He likes to claim credit for it but he would never have come up with the model if it hadn't been for me. Classic case of a pixie promoted to a level beyond his capabilities.'

'Then they need you back in Avalon, professor. That must be worth an amnesty from Oberon. If you went, you could sort this out.'

'Now whyever would I want to do that? Oberon would probably prefer to see the whole system collapse than welcome me back to his court.'

'But we need help. Please, can you not tell this to Oberon at the very least? He's threatening us and the other changelings if we don't succeed in our quest here.' Rick rubbed his palms on his new trousers, hands clammy at the thought. 'He's already got them in dungeons.'

'Lucien?' prompted Dr Ventikos, unexpectedly throwing her weight behind Rick's appeal.

The professor hummed for a moment. 'We can't have another earthquake here like the last one; something's clearly got to be done. But I won't take you young people anywhere near a particle reactor—it would be the death of you. I will go and check on it today and tell you what I find, putting it in language that even Purl-E can understand. How about that, eh?'

'But, sir, we don't have long.'

'I understand, but one doesn't just walk into a particle reactor, you know, there are things I have to do first. Now, young Santiago, come with me for a moment. There's something I want to tell you,' he tapped the side of his nose,'—one Mage to another, you understand?'

Tiago got up eagerly. 'OK.'

'We'll go back to Linette's and wait for you.' Rick tried not to get jealous. He had introduced Tiago to the professor so that Tiago could discover more about his Mage Fey inheritance; he had no right to think the professor owed him more attention than he was already receiving.

'I'll be on my way too, Lucien.' Dr Ventikos got up and kissed a hand to the professor. He sketched a defensive spell in the air to catch it, producing a little glowing shield of power. 'So suspicious still?'

'Naturally.' He bowed. 'Dark Folk survive by not trusting each other.'

Once outside, Roxy turned to Rick. 'What do you think?'

'About her?' They watched the half-Fey as she stepped lightly over the broken paving stones with the natural grace inherited from her mother, weaving in and out of the lengthening shadows. She stopped by a fallen gargoyle. Shaking her head, she moved on. When Rick next blinked, the gargoyle was back in its original high place. 'I don't know. I don't think she means us harm.'

'Not a great recommendation—not wanting to hurt someone.'

'What about you?'

'I think . . . I think I quite like her. More than your professor. She has the royal breeding but without Oberon's coldness. Marmaduke is too fake for my taste—all that friendly-friendly stuff when he clearly despises humans.'

'He said he'd help.'

Roxy folded her arms. 'We'll see.'

Tiago had been gone for hours. Linette had invited them into the little back garden behind the ruined house. The sun had sunk behind the high wall, leaving the lawn a cold and dreary place to wait. They'd played with a small croquet set retrieved from a shed but the game had long since ended.

Linette yawned and rubbed her neck, uncomfortable in her chair.

'Shall we go?' asked Roxy. 'You can tell Tiago to follow on when he turns up.'

'Sorry, I don't want to be rude but none of us got much sleep last night.'

'No problem. We'll head back. Tell Tiago he's a pain for keeping us hanging around for him so long.'

At the entrance to the garden, the gate slammed.

'Hi, Professor Kwan-times-two.' Tiago sounded cheerful—very cheerful. 'Sorry I'm so late. It took longer than expected. Are the others still here?'

A moment later, Tiago's dark head bobbed out from behind the rose bushes. 'You mad?'

'Getting there,' admitted Roxy.

Rick picked up the croquet set to put it back inside the shed. 'Come on, let's go.'

Rick waited until they were on the street before asking Tiago for an explanation.

'So what did the professor tell you?'

Tiago dipped in front of them, jogging backwards as they headed for Broad Street. JCBs were working late, clearing the rubble from the roadway. A crane levered a statue off the pavement and lowered it onto a flatbed truck with a resounding thump. Tiago's silver-grey eyes gleamed in the twilight. 'Can't say. Not yet anyhow.'

'Troll breath, that's not fair!' wailed Roxy. 'I'm gonna die of curiosity now.'

Tiago took her hands and spun her round. 'Unlikely. Not a known cause of human mortality.'

'I'll be the first case.' She smiled as she registered the fact that Tiago, the master of keeping himself separate, had dropped his barriers for once. After their quarrel of the night before, it was particularly pleasing to see him so relaxed with them.

'Was it anything to do with our quest?' Rick asked.

'Nope. Nopedy-nope.' Tiago hopped on top of the railings around the little green oasis of St Mary Magdalen's churchyard and balanced his way along the top, expertly avoiding the sharp spikes.

A couple of students stopped to laugh at his exploits, taking pictures with their phones. Encouraged, Tiago reversed to do the same procedure on his hands, earning himself a round of applause when he somersaulted down.

'You with the circus, mate?' called the Big Issue seller outside the boarded-up supermarket.

Tiago did a little jig on the spot. 'Yep, one of the clowns.'

'You got that right,' giggled Roxy.

Fortunately, the bus drew up before Tiago could make more of a spectacle of himself. Removing the bowing Tiago from his audience, Rick hauled him on by the back of his T-shirt and bought his ticket for him.

'And I thought I was supposed to be the one who didn't blend,' he said to Roxy as Tiago did a little tap dance in the empty disabled space.

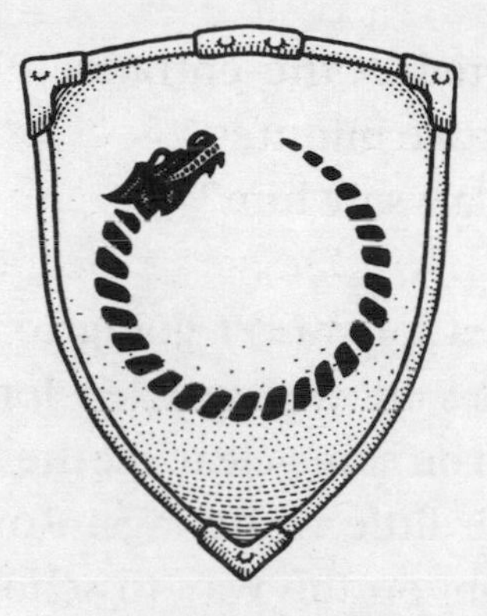

# Chapter 13

'Have you seen Bob?' Tiago stuck his head through the tent flap, waking Rick from deep sleep.

Forgetting he wasn't in a normal bed, Rick rolled over and promptly fell out of his hammock. The jolt brought him to his senses.

'What time is it?'

'Five—in the morning. Does that matter? I can't find Bob.'

Tiago had come down as abruptly from his happy mood as Rick from his hammock.

Rick rubbed his hip, which had taken the brunt of the blow. 'No, sorry. I haven't seen him since yesterday—or was it the night before?'

Tiago hovered in the entrance. 'Twenty hours and twenty-three minutes.'

'Since you last saw him?'

'Yes.'

Rick realized he wasn't going to get any more sleep—not now he was worried for the little dog too. He pulled on some clean clothes, snapping the labels off their little white tags. Roxy had had to do that for him on the way to school the day before and he didn't want to repeat the mistake. He racked his memory to reconstruct the events leading up to Bob's disappearance.

'He came back with us from Linette's, right? On the carpet?'

'Yes. He went out to have a sniff around at breakfast and he didn't come back in to say goodbye before I went to school as he normally does. I didn't worry—everything was upside down then; I thought he was off to see how the clear up in town was going. He's an inquisitive dog.'

'But he hasn't come back.'

'No. It's not like him to do this.'

'I get that.' Rick slid the bracelet off his arm. 'Hey, Aethel, got a job for you.'

Gold shivered into living snake. She wrapped around his neck affectionately, hissing in his ear.

'Love you too, Legless. Now listen: Bob's gone missing. Can you find out if he's got stuck somewhere nearby? Ask the other animals if they've seen a dog in trouble.' Aethel dripped like syrup to the floor then spooled out under the side of the tent. 'She'll find him if he's anywhere close—got great scouting instincts.' He noticed that Tiago was still wearing the clothes he had on the day before. 'You've been up all night?'

Tiago nodded. 'Wanted to tell him what the prof said—didn't go to bed when I couldn't find him.'

Rick could well imagine how distressed Tiago must be because he would react in the same way if he lost Aethel. He'd been with her ever since he could remember; his first memories were of playing with her in the lonely nursery at Dark Lore. She had started life as a precious piece of jewellery, but somehow the magic of Avalon had acted on her and given her this ability to shift from one state to another. Unlike many enchanted creations—usually fickle creatures like the Brazen Face—she was totally loyal to him. He didn't know where Tiago had found Bob but he couldn't remember a day when they had been apart either.

'If Aethel can't find him around here, we'll go into town, OK?'

Tiago buried his face in his hands. 'I feel so guilty. I've been so caught up in solving the Round Table quest, I've not paid enough attention to him. What if something really bad has happened to him?'

'Bob's the cleverest dog I've ever met. I'm sure he'll be fine.' At least, Rick hoped that was the truth.

Linette woke up to the sound of hammering downstairs. The college maintenance crew were working overtime to get a room adapted for her so she could get out and about herself. Unfortunately, that meant she wouldn't get a lie in. Grabbing her crutches, she managed to get up, use the upstairs bathroom and dress without disturbing her parents.

From her parents' bedroom, she could hear the gentle rumble of her father's snores. He was sleeping through the ruckus. Amazing. Spotting Mr Fry in the hallway below supervising the delivery of a stack of plasterboards, Linette waved.

'Could you give me a hand downstairs please?'

Mr Fry and a builder supported her on either side to help her to her chair.

'We'll have a room fixed up for you in a jiffy,' Mr Fry assured her.

'Thanks. I really appreciate it.'

'And I've got a crew on sorting out the broken pavers. Take your chair over the grass for now,' continued Mr Fry.

'Not your precious grass!' exclaimed Linette with a twinkle of amusement in her eye. You knew when Oxford had really been shaken up when the 'Keep off the grass' rule was relaxed.

He winked at her. 'Yes, for a few days. But don't think of making it a habit.'

'I wouldn't dream of it.'

Paths clear for her to go out on her own, Linette decided to visit the Fellows' Garden and see for herself the damage done to the Radcliffe Camera. A light rain began to fall but not enough to deter her. Feeling very wicked, she bumped over the manicured lawn, leaving a track on the green velvet finish. She steered round the remaining obstacles and entered the archway that gave access to the garden. She had to pause for a moment in the shadows to tug a creeper of ivy free of her left wheel. The rapid click of claws on stone alerted her to company approaching. Shifting round, she saw Professor Marmaduke's monster of a dog trotting out for a walk on his own.

'*Bonjour*, Gordon!' Linette called, holding her hand over the side of the chair to invite him for a stroke. He was normally very friendly to her.

The dog looked once then ignored her. She then noticed he had a piece of rope in his mouth. He gave it a tug and Linette then heard a yelp from behind him. Hidden by the huge hound was a familiar black-and-white mutt. He had a new studded collar around his neck, the rope attached to it by a ring, and he was shivering in terror. That was very wrong.

'Bob! Come here!'

Tiago's little dog perked up and tried to bound to her, only to be caught short by the lead. Gordon yanked him back so hard Bob fell on to his back. The big dog put a fist sized paw on Bob's stomach and growled a warning.

'Gordon, stop that! You let Bob go immediately!' ordered Linette. She'd always known the professor's dog was odd, but this was bizarre. Maybe some student had tied up the dogs for a horrid prank? She began to roll towards them, but Gordon dragged on the lead, pulling Bob further away. 'Stay!'

He ignored her and continued to tow the unwilling captive towards an opening set in the wall of the archway—the entrance to the cellars—and the door had been left unlocked for the first time that she remembered. Disappearing inside, the two dogs were swallowed up by the dark stairwell. Only Bob's frightened whimpers could now be heard.

'Gordon, get back here this instant!' Linette shouted, frustrated that she couldn't set off in pursuit. Bob was clearly in trouble and she couldn't do a thing to help him.

'Problem, my dear?' Professor Marmaduke appeared beside her chair.

'Oh, thank goodness you've come, professor! It's Gordon. He's got Tiago's dog on a lead and taken him in there. I expect some students tied them together for a joke—not that I find it the least funny. Bob's terrified and Gordon completely ignored my orders to stop.' She looked up at the old man, expecting him to do something about it.

The professor rubbed his chin thoughtfully. 'So you recognized Bob, did you?'

'Of course. Tiago loves that dog.'

'That's a shame.'

Linette felt the hairs prickle at the back of her neck. That was foolish—she was talking to her friend. The professor had helped her many times over the months since she had lived here so why should today be different? 'Why is it a shame?'

'Because you have just become mixed up in something about which we all would rather you remained in ignorance.'

'What do you mean? You're the one playing a joke on Tiago?'

He sighed. 'I don't want to involve you but I'm afraid the only answer is for you to come with me.' His eyes went misty as he revolved the situation in his mind. 'In fact, this may be even better because the changelings have feelings for you too. It could work in my favour.'

'Changelings? What are you talking about?' Linette put her hands to the wheel rims to back off, wishing someone would come along. No one was about—it was too early for the students to be up at the weekend. The professor was acting so oddly, she was getting seriously disturbed. And if he thought dognapping Bob was funny, then she certainly didn't share his sense of humour.

He put a foot behind her chair, easily stopping her escape. 'Don't worry about understanding, my dear. Just do what I say and everything will be all right—in a fashion.' He fished in a pocket and pulled out two contraptions that looked like large yo-yos. 'How fortunate I slipped these into my jacket this morning. I was going to use them for some heavy lifting but they will do—they will do very well.' He clamped the bright blue discs on the hub of both wheels of her chair. 'To the ring!'

In response to his barked order, the discs spun and split into three-legged prongs, like the symbol on the flag of the Isle of Man. They began to propel the chair to the open door.

'No!' Linette protested. She screamed but the sound was muffled as if she were surrounded by an invisible blanket, a fact that only made her panic worse. 'Stop!' He couldn't mean to throw her down the stairs, could he? She grabbed hold of one of his contraptions to stop it spinning but it was too powerful—it ripped free of her hands and continued to turn. 'You're mad. Stop this now, professor! It's not funny!'

'You'd best hold on tight,' the professor said calmly behind her. 'I think this will work but I've not yet tested them.'

Linette clutched the arms of her chair until her knuckles went white. The leg-things continued to revolve but now took her down the stairs. Her chair was almost as wide as the narrow flight of steps but they managed the manoeuvre without getting stuck or spilling her out, stretching to just the right length for each stair. Finding she was safe, Linette's initial panic was replaced with fury. It was absurd to think the professor meant to harm her, but he had better have a very good explanation for all this. He had at least to tell her why he was playing such a horrid joke on poor Tiago, making Bob a hostage. And what on earth did he mean by changelings?

'I'm not enjoying this, professor. Don't you think you should tell me what's really going on?'

'All in good time, my dear. Don't worry. Bob will be quite all right.'

She decided to wait until they retrieved the dogs; then she'd demand to be taken back. The contraptions on the side of the chair flapped against the floor like soft webbed feet. 'What are these things on my wheels anyway?' she asked.

'I call them triskel. Like them?'

'They're . . . amazing. How do they know how to change to the right length? I've never been able to come down here before. Can I keep them?'

The professor whistled. Gordon barked a response from deep in the cellar. 'We'll see. For now, let's just enjoy our adventure underground.'

'I can't go out without telling my parents.' Linette was still trying to work out how the triskel worked; she couldn't see any obvious sign of computer technology, no wires or batteries—just bright blue extensions that popped out like telescopes.

'Don't worry about them. I'll send a note.' He clicked his fingers over his head. 'Don't you want to explore the college's secrets?'

Linette was sure she didn't want to do anything like that today—and especially not with the professor who was definitely acting strangely. And what if the quake had made the cellars unsafe? 'I don't think this is a good idea. Where are you taking me?'

'Into the secret passage.'

'You mean there really is one—to the library?'

'Oh no, it goes much deeper than that.'

The triskel retracted to be level with the rims, letting the chair down on to the flagstone. They continued to turn so Linette didn't have to propel the wheels as the chair trundled along on a course of its own.

'I want to go back. Is this passage even safe—after last night?' she asked, alarmed to find that the brake had no effect on the professor's contraptions.

'Go back? Where would be the fun in that?' he asked, waving his hand over what looked like a blank wall to reveal a stout oak door. Gordon and Bob waited just inside the entrance. Gordon whined.

'Now, now, none of that. Obey orders!' Professor Marmaduke snapped at the dog, not sounding a bit like his normal jolly self.

'Where did the door come from?' Linette marvelled.

The professor prodded it with his cane. 'Magic, my dear. Magic.'

# Chapter 14

After Aethel reported a fruitless search for Bob, the three changelings agreed to appeal to their handlers for help. When they entered the house, they found Magmell had just got back from Avalon. Sergeant Rotgut was with him. The expected crisis had arrived.

'Soldiers,' barked the ogre, 'the secret police have intelligence that another attack is imminent. You have new orders: prevent anyone interfering with the power ring. As the precise location of the Table had not been found, this means no one is to approach the building from above or below.'

'But we can't!' protested Tiago.

'What!' Rotgut's tusks quivered in disbelief. 'Do

you want me to send you straight to the dungeons then?' He gathered a little portal spell in his palm, ready to fling it in his face.

Rick jumped between them. 'Sir, you don't understand—Bob's missing!'

'What—a soldier down! Why didn't you say?' Rotgut growled. Threatening humans was business as usual; put a Fey familiar at risk and then the Dark Folk got really steamed. 'Since when?'

Magmell stepped forward. 'It makes sense, sergeant. You said this business has a foothold in Avalon too. The Round Table traitors must have found out about our team here and taken the dog as a hostage to divert our attention.'

'Or perhaps he found them and they've silenced him.' Shreddie wrung her hands. 'Poor Bob!'

Rotgut quickly revised his orders. 'Soldiers, we need to split our forces. You humans go to the ring and secure that objective, set up a magical cordon. I will report back to Morgan and tell her what has happened. Magmell, Shreddie, you stand by for further orders. Morgan will want to speak to you.'

Tiago headed for the Rolls Royce. 'Can we get going please?'

Rick didn't follow immediately. 'Wait a second. I'll just fetch my sword.' He had no idea if they could isolate the Camera as ordered—would their magic be strong enough to deny anyone entry?—but he didn't want to face this unarmed if hostile knights might already be on site.

'Not waiting.' Tiago began tugging off the cover.

'I'll only be a moment.' Rick rushed to his tent. Knowing that he couldn't very well go marching around Oxford with a sword strapped to his side, he slung the belt holding the scabbard over his shoulder crossways so the blade was resting against his spine. He could just about draw it over his shoulder in this position—something he had practised to ensure he didn't lose an ear in the process. It made for a straight-backed stance, but his instincts were anticipating trouble of the Dark Folk kind and he felt much better when he had two of his best allies—Aethel and his sword—to hand. He cast a quick glamour over the weapon to make it look like a backpack, then joined Tiago and Roxy just as they got into the car.

'Who's driving?' he asked.

'I've done a guidance spell—should hold until we reach the city centre,' said Roxy, tapping the dashboard. 'You sit in the driver's seat.' On her command, the car jerkily reversed from the drive, then headed out for the main road.

Rick didn't like the feeling of being in the hot seat with no control over the car but it was the fastest way to get to their destination. He set his hands lightly on the wheel, trying not to interfere and make things worse. 'What do you want to do first?' Rick asked Tiago.

'Go to Professor Marmaduke,' Tiago said at once. 'I know he'll help with finding Bob and stopping an attack.'

'He also promised us a report on whether or not the so-called attacks are really down to the ring malfunctioning,' added Rick. 'Fey intelligence might be wrong. Roxy, I asked your robins this morning to look for Bob too. If you see one, can you ask if they found any trace?'

She muttered a word to slow the car for a junction. 'You know, Bob might've just got in a fix all of his own. What if the earthquake opened up a way into the Fey ring he hadn't found before? Do you think he might've stuck his nose down there?'

'I really hope not—the professor was very clear that Fey particle reactors are dangerous.'

'They're OK as long as you don't throw yourselves in the reactor spiral,' muttered Tiago. 'Bob would know that.'

'Reactor spiral?' Rick had an alarming recollection that the Brazen Face on the wall in the professor's study had said something about that.

'Yeah, they work on the golden ratio principle—I thought you knew?'

Rick shook his head. 'I'm rubbish at Feysyks, remember?'

'I suppose I'd better tell you the basics then.' Tiago frowned as Roxy had the audacity to stop the car at a red light. 'The word rings isn't quite right—we call them rings only because we see them from the top, like a cross section. The rest spirals down in loops before joining up again at the top.'

'Er . . . come again, how can it do that?'

'The properties of dimensions beyond four help solve such spacial difficulties. If you add in time, you can engineer it so that the remainder isn't in the same time-phase as the bottom loop. That means it can link to the top without obstruction. I'm simplifying obviously.'

'Obviously,' Roxy murmured, most of her attention on the road.

Rick thought he got it—if you manipulated time you could essentially trick space into doing what you want. Mage Fey claimed to be good at cheating and they had designed the system. 'In that case, I've some not totally good news. Tiago might remember, but the professor's bad-tempered talking head warned me that one of us would meet disaster in the reactor.'

'Oh great—evil prophecies: that's all we need.' Roxy laughed with dark amusement.

'I thought it was remarkable that the face thought any of us would get out at all,' admitted Tiago. 'Fey particle spirals and human survival are not compatible. You get pounded by Fey elements as they interact with this world's green energy—the resulting collision being raw magic. Think chip—deep-fat fryer—and you get the picture.'

Roxy groaned. 'Even better. Wow, you both know how to make a girl feel happy about her day.' She pulled the car over to a parking spot in Broad Street, ending up at a slant but at least there had been no collisions.

'What colour socks are you wearing, Tiago?' Rick asked, afraid of the answer.

Tiago reluctantly lifted the bottom of his jeans. 'Red. My unlucky colour according to the face.'

Rick got out. 'You might want to go barefoot. OK, guys, we're in business: let's leave the car here. We have to find Bob and save the world from the attack on the ring.'

He was rather chagrined to find Roxy's laughter redoubled. 'I love your attitude, Rick: save the world and be home in time for tea. Fantastic.'

'Fantastic or not, are you in?' he asked her seriously.

She sobered. 'Yeah, I'm in.'

'Tiago?'

He nodded.

'Let's go then.' Rick settled his sword between his shoulder blades and headed towards trouble.

Linette thought she must be still asleep because her surroundings were more bizarre than any dream she had ever had, certainly not the stuff of the normal daylight world. Professor Marmaduke had obviously gone mad, talking about magic as if he really believed in it. It made her wonder if he was part of the Dungeons and Dragons group Roxy had been interested in. If so, her friend should steer well away as he had clearly entered crackpot territory. And the passageway was simply not Oxford. She'd been expecting gothic stone flags, cobwebs and flickering torches; instead it was pure white, circular, smooth like marble. It was like crawling inside a seashell, if you were an ant that is. Even the sound and smell reminded her of the beach: there was a whooshing noise as if waves were breaking nearby and the air smelt of salt and earth, recalling sand dunes under a hot sun. Strangest of all was that the whole place glowed even though it was underground. She could not see the source but the tunnel was flooded with light like strong sunbeams filtered through milky glass.

Her chair continued to trundle on with no input from her and by now the miracle of the triskel had begun to annoy her. They might be marvellous inventions but what was the point of them if she could not control what they did?

'Professor, can we stop now?' Linette asked.

'Nearly there.'

That was no answer.

'Thank you for the adventure but I have to get back.'

'Why? Your parents are busy, you have no friends to come calling—indeed, you only have three people who do visit you and they are only there for what you can offer them.' His cane tapped the floor, releasing little green sparks with each collision.

'What do you mean?' Linette rubbed her upper arms, chilled by his callous words.

'They only want you to give them entry here, my dear.' He smiled at her, but it was not a pleasant smile. 'All you've ever been to them is a portal. They know all about those. You can never trust a changeling. We all live in a dog-eat-dog world and you are just one little bone.'

Bob whined, tucking his tail between his legs. Gordon nudged him forward.

'You . . . you're wrong.' Linette's voice shook. What did he mean: changelings?

'Well, look at you, my dear: what exactly do you think you have to offer anyone? I rather pity you—I spent most of the eleventh century laid up with a jousting injury so I can sympathize. But I've lasted as long as I have purely because I relied on myself. I suggest you toughen up and do the same.'

He stopped by a silver-plated door. Her chair came to a halt a few paces behind him. Linette glared at his hateful back. She had no intention of being like him—he was insane for heaven's sake! Talking about changelings as if they existed outside fairy tales. Why take his word on anything?

'OK, I've had more than enough of this. I'm going back now and I *will* tell my dad about you. He'll give you the sack for this! You . . . you are not a nice man, professor.' She could feel herself trembling: for all her threats there was no way she could go back unless she could get her wretched chair under her own control again.

The professor looked into a little peephole in the door for a second then placed his palm over the handle; the glow intensified and the door swung open. He looked over his shoulder at her, puzzled.

'What has "nice" got to do with anything? The word has changed meaning in the last few centuries but I don't think any of the definitions have ever applied to me. I have always preferred the terms "clever", "skilful", and "ruthless"—it is the unholy trinity that buys survival in both worlds.

But most of all I object to being called a "man"—I have not a drop of human blood in me. Now, I would very much appreciate it if you would be quiet: I've work to do.'

Linette couldn't have protested further even if she had wished as she was rendered quite speechless by the view before her. She moved forward on to a balcony. In front of her, in what should have been solid earth under the Radcliffe Camera, was a white version of the building but upside down, a kind of ghost Camera. Peering over the edge, she could see nothing below the roof but stars. Her head spun and she sat back abruptly.

Stars? Impossible.

She looked again. They were still there.

A narrow walkway connected the balcony with the Ghost Camera but it twisted like a strand of DNA so that you couldn't hope to cross without falling off. That didn't deter the professor. Gordon followed, pulling Bob with him.

'Wait! No!' Linette called.

The professor paused at the point where the bridge began to twist. 'Really, my dear, I asked for silence, did I not?' He pointed at her and she felt a gag form in her mouth. She put her hands to her face but there was nothing there. Panic-struck, her breathing accelerated—she was going to suffocate!

'Now, now, don't be like that,' the professor said sternly, seeing her eyes go wide. 'If you promise to behave, I'll take the silencing spell off.' He held her gaze with his own, a cat with a mouse trapped under a paw. 'Do you promise?'

Terrified she was going to die, Linette nodded. He waved his stick and the muffling sensation eased. She rubbed her mouth and throat.

'You can wait there if you wish,' the professor called cheerfully as he continued his passage across. 'But if you decide to follow, just tell your chair to go forwards and it will take you over.' He was now walking upside down—but his hair and clothing were not hanging past his shoulders, no dangling tie or loose change falling from pockets. It was as if gravity no longer controlled him. And the two dogs were able to trot along like a slow moving roller-coaster on a corkscrew.

How were they doing this?

Then Linette remembered the professor had said the chair would obey her. She had to escape this madness.

'Go back!' she whispered to the triskel.

Nothing. Naturally the devious inventor would not give her complete control of the programme. That left her the option of sitting here for who knew how long while Tiago's dog got dragged off to some terrible end in that impossible building.

She wouldn't be much of a friend to Tiago if she let his pet go without a protest. That meant following.

Her gut feeling told her that it would be horribly dangerous, but that wasn't enough to stop her. 'Go forward.'

The triskel immediately spun and propelled her on to the narrow walkway. It was just a few centimetres wider than her chair, a thought she had no wish to dwell on. Closing her eyes (there was only so much weirdness her brain could stand) she let the triskel take her across.

# Chapter 15

There was no answer from Professor Marmaduke's rooms.

'I'll search the gardens,' offered Roxy. 'That'll give me a chance to find a robin.'

Ignoring the rain, she headed off under an archway and on to the tree-lined pathway that led to the walk with a view of the Radcliffe Camera.

'Let's go and call on Linette,' suggested Rick. 'She might've seen the professor—or Bob for that matter.'

Tiago gave a tight nod, his anxiety for his dog having reached epic proportions.

Mrs Kwan was busy making coffee for the workmen when the two boys knocked on the front door of their temporary accommodation.

'Oh, hello. Horrible weather today, no? Come into the dry.' She stood back to let them in. They followed her to the kitchen where she returned to her task of setting out a tray of mugs. 'Linette's not here just at the moment. She's gone somewhere with Professor Marmaduke. He left a note for me to say he'd fetched her.' She gestured to a piece of paper on the table; spidery writing crawled across the page. 'You can wait here in the dry if you like.'

Rick touched the corner of the paper. It was slightly hot—a sign that it had got here by magical transfer rather than more conventional hand delivery. Odd.

'We're in a bit of a hurry. Any idea where they've gone?' Tiago asked.

Mrs Kwan frowned. 'Now you mention it, I don't. Try the professor's rooms—he sometimes helps her with her homework.'

'Been there. No one in.'

She shrugged. 'Then I'm afraid I'm out of ideas. Linette left her phone behind so she won't have gone far—she knows not to leave the college without it.'

Tiago tried to peer over her shoulders further into the house. 'Have you seen my dog?'

'What, the little black and white one you had with you the other day?'

Tiago nodded. 'Yes, that's Bob.'

'Sorry no, but I'll keep an eye out for him.' She patted Tiago on the shoulder. 'You should keep him on a lead in town, *chéri*.'

'Thanks. We'll go and look for Linette.' Rick beckoned Tiago away. 'Come on, let's find Roxy.'

They didn't have far to go as Roxy ran into them as she hurtled round the corner. 'Bob!' she gasped. 'The robins saw him!'

'Professor Marmaduke has him, doesn't he?' Rick said. Things were beginning to slot in place for Rick. The Mage Fey had been the only real candidate for meddling with the ring once human interference had been ruled out. Dr Ventikos, the other known Fey on the spot, did not have the skills. Marmaduke had just not trusted them enough to let them in on the secret of the new Round Table. But what part did Bob have to play in Marmaduke's revenge on Oberon?

'It's been him all along—for all of it.' Rick pulled them into an alcove by the chapel decorated with sword-shaped stained-glass windows. 'I dismissed him too quickly as a suspect when he said it was probably a malfunction. I liked him too much to think he'd hide the truth from us.'

Tiago ran his hands through his hair and tugged at the roots. 'I hate not knowing—not understanding! Maybe he needs Bob for some reason?

Maybe he does have a good plan that will defeat Oberon?'

'But why lie to us?' asked Roxy.

Tiago shook his head vehemently. 'He's not lied—he's just kept his plans secret. He wouldn't lie, not to me. He's going to tell us, I'm sure.'

'Why?' Roxy peered at him curiously.

'Trust me; he just wouldn't.'

'Tiago, my robins saw Gordon pulling Bob down into the cellars—that doesn't sound as though Bob wanted to help.' Roxy gulped. 'And they said Professor Marmaduke followed with Linette soon after.'

'What!' exclaimed Rick. 'Was she all right?'

'The robins didn't see. She's not come back up.'

Tiago kicked the wall. 'He wouldn't harm her. He wouldn't.'

Roxy frowned. 'Oh, Tiago, I know he's a Mage and everything, but haven't you always said you're from a trickster people?'

Tiago shook his head.

'And he's not likely to hurt Bob, not when he knows how important he is to you.'

'It's still possible that we're on the same side as him—against Oberon's tyranny I mean,' suggested Rick, trying to find a bright side. 'We should go after him—find out what he's doing, if it is a new Round Table to divert power or something else he's up to.'

'We have to follow—Linette's with him now,' added Roxy. 'I really don't like that.'

'You have to admit, Tiago, he might not do anything to harm Bob, but I'm not convinced he'll be so careful of a human.'

'I bet you are wrong—I bet he has a good reason for all of this,' Tiago said mutinously.

'Well, let's catch up with him and prove it. So, how are we going to find him?'

'I can take you to where my robins last saw him.' Roxy led the way out of the alcove. 'Follow me.'

There were many doors leading off the quad where the robins waited for Roxy.

'We can't afford to make a mistake—we'll get thrown out if we're caught,' said Rick, glancing over at a porter by the front gate who was watching them suspiciously.

'We won't go wrong—you can find him.' Tiago tapped Rick's chest. 'Remember—you are magnetized magically to each other.'

'How does that work exactly?'

'I guess you need to look inside and see which way you want to go.'

'As simple as that?'

'We'll soon find out,' muttered Roxy.

Rick closed his eyes. His magic was strong, fully charged on the green energy of Earth. He could feel a tug somewhere in the vicinity of his breast bone, almost as if he was hooked on to another magical presence that was towing him in a certain direction. 'OK, take my hand, I'm not going to open my eyes. Let's see where this goes.'

With confident steps, he led them out of the sunshine into the shadow of the archway.

'Ow!' He collided with a heavy wooden door half hidden by ivy. 'You were supposed to stop me when we got here!'

'Sorry—didn't want to break your concentration,' said Roxy. She tried the door, expecting it to be locked, but it opened smoothly. 'Seems as though you're right: someone has been this way recently.'

Down the steps, they found a cellar with cobwebby racks of wine. Rick let his magical sense lead him to a place in the corner between two wooden shelves.

'There must be a hidden door.' Anyone with a basic grasp of spells could uncover it with a revelation spell that was attracted to any magical object and would settle on it like a silvery net. Rick quickly exposed it. More complicated was the locking mechanism—that was unlike anything they had ever encountered at Dark Lore.

'Any ideas?' Rick asked.

Roxy pulled a couple of lock picks from her pocket.

'You just happened to have those with you?' Rick marvelled.

'Raised by pixies, remember. Never leave home without them.'

Unfortunately, the professor must have anticipated pixie ways: the picks melted in the lock, burnt to a stub by magic.

Tiago clicked his fingers. 'Rick, I've been thinking—Brazen Face.'

'You mean that totally useless prophet of doom in the professor's office.'

'Useless but maybe not totally. Remember what he said—everything he said?'

'That one of us would meet with disaster?'

'No, not that. No, the other thing he said, besides the stuff about socks and you changing the fate of Avalon.'

Rick searched his memory. 'Something about Mage Fey being defeated by their arrogance?'

'What if the professor thinks he's the only Mage Fey who can open the door?'

'That doesn't help us.'

'It does—the only Mage Fey, get it? He's not expecting another one down here.'

Roxy cottoned on before Rick. 'Oh, that's good. Go on, Tiago, peer through the peephole.'

Now Rick understood—magical iris recognition.

'Now grasp the handle.' Mage palm print.

There was a pause and Rick had time to think they had failed, before the door swung smoothly open.

Tiago grinned. 'Cool. I'm Mage enough, it seems.'

Rick was already advancing into the tunnel. 'Come on.'

Roxy and Tiago followed swiftly, their feet hardly making any noise on the smooth white floor.

'Do we have a plan?' asked Tiago.

'Not really,' admitted Rick.

'Yeah, we do, guys.' Roxy grinned at them. ' "Fly by" and "seat of the pants" feature very heavily.'

Tiago sniggered.

'You know, I like working with you two.' Rick drew his sword out of its scabbard with a soft whoosh.

'Yeah, go Team Changeling.' This time Roxy said it as if she meant it. She took a place at his right-hand side.

Tiago joined them on Rick's left. 'Let's get Bob and Linette back.'

# Chapter 16

The wheelchair came to a gentle stop the other side of the bridge in a doorway. Linette opened her eyes gingerly—she couldn't really believe she had just crossed that impossible twisted structure but she had felt nothing, no rush of blood to the head, no pull of gravity. Shelving that experience in the 'too difficult to comprehend' file for the moment, she surveyed her new surroundings. She had been delivered 'upside down'—if such categories worked here—so that the ghost Radcliffe Camera was the right way round. With the sky overhead, she felt as though she had gone outside rather than deeper into the earth. How peculiar—she could swear there was a breeze. The air smelt salt-fresh and bracing, not the traffic-infused stuff above ground.

'You have to face it, Linette,' she muttered to herself, 'you've probably gone mad as none of this can exist.'

Ordering the triskel to take her inside, she glided into the building. Here the resemblance to the Oxford Radcliffe Camera stopped: no shelves, no scholars, no books: just a smooth spiral winding upwards (or was it downwards?). The slope curled round and round to what was the roof of this building and out of sight. The whooshing sound she'd noticed earlier was much louder here, uncannily like the breathing of a great monster. The walls appeared to squeeze then rise slightly, reminding her of the concertina effect she'd spotted that time in the Fellows' Garden.

'Ah, you chose to join us.' The professor appeared above looking over the rail of the spiral about halfway up. 'Now you're here, you might as well come and see what I've been up to.'

'What about Bob?' she called, not convinced that joining the mad professor was the best plan at all.

'He's safe. Gordon is looking after him.'

*Looking after him?* Bullying him into submission, more like.

Deciding she was doing no good staying where she was, Linette let the triskel propel her up the slope.

'Are you going to explain to me what all this is about?' Linette asked when she reached the professor. He was in a chamber two-thirds of the way up, a thick transparent partition separating the room from the spiral. The walls also seemed to be lined with glass; the place shone, giving the impression they were slightly wet. A bay window gave a view only of darkness—all the light was inside.

It must be a bit like this inside a crystal, Linette thought, as her wheels glided soundlessly across the slippery floor.

A spherical object with a definite similarity to an astrolabe she'd seen in the Museum of the History of Science sat on a large round table under the window. Within the golden grid of the globe was a track bent in a spiral shape; a series of tiny glass balls were set ready at the top to run down the gold wires like an elaborate helterskelter.

'Hmm, what's that?' The professor was clearly not paying her any more attention, concentrating on the fiddly task of lining up the little spheres.

'What's going on?' Linette repeated in blunter language. 'What have you done with Bob?'

Satisfied with the alignment he had achieved, the professor stood up and turned to her. 'Look out of the window.'

Linette rolled closer to the desk.

'Careful! Don't jog the instruments or . . . well, the result would not be good for either of us,' he warned.

Mindful of where she was putting her chair, Linette leaned forward to get a glimpse of the view. She swore under her breath. 'Where are we?'

'Congratulations, my dear, you have crossed into the Fey realm of Avalon.'

He really was insane. Or she was.

Linette rubbed her eyes, but no, the distant snow-capped mountains stayed where they were, gleaming in the light of millions of stars that stretched in swirls and sweeps in the midnight-blue sky—a sky as Van Gogh would have painted it. If she craned her head to the right, she could see the ocean washing into a rocky bay, ink-black waters tipped with quills of foam. The white Camera appeared here to be situated like a lighthouse on a peninsula.

'Avalon?'

'That's right. To be exact, you are looking out on the part of Avalon called the Land Under the Waves. Forget everything you think you know about Feys, Linette: we are not in Tinker Bell territory. The Dark Folk, Feys and other fey bloods, are the oldest people alive in this universe, living in parallel to your world on a slightly different physical plane so, obviously, your physicists are yet to find us. They've theorized we might be there but can't detect us.' He nudged one glass bead with the edge of a fingernail to stop it slipping from its place.

'I see,' Linette murmured. Her brain felt as if it had been left back on that bridge because she could not think what she should do or say in such extraordinary circumstances.

'Our magic, as you see it, is really a form of advanced scientific knowledge. We manipulate the elements at the quantum level in dimensions beyond those with which you are familiar.'

'Uh-huh.'

He appeared amused by her stunned state and could not resist piling on the impossible. 'I am King Malduc of Misty Lake, once ruler of this realm—soon to be in charge again.'

Yes, and she was the Queen of Sheba. He had obviously completely lost his sanity along the way. Linette tried to get a grip on the situation. 'OK, I'm not even going to mention that Fey business but I can accept we are somewhere else—not Oxford. Why?'

He folded his arms. 'I suppose I can tell you—after all, you can do nothing with the information now you are here. I've used this sphere to drain Avalon of power. With that power I have made a door.'

'Should I say "well done"?'

He laughed. 'Yes. It was quite a feat, even for me. I think I've also cracked how to avoid the unfortunate tremor side effect so Oxford should survive. The Fey make portals all the time—brief intersections between the two worlds, but no one had made a permanent passage before.'

'Is this like some kind of worm-hole?' Linette asked, thinking of the Sci-Fi films she'd watched.

The professor dismissed the concept with a scornful snort. 'No, no, far more complicated than that—worm-holes involve collapsed stars and black holes—simple stuff. To keep my connection open, I have had to use a billion dimensions in Hilbert space.'

'Pardon?'

'Ask your mother—it is a concept human scientists are only now beginning to discuss, but I have actually been there. And now so have you.' He rubbed his chin. 'And the two dogs. The trick is to stop the universe imploding at the collision of the two worlds—it doesn't like the Fey matter of Avalon mixing with the atoms of yours—rather like gunpowder and a match. It takes excessive amounts of power to achieve but I have managed to isolate the match to prevent it igniting the powder, if you follow me.'

No, but that wasn't important. 'I still don't understand why you've done this . . . this thing.'

'No, you wouldn't. There's only one person who managed it before on a smaller scale and that was Merlin. He would understand how I have developed his idea of a Round Table and made it so much more powerful, diverting huge flows of magical power into my doorway. Your friends would comprehend too. Tiago anyway.' He took a silk handkerchief out of his breast pocket and cleaned a speck of dust off the desk. 'He'd appreciate my Sphere. Inside is a miniature of the Fey reactor. It steals the magic it needs, but having more dimensions than the old Round Table, it is much more powerful.'

'Why would my friends understand?'

'Because they are from the Fey realm of Avalon. I told you: they are changelings. You must have heard the tales of the children swapped for Fey offspring?'

'But they're just stories.'

'Everything is story if you think about it—the Big Bang, discovery of gravity, your own birth as your parents tell you about it. People shape their existence by story.'

'I meant they can't be true—they're fantasy.'

He quirked an eyebrow. 'Really?'

Inside this fantastical building, Linette felt on very shaky ground with this claim. 'I thought they were.'

'Think again, my dear. Life as you conceived it is the fantasy—this is the reality.'

'So what are you going to do with this passageway?' She gave a frail laugh. 'Start a new form of tourism?'

He shook his head. 'Oh no. I'm planning an invasion.'

'Of what?' When would her head stop whirling?

'Your world, of course. Avalon has been ruled for centuries by a tyrant. I learned to my cost that you can't challenge him while he retains his magic. If I own the human world and have the source of Fey magical power in my hands, I will then be strong enough to challenge Oberon.'

'But isn't he a character in a play?' Linette wobbled back to thinking that this must be some very strange hallucination, parts of her subconscious doing a tango across her brain.

'Funnily enough, it was I who whispered his name to Will Shakespeare down the tavern one evening—an excellent piece of negative propaganda, *A Midsummer Night's Dream*, when you read it carefully. Oberon is quite the monster—all those demands and meddling where he shouldn't.'

Going down the pub with Shakespeare! Marmaduke would have to be over four hundred years old to do that—but then he had already claimed to have been injured in a joust a thousand years ago.

Could anyone be that old? 'You are talking non-sense—you have to be.'

'If you don't believe me, Linette, then why not take a proper look outside?' The professor turned back to his instruments. 'You have only two choic-es now: stay in this isolation room with me while I run my Feysyk particle reactor at full power and draw the magic off for my Sphere, or go beyond contamination range.' He gestured to the rocky shoreline.

'I'd prefer to go home.'

'Not possible.'

Linette rubbed her legging-clad thighs nerv-ously, wishing she could get up and go wherever she wanted. 'Can I take Bob with me?' She didn't fancy the idea of leaving him exposed in a build-ing where an isolation room was required.

'Fine by me.' Professor Marmaduke checked his pocket watch. 'Bob and Gordon will need to stretch their legs by now.' He poked his head out of the glass door. 'Gordon! Walkies!'

Linette pushed past him. 'How do I get outside?'

'Go through the door opposite the one you came in. Don't come back in until Gordon tells you it is safe to do so—that's very important.'

'How will he tell me?'

The professor shrugged. 'Frankly, my dear, if you can't read clear signals from a Gabriel hound then you deserve to be irradiated with a fatal dose of Fey particles.'

'Thanks for nothing,' Linette muttered.

'I could've just killed you, you know. I think I am being extremely generous under the circumstances. Almost the perfect host.'

'Apart from the not-letting-me-leave-taking-Bob-captive part.'

He chuckled. 'Ah, I hoped you would overlook such minor transgressions. After all, I am going to be your new king by the end of the lunar month.'

More like *lunatic* month, thought Linette.

Gordon appeared with Bob still attached to his tether. If Linette knew anything about dogs' expressions, she could've sworn the Gabriel hound was looking a bit sheepish about dragging the little terrier around.

'Come on, boys; let's go visit "Avalon"—see if we can escape from this madness.'

First she tried the door she had come through. Locked. She hadn't really thought that there would be escape that way—far too easy. Following the curve of the wall she travelled to the opposite door and turned the dolphin-shaped handle. It opened smoothly, revealing a flight of steps running down to a beach. Hopefully the professor's clever device would solve the problem of travelling over sand for her as they had had no difficulty with stairs.

That left her to puzzle out the unavoidable mystery that she was facing a starlit sea that looked real, sounded real and, from the wet spray whipped off the choppy surface, tasted real. Her only sense in denial—common sense—still screamed at her that this could not possibly be there.

'OK, test the theory by experience,' Linette murmured, setting her chair on a collision course with the surf.

The dogs bounded away to mark their territory. In his excitement at being outside, Gordon barked, dropped the rope and leapt in the air, chasing a silver-backed seagull that had made the mistake of landing on this particular stretch of sand. He bounded a few huge paces, almost as if he could fly. Bob turned tail and ran for Linette, jumping on to her lap for a hug. Linette slipped the rope and collar off his neck and gave him a good scratch under his chin.

'OK now?'

He licked her face.

'Stay with me. I won't let anything happen to you if I can help it.'

The triskel adapted to the uneven surface by changing shape to flat paddles, rather like diver's flippers. A few grains of sand flicked up at each revolution, but unless someone was standing directly behind the chair that was no inconvenience.

Putting Bob on a flat-topped stone next to her, Linette pulled off her shoes and socks.

Bob cocked his head.

'I'm going in,' Linette explained. 'I'm not going to believe in any of this until I feel it.'

He whined.

'I'll be fine. I'm a good swimmer. Guard my jacket for me.' Stripping down to her T-shirt and leggings, Linette ordered the chair to go deeper. The waves rocked it and splashed water into her face, provoking a startled laugh—it was cold, but not unbearably so. Once the wheels were submerged, she knew she had gone far enough. Pushing off with her arms, she began to swim away from the chair, using breaststroke so she could look about her.

Yes, the sea was still there: cool as marble, black like a rook's wing, except where the starlight caught on the crest of the waves. She pulled down strongly with her arms to touch the sandy bottom, fist curling around an odd shaped object. Bringing it to the surface and shaking hair from her eyes, she saw that she had retrieved a pale blue and lemon razor shell. Turning on to her back, she floated, shell resting on her chest, and gazed up at the pinpoint bright stars. She couldn't trace any of the familiar patterns—no Plough or Pole Star, not even a Southern Cross—but they were there and she was here (wherever that was) and she could no longer be in denial. Somehow, some way, she had crossed from land-bound Oxford to a coast where a white twin to the Radcliffe Camera dominated the shore. If it had existed in her world, surely she would have heard about it? And if it wasn't Earth, then that left the professor's claim for Avalon the front-runner in the explanation race, no matter how absurd that seemed.

She felt a touch on her waist. Linette shivered. Drifting seaweed? Dropping the shell, she flipped over and swished her hands through the water. Her fingertips brushed against something sleek and flexible. A fish? Please, not a shark! This place might even have sea monsters!

Heart thumping, she pulled for the shore. Gordon started barking hysterically on the beach—his great booming voice echoing off the cliffs. He was joined by Bob who was yipping so hard he was lifting off his rock with each effort.

'What is it? Can you see?' Linette called, swimming for the shore as smoothly and as quickly as she could manage. Sharks go for splashing, she remembered.

Bob crouched in a growl, then exploded into another round of barks that had begun to sound an awful lot like 'Linette! Linette!' to her ears.

She had to get to safety. Stretching out in a powerful front crawl, she swept her arm through the water.

Only to have her hand caught at the lowest point of the stroke. Fingers seized hers and pulled her under.

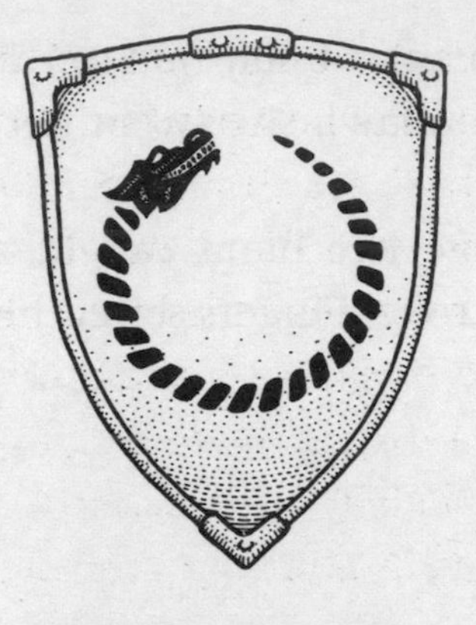

# Chapter 17

Passing through the second door at the end of the white corridor, Rick, Roxy, and Tiago reached the balcony and looked across at the ghost Camera.

'What is it?' Roxy wondered. She tapped her nails on the rail nervously. 'I mean, I know what it looks like, but what does it do?'

'Must be the Fey particle reactor.' Rick moved to examine the bridge. 'The professor is definitely over there. I can feel him. How do we get across this?'

Tiago crouched down and placed his palm flat on the first twist. 'Can you do another revelation spell, *amigo*?'

'OK.' Rick knelt beside him. 'You want to see what sort of charms he's used on this?'

'Yep. But I think we should stand back.'

Rick took his sword in a two-handed grip and pointed it at the centre of the bridge. Reaching for a thread of magic, he spun it into a fine web then used the sword like a fishing rod to cast it over the structure. It immediately twisted in echo of the bridge.

Tiago rubbed his chin. 'Interesting. I think he's bent gravity.'

'Can you do that?' asked Roxy.

'I didn't think it possible except for something really powerful like a black hole, but look at Rick's spell-net: it's caught on the charm boundaries.'

'So we can . . . what? Walk across?'

'Theoretically.'

'OK.' Roxy closed her eyes and took a first step. 'I'd appreciate it if one of you would pull me back with a clever charm if this fails.'

'Let me go first.' Rick tried to catch her before she committed to the crossing.

'No way. I'm the lightest—let me test it. Plus you're better at spells than me—I might need you.'

Rick watched reluctantly as she made her way across the bridge. She reached halfway to a point where she was upside down and then looked back at them.

'Amazing—you're the wrong way up!' she called.

'How does it feel?' Rick asked.

'Completely and utterly normal—it's awesome.'

Before her words had died away, the building began to shimmer and creak as the professor played with the reactor. The white light that suffused the air flickered off—on—off. Roxy vanished in the darkness.

'Oh sprites!' she shrieked.

'Quick! We need light!' Tiago told Rick.

Rick drew on his power, bringing magic to the surface and letting his skin glow with searchlight intensity. Roxy was hanging on to the edge of the bridge, her feet dangling over the star-filled abyss.

Tiago was already pulling off his shoes—he'd already ditched the red socks. 'Hang on, Roxy! I'm coming!'

'How?' asked Rick. The effort of sustaining such a bright light spell to fill the cavern was rapidly draining him.

'Glue charm. I use it for playing tricks. If you put it on your palms and soles, you can make like Spider Man.'

'Hurry!' Roxy wailed. 'I'm slipping!'

On all fours, Tiago moved out on to the bridge. The spell took a lot of concentration as he had to remove the glue each time he wanted to lift a hand or foot and he couldn't afford to get it wrong and lose his connection. Despite the difficulties, he was travelling swiftly and reached Roxy before her grip loosened.

'Grab my wrist, *amiga*.' He planted his palm by her white knuckles.

'Oh pixies, I hate this.' She let go of one side and made a lunge at his arm. From Tiago's 'ouch!', Rick knew she had hit the target perhaps a little too enthusiastically.

'OK, got you,' said Tiago. 'I'm going to drag you up and we'll climb this thing together to the other end.'

Tiago was right: there was no point going back when Bob and Linette were in there. As he watched the two inch over, Roxy clinging to Tiago's back, Rick searched his memory for a spell he could use to make the journey across.

'We're safe!' called Tiago, once they'd reached the far side.

'Good. I'm going to have to let the light go so I can spell myself over. I think the professor must be messing with the power switches so we can't trust the bridge.'

'OK.'

'Be careful, Rick!' shouted Roxy.

'When am I not?' Rick released the thread pulling on his magic to produce the glow, letting his skin subside to normal.

Roxy gave a hollow laugh. 'Do you really want me to answer that?'

Rick smiled wryly. OK, he needed to cross but he didn't think he could learn that spider charm of Tiago's so quickly. He would have to do it by more conventional means and forget the bridge entirely. Slipping the belt off his jeans, he muttered a transformation charm, transforming it into a hank of rope. Tying one end round the balcony rail, he threw the other in the direction of the other two.

'Incoming!' he called—a shade too late.

'That hob-snot of a rope hit me!' squawked Roxy.

'Sorry. Can you find something to tie it to?'

A gentle glow lit up the other side: Roxy had conjured a flame in the palm of her hand; it looked odd with the flame burning downwards. 'Yes, there's a rail over here by the door. Are you going to do what I think you are going to do?'

'Yep. Tiago is not the only one with circus skills.'

'Rick, are you sure?'

'No, I'm not sure. But I haven't got anything else to conjure to make another rope. Do you?'

They were woefully under prepared for this quest—neither of them had so much as a belt.

'No, sorry!' Roxy called. 'Do you want us to look inside the building for something we can use?'

'Best not split up yet. It's OK. I think I can manage with one.' Rick muttered another spell to transform the sword into a pole. 'Theory is, if I use this, my centre of gravity goes below the rope so I can't fall off easily.'

'Don't talk to me about gravity,' shouted Roxy. 'It must flip somewhere in the middle to make your up our down. What are you going to do then?'

'Improvise.' He took off his shoes and strung them round his neck. 'Can you keep the light going so I can see where I'm putting my feet?'

His answer was a second flame as Tiago joined the candle brigade.

'Coming over.' Rick climbed up on to the rail. His head was spinning already as he looked down at his pale toes curled round the edge.

I can do this, he told himself.

Feeling out with his right foot, he found a spot where he felt balanced and took the first step. The rope pressed reassuringly against his sole.

'As long as I don't think too much about what I'm doing, this will work,' Rick muttered.

The silence was the worst thing—he could feel the others holding their breath waiting for him to make a mistake. His heel slid, leaving him wobbling in the middle of the rope. Roxy shrieked then clapped her hand over her mouth. Sweat ran between his shoulder blades as he struggled to level the pole again. OK—he was back in balance.

Leaning forward slightly, he suddenly realized that the perspiration on his brow was tickling upwards into his hair. Tilting back, it ran down his cheek. That must mean he had reached the trickiest spot, the point where gravity flipped to the other world.

'What are you going to do, Rick?' called Roxy.

'Suggestions?' His voice sounded calmer than he felt.

'If you find the very centre, you should be able to float round,' Tiago offered. 'But it's only a billionth of a centimetre wide so it might take a while.'

'Any *other* suggestions?'

'Grab the rope with your hands and feet and make like a sloth,' said Roxy.

He preferred her idea. The difficult bit was making sure he didn't lose his transformed sword as he transferred his grip to the rope. 'Aethel, grab my sword when I let go.'

The snake slithered down his right arm and formed a loop around the pole.

Rick slowly lowered himself so he was crouching over the taut rope 'Now!'

As the snake took the weight of the rod, Rick lunged forward and grabbed the rope. It was the weirdest sensation: his torso was pulled one way, his legs another, leaving him firmly wedged on the rope.

'Ow!'

'You OK?' called Roxy.

He decided not to tell her that he might be singing only high notes until he recovered. 'Yep, fine!' He edged forward, hanging 'below' the rope in the new gravity field. Once he was in reach of the other side, Tiago grabbed the pole from the snake and Roxy helped haul him on to the platform.

Roxy flung her arms around him. 'You did it—you're safe.'

He ruffled her hair. 'So are you.'

Tiago saluted Rick. 'Way to go, Sloth-Man.'

Rick bowed. 'Thanks.' He turned the sword back to its original form and sheathed it. 'So how do you think we get in there?' He nodded to the entrance ahead.

Tiago took the handle and turned it. The door opened. 'I think we just do this.'

The last bubbles of air slipped from Linette's lips as she struggled in the arms trapping her under the surface. If she took a gasp, she would be on the way to drowning, but nothing seemed to work—she could not squirm free. Then with a heave of parting water, she was in the air, clutched against the chest of a creature with dark blue, scaled skin, clad in a tunic of seaweed. His green hair lay flat against an oval skull, lank like pond weed out of the water; black eyes bright like pebbles shining in a rock pool; mouth curved in a shark's grin, sharp double row of teeth visible in the gap.

'*Mon dieu.*' Linette wished she could summon a faint. She was in the arms of some kind of alien species. Arms that ended in webbed hands and feet.

The creature looked down at her, his grin widening. 'You are not a mermaid.'

'You're not either,' she whispered, rather surprised she could talk at all. She then realized he was not alone. Striding out of the sea along the full stretch of the beach were hundreds of others like him. 'What exactly are you?'

He raised an amused eyebrow. 'We are the nixen. And what are you?'

'Human. A girl.'

He looked more closely at her, studying her hands with particular interest. 'How do you swim with no webs?'

'I simply do.' Linette really didn't think this was the most important question that needed answering right now. 'Why are you here?' The water was only ankle deep now. The blue creature made to drop her on her feet. 'Don't! I can't walk!'

He paused. 'Humans do not walk?'

'This one doesn't. I've a wheelchair—somewhere.' She looked desperately about her and spotted the two dogs guarding it from the attentions of the advancing nixen. 'There.'

The creature shifted her in his arms. 'You are no burden for me. I could carry you for the invasion.'

Her heart sank. 'You're the professor's army?'

'Professor?'

'Professor Marmaduke.'

'You mean *King* Malduc of the Misty Lake?'

She nodded.

'Yes, we are part of his forces. Aren't you? We were ordered to gather here.'

'No, I'm just a . . . a visitor. Please, can you put me in the chair, Mr Nixen?'

He shook his head. 'You must learn, human: one nix, two nixen. You should call me Mr Nix—or you could call me by my given name, Prince Litu.' He lowered her with surprising gentleness into her chair. 'So, you are one of our new subjects?'

'What?' Linette reversed out of the water to a dry patch of sand.

'When we rule the human world, King Malduc explained that we would have command of the humans.'

'He did?'

'You are frail creatures, he said, easily defeated as you have no magic.'

'Might not be as easy as all that,' mumbled Linette, squeezing out her hair. Her clothes felt uncomfortably soggy.

'Is that right?' Prince Litu sketched a shape in the air and she found she was dry, no longer shivering with the cold. He beckoned his soldiers to join him.

Bob brought her socks and Gordon dragged her jacket and shoes within reach. Linette dressed quickly.

The nixen gathered around Prince Litu, checking their weapons and confirming their orders. Each soldier carried a trident and a net like an ancient gladiator. These tools might not look very formidable when compared to semi-automatic rifles, but there was something in the cold expression in the nixen's faces that made Linette think twice about dismissing them as a fighting force. What they could do with these tools combined with magic she could not guess.

Bob cocked his head intelligently at Linette, as if expecting her to come up with a plan.

'OK, boys, we've sea creatures planning an invasion of Earth. What now?' she muttered to the dogs. 'Is it safe to go back in yet?'

Gordon whined.

'I'll take that as a "no".'

A horn sounded in the distance. Prince Litu stood up straighter, revealing his full height to be nearer seven than six feet.

'The Wild Ride approaches. Nixen, fall in!'

The sea creatures formed up in ranks, not straight lines like human soldiers, but curved ones of waves creeping up a beach.

'What's happening now?' Linette asked.

Prince Litu patted her on the head. 'Stay.' He seemed to include the dogs in the same order, confirming that he thought of her as some kind of harmless pet. He did not regard humans as top species on Earth, but had filed them in his mind as fairly low down on the scale. Now she knew how Bob and Gordon must feel.

She had no time to dwell on this because the Wild Ride was rapidly approaching from over the mountains. It appeared first as a gash of silvery light on the night horizon. The glow increased until Linette could see the individuals making up the Ride. The soldiers were human in form but elongated, like the shadows cast by bodies in the late afternoon sun. Their skin was ghostly white, stretched tight as if it had already begun to desiccate and shrink on the skeleton beneath. White-blond hair whipped behind them, strands plaited and dressed with feathers and scraps of cloth forming a fluttering mane of dreadlocks. Each warrior rode a grey horse, but they were like no horses she had ever seen before. Their coats shimmered as if they weren't quite there, a mirage in a desert. Flames flickered in their eyes and sparks flew from their hooves even though they appeared never to make contact with the earth, gliding along on an invisible road of their own making.

The lead horse hurtled to a stop a few paces from Prince Litu, sending an explosion of metallic sparks jetting into the air. The rider, a woman with feral eyes, her armour made of bones, nodded once to the sea creature.

'Prince Litu, you are also in time, I see, to join Malduc's Sphere.' The men and women of the Ride spread out on the shore around her. Their horses moved restlessly, never letting their hooves rest on the sand for more than a second. It was hard to count their number but Linette guessed there were at least as many as the nixen.

'Hail, Arianrhod.' Prince Litu bowed.

'Are we all gathered?' The lady scanned the surroundings. 'Air and water are come, but what of earth and fire?'

'Earth remains loyal to Oberon. He has granted the hobs and the dwarves all rights to mine the underground treasures of his kingdom—they were not to be swayed.'

'And the People of Fire?'

'They will come at sunrise when we have already passed through.'

'Ah yes.' She pulled off one black glove. 'I forgot that they prefer to move by daylight.' She now noticed Linette and the two dogs. 'And who are these creatures? What part do they play in this?'

'I do not know—I too have only just arrived. The two-legged one is a human.' Prince Litu summoned one of his warriors with a whistle. A tall nix with a fine head of bottle-green hair stepped forward. 'My son, go enquire within when exactly the pathway created by the Sphere is ready for us to cross. You know what to do?'

'Yes, Father.' The nix saluted and took a step towards the white Camera.

Gordon growled and stood between the nix warrior and the entrance.

'I think that means it is not yet safe to go in,' Linette offered.

Arianrhod turned to her in surprise as a person would if their cat suddenly started talking to them. 'How wonderful—the human can speak intelligently.'

Litu smiled with what might have been meant as encouragement at Linette but instead looked terrifying with all those teeth. 'Yes, she is quite talented. I think it must be the magic of this place aiding her in understanding. Humans are said to be quite stupid.'

If that was what they believed then they were going to be in for a big shock when they went ahead with this invasion idea. Linette knew she couldn't let it happen without a protest. They might not get far against the combined armies of the world but the initial attack would be unopposed. Oxford was simply not ready to find itself at the centre of an unearthly onslaught—and her parents were living right on top of the invasion route.

'You can't do this, you know,' Linette argued as Litu waved his son to ignore the dog and take his message inside. 'There are seven billion humans—we won't let you just take over without a fight. One little force like this,' she gestured to the troops on the beach, 'will not succeed.'

Arianrhod bent low over her mount's shoulder and picked up one of Linette's hands to study it curiously. 'They don't have many defences, do they? No claws.' She peered at Linette's mouth. 'No teeth to speak of.'

'But they show signs of developed brains.' Litu stroked Linette's hair absent-mindedly, his gaze fixed on the white building. 'I think we could get rather fond of our new subjects once they are trained.'

Linette pushed his hand away, anger bubbling. 'Aren't you listening? I'm trying to stop you heading off on some kind of suicidal mission for that madman in there!' She stabbed a finger at the Camera. 'Professor Marmaduke—your King Malduc—is crazy—and you need to forget anything he's told you and stay here in your own world. We've got bombs and guns and tanks—we won't just let you take over because you say so!'

'I might keep this one with me,' Prince Litu continued as if her outburst had been no more than a round of barking. 'She swims well even without webs. I first thought she was a mermaid until I saw she had no tail.'

'Lucky for her.' Arianrhod secured her dreadlocks with a ragged scarf, preparing for the serious business of invasion. 'I thought your kind feasted on merpeople.'

'Only very occasionally—when we're particularly annoyed with them. I imagine they've all found very urgent reasons to keep away from the other sites where our armies are gathering.'

Other sites?

'Please tell me this isn't happening in other places?' said Linette. Prince Litu didn't look as if he was going to answer so she tugged at his tunic to get his attention. 'I need to understand. It's my world that's at stake.'

Prince Litu gave her another of his condescending smiles. 'No need to worry your little brain with the details, human.'

Arianrhod unsheathed her pale sword. 'Is it true, Prince Litu, that King Malduc has succeeded in breaking the power flow to every major ring and diverted it to build stable crossing points?'

'Yes. This one is the lynchpin—he has been able to create pathways to nine fey power rings from here. Humans will be overwhelmed in a short, sharp campaign, coming at them from all directions.' The prince took his trident from his standard bearer.

'It is truly astonishing—after all these years of believing it impossible,' the warrior-woman marvelled.

'Indeed. King Malduc has finally mastered the process started by Merlin of balancing the exchange between Avalon and Earth so we can come and go without causing the collapse of the universe.'

Arianrhod tightened her grip on the metal studded bridle. 'And if not? If he's got it wrong?'

Prince Litu's eyes gleamed with a fanatic's fervour. 'Then we all go down in one glorious implosion of the universe as the Fey matter reacts with Earth's particles. But what an end that would be! Do you not agree?' He held up a closed fist, expression hard, judging the sincerity of her response to his challenge.

Arianrhod leaned over from her saddle and knocked her knuckles against his—a fellow soldier's salute. 'Yes, warrior, a worthy end. Anything to defeat Oberon.'

Linette hugged Bob. How could these magical creatures risk so much in a stupid power struggle? More to the point, what could she do to stop them?

# Chapter 18

It was completely dark in the building. Rick reached out to catch Roxy's arm, not wanting to bump into her by mistake, not when they could not see what lay before their feet.

'Light?' Roxy whispered.

'Let me,' offered Tiago. He cupped a flame in his palm.

'Why is it so dark?'

Tiago nurtured the light until they could see the whole of the bottom section of the building. 'I think he's cut the power again. Dark Lore will be melting.'

'But what's the point of that?' Rick moved towards the spiral slope. 'If he's already draining the power with his Round Table technology, what's he doing with it?'

'Let's go ask him,' suggested Tiago, still holding on to the hope that this was a good idea.

'Where do you think he's keeping Linette and Bob?' Roxy peered into the gloom. 'There's another door over there.'

'He's not outside.' Rick hated the uncertainty. 'I can feel him—he's above us somewhere.'

The handle on the second door pressed down, dolphin nose bobbing.

'Someone's coming—quick!' Rick pulled Roxy and Tiago down into the shadows under the spiral. Tiago snuffed out the flame.

A warrior nix marched past them, heading straight up the slope, his way lit by the strange phosphorescent glow that came from his scaly skin. With weapons strapped to his side, he was armed for war.

What was a nix doing here? At least that gave them a clue where the other exit led: the nixen were never found outside Avalon, liking their sea-realm far too much to stray into human waters. This building must be a crossing point.

Tiago prodded Rick. 'I can hear Linette's voice—out there.'

His part Fey senses had to be far better than human because Rick couldn't hear a thing. 'You sure?'

Tiago hissed in annoyance.

'OK, you're sure.' Rick flicked his gaze upwards. They could all now detect the rumble of voices above and the light was growing stronger.

'. . . lucky young nix. Thirty seconds later and you would've been pounded by Fey particles,' the professor exclaimed.

Hobspit. They had to move.

'Roxy—go and find Linette. Tiago and I will get the professor—discover what he's planning.'

With a nod, Roxy darted from their hiding place and made for the door. The two boys rushed up the slope.

*15 . . . 14 . . . 13 . . .* Rick counted down in his head. They were on the point of being crispy-fried and he hadn't a clue where they were going.

'We've got to get out of this spiral!' Tiago shouted. 'He must have somewhere out of the particle stream.'

'What would it look like?' Rick let his magic blaze out—no point hiding if you are about to be plunged into a cauldron of magic. *8 . . . 7 . . . 6.*

'We'll know when we see it.'

Rounding a bend, Rick spotted the glass doors and the two figures inside. 'I see it.' He put his shoulder to the door and forced his way through, Tiago tumbling in on his heels.

'What in the name . . . !' roared the professor—but he was no longer the professor. His glamour had dropped away and he stood tall and straight—not a wizened old man but a king in the prime of his years, long chestnut hair, robes of gold cloth, but still the same silver eyes of one of the Mage Fey. 'Shut the door!'

With a kick of his feet, Rick slammed the glass door closed.

'Too close, too close.' Marmaduke clutched his chest, leaning heavily on the desk for support. 'Troll claws: now you've done it!' His move had nudged one of the tiny silver balls off its perch to lead a cascade down the model—a mesmerizing trickle that became a waterfall. With a shimmer they winked from sight at the bottom and reappeared at the top to begin the descent again, perpetual motion made possible by a clever manipulation of extra dimensional space.

Beyond the doors, the spiral exploded in a blaze of green light. The noise rose to excruciating levels even in this protected place, like thunder on a mountaintop. Silver balls the size of millstones whizzed past, gathering speed until they could no longer be seen by the human eye.

Tiago flopped on his back. 'I guess that's the Fey particle reactor reacting.' He gave a wild chuckle, celebrating their narrow escape.

Rick stood up. The sphere on the table was glowing brighter and brighter as it fed on the power outside. A ring of large shallow bowls surrounded it, the surface of each sparking with blue lights.

'Who are these intruders, your majesty?' the nix snarled, stepping in front of Marmaduke in a protective gesture, trident pointed towards them. Rick drew his sword.

'Students of Dark Lore—Oberon's agents but possibly now our allies. We will have to see.' Marmaduke dismissed them by turning his back to crouch over his instruments. Rick found it hard to reconcile this majestic presence with the frail Oxford professor Marmaduke had pretended to be. He still looked more ancient than any Fey blood Rick had seen, but it was age combined with strength, the walking stick now a laughably unnecessary prop, lying unused on the floor.

Marmaduke had set up nine water-filled bowls on the table and now consulted each like a chef in the final stages of preparing a feast.

The nix was not so ready to let the boys' presence in the room pass without further comment. 'Shall I kill them for you?'

Tiago jumped to his feet, 'Hey!'

'No, leave them,' Marmaduke ordered, not bothered by the brewing confrontation. 'We've far more important things to consider just at present.' Marmaduke folded back his long sleeves and breathed on the water of the first basin. The New York skyline shimmered into view.

'Is that the Yankee Stadium?' Tiago asked.

'Of course. One of my North American rings. The drac are leading the charge there.'

The warrior nix spat: the nixen were famous for their hatred of their smaller rivals, the water drac, jealous of their ability to shapeshift at will.

'Professor, is this a Round Table?' Tiago gestured to the strange instruments set out before them.

'A Sphere—more dimensions than a Table.'

Rick felt a spark of hope that this might be the new Round Table he'd dreamed of joining.

'So able to divert more power,' concluded Tiago. 'Awesome. So, you are planning to overthrow Oberon; how?'

'By seizing control of magic.'

'Invading Earth?' Tiago frowned.

The professor nodded.

'How many armies do you have exactly?'

'Nine—to start with. To divert Fey power you need enough warriors at your Table, or in my case, Sphere, to act as channels. Merlin thought too small: he made the places at the Round Table for single knights to occupy; I have built mine using the distinctive characters of each race in my army. He managed a small diversion to his knights; I am about to re-route the entire river.'

'But what about the impact on Earth?' asked Rick. His hope that this would be a plot he would want to support was rapidly diminishing.

Marmaduke breathed on the other bowls; images rose from the depth: the mound hiding the first Chinese emperor's tomb surrounded by his terracotta army; Ngorongoro crater in Tanzania; the Jantar Mantar observatory in Delhi; a patch of outback near Uluru, the red rock; the Moscow metro; the vast monkey with curled tail etched on the Peruvian desert; the interior of the Radcliffe Camera and . . .

'Is that a motorway?' Rick watched the little cars zipping at high speed through the picture shimmering on the water's surface.

'Yes, the Capital Beltway circling Washington.'

Tiago glanced at Rick, both puzzled. 'How's this going to work exactly?'

'Ah, that's the quite brilliant part. As you will have gathered from the bowls, Tiago, I'm sending hundreds of thousands of Fey warriors into your world. A couple of individuals crossing the boundary are one thing; a whole army is another, so I had to do something to stabilize the exchange. The portals calculate and, on my order, take the balance from the human world and put it in Avalon.' He tapped his lips with a long index finger. 'Let me see—that human girl, Linette, has already passed that way so we have already disturbed the balance; I can show you how to even it up.' He pointed his walking stick—now shivering into its true form as a wizard's staff—at the warrior who, while they had been caught up in their argument, had silently advanced on the table to take a closer look at the instruments. 'Be proud, nix: you have the honour of being the first.' The nix flashed out of the room, reappearing in the basin showing the abandoned reading room of the Radcliffe Camera. Oberon's ice throne materialized beside him.

Marmaduke raised his hands in a victory salute. 'Excellent! I could not have chosen better myself. I hope Oberon was sitting on it when it disappeared.'

'Why did—?' began Rick.

'Linette's chair,' explained Tiago, catching on swiftly. 'This reactor must weigh each particle and compensate one world for the loss to the other.'

'What? At random?'

'I've set the parameters quite close in your world—just the surrounding area to each ring. In Avalon, I've targeted Oberon's court as the exchange for any materials I bring over from Earth. He'll be most annoyed as inanimate objects start vanishing without explanation. It will rapidly destroy his riches and citadel without me having to lay siege.'

This wasn't Rick's dream: it was his nightmare. 'You can't do this!' This new Round Table—this Sphere—would catapult confused Yankee fans, Oxford students, Tanzanian tribesmen, Aboriginal people, Washington motorists, Russian commuters, Indian scientists, and Chinese tourists out of one world and dump them in another. In effect, Marmaduke was destroying the differences between the worlds, making all people potential changelings.

'And who is going to prevent me? Not my fellow Mage here—Santiago sees the need for Oberon to be defeated, don't you?'

Tiago wouldn't meet Rick's eyes. 'I suppose so.'

Marmaduke nodded with satisfaction. 'Oberon won't fall without a major shift in the balance of power—I've learnt that to my cost over the centuries. My more subtle plots to undermine him have failed; I needed a big gesture to destroy his grip on Avalon. Tiago, have you considered my offer?'

Shocked, Rick turned to look at his companion. What was this?

Tiago shuffled, head hung. 'Where's Bob?'

Rick didn't like the thoughts his mind was entertaining. Tiago had been on his own with Marmaduke the day before.

'Your dog is quite safe. He's on the beach. So, Tiago, what's your answer? Be quick—there's much to be accomplished this day.'

Rick grabbed his friend's arm and pulled him aside. 'What's he offered you?'

Tiago couldn't have looked guiltier. 'There's so much going on here that you don't understand, Rick.' He tugged free.

'Yes—because you kept it quiet!'

'It's difficult—look, I'm part Mage too.'

'But he took Bob!'

Tiago scrunched up his face in pain. 'Yeah, I know—but he's . . . he's . . . '

'I'm his father.' Marmaduke placed a hand on Tiago's shoulder, guiding him to his side. 'Forget the humans. We need to start afresh, you and I.'

Well, that certainly changed things, thought Rick. Fey-bells, he was in trouble now.

'And you were going to tell us this when exactly, *amigo*?' hissed Rick. Had Tiago invented all this stuff about Bob to get them here? Had he set them up?

'I was going to tell—when I was ready.' Aware he had let his friends down badly, Tiago took refuge in anger. 'Look, it was my secret, all right? I wanted time to get used to finding him.'

'So Bob never was in danger.' Rick shook his head in disgust.

'Yes—I mean, I thought he was. I really thought he was.' Tiago turned to Marmaduke. 'He's OK, isn't he? And Linette?'

'I've not harmed them, though it was unfortunate your friend got involved. She won't be able to go back now, not until I'm victorious—she knows too much.'

They'd see about that, thought Rick grimly.

'So, are you going to join me, Tiago? I have need of an heir to my kingdoms; there will be too much for one king to rule when I add Earth to my old realm of Avalon.'

Tiago's expression showed his anguish. 'I . . . um . . . I would just prefer a dad really. I'd like to get to know you first. I didn't understand that you planned all these exchanges.'

Marmaduke let his arm fall from Tiago's shoulders. 'I see. My life has taught me that there's no pleasure being on the losing side; that's something you must learn, Santiago. I rather thought you might need encouragement to claim your inheritance after meeting you in the company of this human—that's why I borrowed Bob. He is a guarantee of your good behaviour.' He seized Tiago's shoulders and gave him a little shake. 'Open your eyes: it is time you woke up to your Mage blood. It's calling to you—asking you to seize this chance.'

'So you only want a son for what he can do for you? You're more of a monster than Oberon!' said Rick accusingly. 'At least he didn't pretend to care!'

Tiago brushed his father's hands off and moved to stand alone. Rick understood why he was torn: he had a chance to recover his past, find out what it meant to be a Mage, take part in the rebellion, but that was at the expense of his present friendships. 'What do you want from me?'

Marmaduke smiled, pleased he'd got this much: the half-Mage standing apart, no longer backing the human. 'Not more than you can bear, Tiago, you'll see.'

'I bet your idea of what's OK doesn't match Tiago's,' argued Rick, not at all sure which way this argument was going. His closeness to Tiago had been a very recent thing—and even then he hadn't really known him, had he?

'Maybe,' said Tiago with a shrug, 'but I am as much Mage Fey as human—I can't forget that. I don't belong in the human world any more than I do at Dark Lore. And the professor—well, he's really King Malduc.'

'What!'

'That's what he told me yesterday. He ruled Avalon from his old seat at Dark Lore. I could be a prince too, he says. That's got to be pretty cool. So you see, there has to be something else, something better for me than being Oberon's prisoner.'

'Exactly!' Marmaduke checked his pocket watch. 'About now, the Fey particle reactors in these nine sites should have reached critical mass. My armies are about to move. You have to choose your side.'

Losing Tiago to Marmaduke would be fatal. Rick couldn't fight two of them and it looked rapidly as if they were going to come to a battle. 'Tiago, don't listen to him. He's just making thousands more like us—out of time, out of place. You know that can't be right.'

'He won't listen to you, human, because he won't risk Bob. That leaves you—and frankly, no one needs an Anglo-Saxon prince these days.' Marmaduke gave a cruel laugh.

Rick settled his grip more tightly on his sword hilt. 'No, I won't—I can't allow this. Tiago?'

'Rick, I dunno . . . it's not that I think he's right, I just don't know what's best. We talked about overthrowing Oberon—isn't this it?'

'Not his way—there has to be another.'

Marmaduke raised his staff. 'You are far too late, Elfric. I'm sending in my armies. The second reign of King Malduc is about to begin.'

'Not if I can do anything about it.' Wishing he knew on which side Tiago would fight, Rick raised his blade and swung, aiming his stroke at Marmaduke's staff.

'Oh, for goblin's sake, boy! You're wasting my time!' Marmaduke whirled his staff expertly, deflecting the blow. He carried through the parry to bring his staff down towards Rick's head. Rick let the momentum of the deflection carry him round, spinning out of reach.

The staff shimmered in Marmaduke's hand, transforming into a long sword with a black leather hilt wrapped with silver wire. 'If you insist on a fight, then let's see what you've learned, changeling. Remember, I had lessons from your father—you don't think you stand a chance of beating me?'

That was exactly the wrong thing to say, reminding Rick of all his reasons to resent the Mage. A red rage gripped him. His vision narrowed. He chopped at his opponent's sword, the edges meeting in an arm-juddering clang.

'Clumsy. You'd dull our blades if they were not magical,' jeered Marmaduke.

Rick felt angry with himself—angry with the whole hobspitting situation. He didn't actually want to kill Tiago's father. He just wanted to stop his plan from going ahead. But how?

The blades met again, letting out a shriek of metal on metal. Marmaduke was driving him back, away from the table on which his equipment sat. The chamber began to shake.

Marmaduke's face set in a furious scowl. 'Santiago!'

Tiago rushed to the table and checked the instruments. 'Rick, he's right: there's no time—the power's building up. We have to release it or this whole place—possibly the fabric of time too—is going to blow! There are barely minutes left. We've got to let the armies go through.'

'I. Will. Not. Let. Him. Invade. Earth.' Rick took a stroke with each word forced between his teeth. He was holding his own in this sword fight and Marmaduke knew it.

Then Marmaduke clenched his fist and threw a ball of magic at Rick—an elfshot. Calling on his reflexes, Rick brought up his sword to deflect it in time but the impact jerked him back against the wall. His head clipped the edge of the window embrasure. Stars wheeled before his eyes.

The flat of a sword knocked his weapon from his numbed fingers.

'Finally,' panted Marmaduke. He swept Rick's legs from under him, leaving him sprawled on the floor, then kicked his stomach for good measure. 'Enough is enough, human. You've angered your last Mage Fey. Santiago, come here. Deal with him while I sort out the Sphere. You need to learn the first lesson of a leader—even those who you once counted as an ally must be sacrificed. Take my sword and put an end to this miserable creature's life.'

Rick lay with his face pressed to the cold tiled floor, barely conscious, but aware that his fate now rested in the hands of someone he had once foolishly considered a friend.

'You're joking?' asked Tiago in a horrified voice.

The icy touch of steel pricked the back of Rick's neck. 'I'm deadly serious. Kill him or I'll summon your dog here and slit his throat to show you how it's done. Choose: the human or Bob? Which is it to be?'

# Chapter 19

The nix warrior had only just entered the white Camera when the door reopened and Roxy flew down the steps. Bob charged towards her and leapt into her arms, licking her face.

'Yes, yes, Tiago is fine. He's in there,' Roxy told the ecstatic dog, not breaking her stride.

As she ran towards Linette, the building flashed white hot behind her, light blazing from the windows. The gathered armies watched, shading their eyes against the glare; everyone could see the vortex whirling in the spiral reactor. It seemed impossible that the building could contain it, the sides rippling as if stone had turned to water.

'They're in there?' squeaked Linette. 'They'll never survive that!'

'Fall back!' ordered Prince Litu. His army retreated into the waves, taking refuge in the sea. Arianrhod gestured to her cavalry. They turned with the crunch of hundreds of hooves on pebbles and streamed away to the furthest point of the bay.

Roxy reached Linette and dumped Bob on her lap. 'Let's go. We need to take cover.'

'What about Rick and Tiago?' Linette set the wheelchair in motion.

Roxy grimaced. 'They have to be OK. They'll be with Professor Marmaduke—he'll have some where safe.'

Linette risked a glance over her shoulder. The building looked like a rocket on lift-off, energy on the point of blasting out from any weakness. 'I hope he knows what he's doing with that reactor thing.'

Roxy jogged beside her, Gordon at her heels. 'Are you OK? You don't look as shocked by all this as I expected.'

'I haven't had time to be shocked. I'm working my way up to it. Do you know what's going on?'

'Not really. We're making guesses—something to do with the revenge that Professor Marmaduke has been planning against the ruler of Avalon.'

Linette shook her head. 'I can't quite get used to that name—it's out of Arthurian legend isn't it—not real life? And the Fey, they are fairies like in sugar plums and tinsel, no?'

'You think that because you've not met any real Feys. Other than Magmell.'

'He's a fairy?' Linette gave a shocked laugh at the absurdity.

'Yeah, but "fairy" is an English corruption and massive misunderstanding. He's quite typical. The professor is one of the Mage Fey, a minority, with a big chip on their shoulder for having invented everything, then been pushed out when they got too powerful.'

'That blue sea creature—Prince Litu—claims the professor is really someone called King Malduc.'

Roxy pulled Linette to a stop behind a rock. 'Are you certain he said that?'

'As much as I can be sure of anything here.' Linette didn't like Roxy's expression—it meant she had passed on some very bad news without realizing.

'Marmaduke.' Roxy closed her eyes. 'Malduc, the name for the old king before Oberon—yes, I see. Not really a false name.'

'Who is he?'

'Oberon's most bitter enemy. Their last battle ruined Mag Mor, the Great Plain, turning it into a wasteland. Malduc was forced out, and then he simply disappeared from stories. If Oberon and Malduc are going head to head, we can expect thousands, if not millions, of people to suffer.'

Linette only understood the gist of what Roxy was saying. 'When did all this happen the last time?'

'A few decades ago—or two millennia—depends on your perspective.' Roxy shivered, gazing back at the Camera. 'But it's not good. This keeps getting much, much bigger.'

'Well, Professor Marmaduke has got armies poised to invade the human world. Is that big enough?' Linette hugged Bob, wondering when her normal life would resume, if ever.

'King Malduc wouldn't care about controlling the Earth,' said Roxy. 'He must have a plan to take over from Oberon. Of course: the magic supply! Control that and you control everything!'

'So how are we going to stop him?' Linette frowned. 'We do want to stop him, don't we?'

Roxy caught Linette's suspicious tone and gave her a flicker of a grin. 'Course we do, you twit. While I'd cheer to see Oberon defeated, I wouldn't want it to come at so high a price.'

'But you're . . . '

'A changeling. I know. So's Rick. But hey, not our life choice, remember? We're here just because we want to stop people getting hurt. Swapping leaders of Avalon is not on our agenda. Not today, at any rate. Sorry, we couldn't tell you—didn't think you would believe us.'

Linette looked down at the beautiful pale sand flecked with blue and yellow specks from crushed seashells. Strange how the natural processes of the sea still ruled in a place as unnatural as this, turning shells to sand over the years. 'Still not sure I do believe you—or any of this.'

Roxy patted her arm. 'It's OK. Just pretend for the moment—we'll sort it all out later. Tell me: what have we got here?' She gestured to the waiting army.

'Something called the Wild Ride and nixen.'

Roxy nibbled her fingernail. 'Yeah, Wild Ride—that follows. They were always allies of King Malduc, an ethereal race of fey riders on flame horses. They are the closest Avalon gets to ghosts. But nixen? That's odd. I thought they had no desire to leave their seas. Oberon gives them pretty much a free hand to do as they like.'

'Prince Litu wants our world too—thinks he'd do a better job looking after it. He also seems to think humans are dim. He wants a few pets, he says.'

Roxy shook her head. 'No, nixen are ambitious but they just aren't that interested in land creatures. Something doesn't add up.'

'But I heard him tell this to the woman who leads the Wild Ride.'

'Still . . . ' Roxy stood up. The Camera had stabilized, now glowing with an intense white light like a burning magnesium flare. The nixen emerged from the waves, water streaming down sleek skin and shiny green tunics, Prince Litu at the front having put on a helmet of starfish and coral, a turtle shell breastplate strapped to his chest. Rather than look at the beacon of a building as everyone else was doing, he was gazing over the heads of the Wild Ride, scanning the skies.

'Is it almost time to pass over to the human world?' asked Arianrhod, spurring her mount to within speaking distance.

On the horizon, an arrow formation of great flying birds appeared, heading their way. No, not birds, Linette realized. Now she really was dreaming because she thought she saw dragons. And on their backs were riders in armour. Behind them flew a mass of tiny helicopters, but they only seemed to carry one soldier like a personal parachute.

'Captain, it's Oberon!' shouted one rider from the rear.

All heads turned.

'We've got to run.' Roxy pulled on the chair but it had sunk in the sand.

Linette was too shocked to give the triskel the order to move. Arianrhod took one look at Prince Litu's proud smile and understood.

'Traitor! You've betrayed our plans to Oberon!' the wild rider shrieked in fury. 'You were never part of the rebellion!'

Prince Litu swung his trident to his shoulder. 'To my shame, I was at first, but no longer. You—you are the traitors—following that usurper, meddling with the stability of Avalon. Malduc's willingness to risk all planted the seeds of doubt but as soon as I heard yesterday that he brought the drac, our enemies, over to his side, I knew I had to stop your rebellion.'

Arianrhod swung her sword, her cavalry drawing their blades with a soundless sweep. Her feathery hair fluttered like a ragged banner in the breeze. 'You will regret your choice, shark!'

The prince lunged forward, trying to skewer her mount with his weapon but the prongs were kicked away with a clang by iron-shod hooves. He stood back, not really surprised his initial attack had not beaten her guard. 'The regret will be yours.'

'We'll see who will die here!' howled Arianrhod, her bone armour clicking as she spurred her horse forward, intent on running him down. Litu crouched, trident held forward, braced against the earth. The horse was forced to leap clean over him to avoid being disembowelled.

On this signal, the two armies clashed, nixen pitted against horsemen on the very edge of the water. The air was full of the screams of hatred, curses and howls as blades found their target. It was like watching a stormy sea beat at bone-hard rocks, neither willing to give an inch, bolts of magic blasting a path when weapons struck.

Roxy tugged at the handles of Linette's wheelchair. 'Get this thing to move! We've got to hide.'

Linette whispered an order to the triskel, bidding them retreat up the beach to the sea cliffs. They could take refuge in the caverns hollowed out by the tides while the two races of Dark Folk battled it out on the strand.

'Why have we got to hide?' she asked the panting Roxy as they scrambled up the tiered beach, dogs outstripping them in their race for cover. 'No one was fighting us.'

'Dragons!' gasped Roxy, holding her side against a stitch. 'They're Oberon's shock troops. They don't distinguish between friend and foe—hating all Dark Folk equally. Just watch—the nixen will clear out when the dragons land. Second thoughts—don't watch: it's going to be horrendous.'

The dogs had found a cave for them all to fit inside. Linette had a grandstand view of the ugly fight on the sand as the Wild Ride fought for its survival. As the first of the battle-scarred dragons swooped, Prince Litu ordered the conch horn to be sounded to signal his troops to retreat. They hurried to sink back into the water, leaving their wounded where they lay. But Linette only had eyes for the airborne menace. The dragons swept through the horsemen like a combine harvester through a cornfield. They weren't the beautiful rainbow colours of fairytale dragons; their black or grey skins were knobbled like solidified lava flows and as hard. Magic faded before it reached their hide and any arrow bounced off with no harm done. It took Linette a few seconds to see that each dragon had a Fey rider on its back, clinging to a black leather and chain harness. Blinkers covered each dragon's eyes, rendering them nearly blind.

'That's how Oberon controls them,' Roxy explained, grimacing as a rider's arm was slashed in two by a claw. 'They would never obey otherwise.'

'But they're so ugly!'

'They've been that way ever since they were forced into servitude. They blend into their background—a kind of camouflage as they have chameleon blood—and they're kept in dungeons by Oberon's castle. No colour there.'

The Fey-captors whipped their mounts into a frenzy with iron-spiked crops, showing no mercy. The dragons roared, dashing horses and riders from the Wild Ride to the ground, trampling on the fallen. Little blood was spilt—the horses once crushed crumbled and blew away like ash from a funeral pyre, their spark extinguished. The Fey riders snapped apart, their thin silvery blood leaking slowly into the sand. Arianrhod managed to rally part of her troops for a concerted strike against one of the smaller dragons, fatally injuring it with a sword through the throat, but their temporary victory was reversed when a massive grey dragon landed in their midst and set about slashing them into fragments. Those who tried to flee were caught by the soldiers zooming in on their helicopter wings like a swarm of wasps.

Even though the members of the Wild Ride weren't human, or even a species she knew, it was still horrid to see living creatures annihilated with no mercy. Linette couldn't bear to watch any more as Arianrhod was thrown from her horse, propelled into the sea to sink from sight in the midst of the nixen army. She heard Roxy curse again.

'Oh goblin-sliming hobspit! Oberon's here.'

Linette dropped her hands from her eyes and followed Roxy's pointing finger. The biggest of the dragons—an ugly brute the colour of pumice stone—had a silver-clad rider on his back. On a sleek black dragon beside him rode a female warrior dressed in purple.

Roxy groaned. 'And Morgan.'

'Who's Morgan?'

'Our commander, runs Dark Lore.'

'Your old school?' Linette gasped. The wicked looking warrior-rider didn't look like any headteacher Linette had ever met. She was certainly not in the practice of handing out detentions because she had just run a rider through the gut. 'Remind me not to apply there.'

'It's not a school—it's a prison. Don't worry—you have to be a changeling to get in.'

'And her being here is bad news because . . . ?'

'She's ruthless—like our king. We'll try and sneak you back without them noticing you when the crisis is over.'

'But Prince Litu has met me.' Linette gestured to herself. 'Don't really pass for a Fey, do I?'

The battle on the shore was winding down. A few riders managed to flee but the rest lay dead, littered along the sand like bones scattered by grave robbers. With a flick of his hand, Oberon released four shackles from his saddle; the ends flew wide to stake his mount to the ground by each limb. The dragon roared in fury, beating its wings in helpless anger, but Oberon ignored it. He jumped down, pulling off his gauntlets. After securing her dragon in similar fashion, Morgan leapt to the sand and joined him at the water's edge. The soldiers landed further off, forming ranks across the shingle, wings of their helicopters folded flat. Prince Litu emerged from the sea with Arianrhod's sword in his hand. He knelt and presented it to the king.

'Your enemies are vanquished, sire,' said the nix.

'Not so.' Oberon stared at the glowing building. 'When you decided to betray your fellow conspirators and return to my favour, I told you there was a price for my forgiveness. I thought you were supposed to have a nix inside by now.'

The prince shifted anxiously. 'I do, your majesty. I will not make the mistake of betraying you again. I sent my best soldier. He had orders to break the Sphere powering the doorways once the other armies were in the process of crossing between our worlds, thus destroying them.'

'Clearly something has gone wrong. That means there are still eight armies waiting to pass over to Earth, including the drac.'

Prince Litu spat on the ground at the mention of his enemies.

'Traitor Malduc could still launch his onslaught on the humans and hold my source of power to ransom.'

Prince Litu gestured to where the girls were hiding. 'One of the humans came out just before the Sphere was activated. She might know what's happening inside.'

'I wish he hadn't done that,' mumbled Roxy. Squeezing Linette's hand, she left their cave and slid down the beach to reach the king in double quick time. 'Your majesty.' She curtsied stiffly.

Linette looked at Bob. Bob cocked his head as if to say 'you're not going to leave her alone with those three, are you?'

'You're right. Come on, Bob. We've an audience with a king.' Linette directed her chair to follow Roxy.

# Chapter 20

With the sword pressing into his skin, Rick was unable to move his head, not even able to glimpse Tiago's face so he could make an appeal eye to eye. All he could see was the hem of Marmaduke's robes.

'I can't kill my friend,' said Tiago. Rick heard him retreat to the far end of the room, coming now into view to one side of the Mage.

'Then your dog dies. I'll say the summoning spell and he can come to perish in the human's place.' Marmaduke left the point of the sword against Rick's neck but shifted to face Tiago.

'That's not fair! You can't make me choose between them.'

'I'm not here to be fair, Santiago. You have to remember you are my son first or you are no use to me.'

Tiago hunched over as if he'd just been kicked in the stomach.

Professor Marmaduke laughed mockingly. 'Look at you! You're pitiful. Not a scrap of ambition. You truly are your human mother's child.'

Wrong thing to say. Tiago shot him a poisonous look, standing straight again. 'I owe you nothing. You didn't stay around when I was born—you let my mother die in slavery at the hands of the Spanish conquerors and me be raised in a Spanish orphanage until I was taken to Dark Lore.'

'I was one of the conquerors, *mi hijo*. Why do you think I made sure you ended up in Spain? I thought that race superior to the dying Aztecs.'

Tiago shook with rage.

'It was regrettable that the Fey found you where I had hidden you. They rounded up so many of my children. Fortunately, they never found out who was your father or you would be dead. I did that much for you.'

Tiago and Marmaduke were so absorbed in their argument that Rick could risk slipping Aethel from his wrist. The golden snake slithered to his fist, forming on his whispered command into the bent and slightly flattened shape of a boomerang.

'You know, professor, you don't understand humans even though you've lived here so long,' Tiago continued, bitterness dripping from each word like venom from a dragon fang. 'You're not offering me what I really want.'

'Don't be ridiculous: I'm offering you a kingdom,' Marmaduke said coldly.

'What-e-ver,' drawled Tiago, giving him a full blast of twenty-first century teenage disrespect.

What was Tiago doing, purposely baiting the professor? Did he want to be killed too? Rick gripped Aethel, waiting for his moment, movement restricted by the little detail of the sword pressing at his throat. If he shifted too quickly, he'd only succeed in cutting his own neck.

'Every word you speak proves that you are not ready for the position of honour I've offered you. You need a few years—perhaps a few centuries—to cool that temper of yours. You are only getting in my way here.' Marmaduke muttered some words under his breath and the sword went hot for a second, scorching Rick's skin. 'A stay in my dungeons in my old palace should cure you!'

As Marmaduke lifted the sword-wand to aim his spell at Tiago, Rick sprang, launching Aethel from his knees. Hampered by his awkward position, the boomerang only clipped Marmaduke on the temple. He didn't crumple but he did release his grip on his sword to clutch his face. Marmaduke shrieked, groping half-blind on the floor for his weapon.

Rick jumped to his feet and snatched Aethel from the air as she circled back. He looked round for his weapon but the sword had been kicked too far for him to reach in time.

A hand grasped the leather-and-silver wire hilt of Marmaduke's blade and pointed it straight at his target. '*Gán*!'

Professor Marmaduke vanished, leaving Tiago the new owner of his sword.

'Thanks,' said Rick, snatching up his sword, heart still pounding. 'What did you say?'

'Old Mage word meaning "begone". I figured he would've made his wand respond to his native tongue.'

Rick wasn't surprised that Tiago had proved a true friend; his instinct had never whispered that Tiago would go so far as to kill him. Try to reconcile enemies, yes; murder him, no. Still, it wasn't an easy thing to do: banishing the newly discovered father who had promised you a world. 'Where did you send him?'

Tiago shrugged. 'Wherever he was going to send me. His dungeons, I suppose. I didn't have time to work out how to change the destination.'

'He can get out then?' Rick half-expected Marmaduke to pop back into the room and blast them to oblivion.

'Nope. His old citadel is still under Oberon's control, isn't it? Only it's called Dark Lore House now. I guess Morgan has a new prisoner.'

'Yeah.' Rick sheathed his sword and stroked Aethel back into her place on his wrist. 'Drastically bad father you've got there, Tiago.'

'Yeah, he's a disaster. I dunno why I ever listened to him.'

Rick knew: because as orphans they all wanted to belong to someone. He would have done the same. 'Can say one thing for him: he's not short of ambition. He really thought he'd get to rule all worlds before what . . . ? End of today? Shows a man of vision.'

'*Mage* of vision, please.' Tiago touched his heart and bowed in mock respect. His expression suddenly sobered. 'Troll farts—his armies. They're still poised to invade.' He glanced at the Sphere. 'And this thing is exceeding all safety levels—it'll blow up in a minute. We might just have to do the exchange to get rid of the excess power he has diverted to the Sphere.'

'Then, genius, you'd better work out how to disarm the thing without causing the Earth to be overrun.'

Tiago scowled. 'Why me?'

'I'm not the one to get an A star in my last test. I'll have a go if you like.' Rick rolled up his sleeves and approached the table of instruments.

As he expected, Tiago leapt in his way. 'No. You stay away—far, far away.' He closed his eyes and the sword shimmered back to staff. He placed it flat on the table. 'OK, I can do this; I can do this.' He studied the model with anguished concentration. 'I'm just not sure how.'

The building began to creak. A crack snaked across the containment doors.

Rick could imagine how long they would both last if their barrier failed: no time at all. 'I'm going to have to push you for your best guess then.'

'Can I phone a friend?' Tiago rubbed his forehead. 'Look, either I try to slow the silver balls down so I can remove them one by one—it could take a while though.'

A panel in the glass doors fractured into a crazed pattern like a shattered windscreen.

'Or?' Rick tensed, waiting for the bath of Fey particles to flood the room. He imagined the end would be painfully quick.

'Or this. Pray that I'm right.' Tiago seized the staff and smashed it down on top of the Sphere. In a burst of white flame, the silver balls shot around the room, pinging off floor and walls like some demented pinball game. Link to the reactor abruptly broken, the machine slammed to a halt. The glow beyond the doors vanished.

Silence.

Tiago began to laugh hysterically. 'It worked—it worked! It was just a theory but it worked!'

Rick sagged against the wall in relief. 'Do I want to know how close that was to our complete destruction?'

Tiago did a somersault on the spot. 'Ta-dah! Engineering genius takes a bow!'

Rick laughed wearily and gave him the applause he requested. 'What did you do, O Genius? It didn't look very subtle.'

'I took a guess based on what Morgan did to the Round Table—split down the middle. If that worked to break Merlin's spell, then I guessed that if we smashed the Sphere and caught the Fey particles as they passed through the seventh dimension then they would not reappear in our reality and blow us to bits.'

'Come again.' Rick peered into the basins. Each human location looked blessedly normal—no invading armies in Red Square, no citizens fleeing their cars on the Beltway.

Tiago chuckled. 'You really suck at Feysyks, don't you?'

Rick let that one pass: Tiago had just saved them, after all.

'I told you before that to circulate from bottom back up to the top the reactor passes the material through the other dimensions beyond four. In a sense, the particles are everywhere all at once. If you crash the machine, the information as to where they should be gets wiped and they are dumped elsewhere—elsewhere normally being the seventh dimension.'

'Elsewhere is a place?'

'Yep. Home of all lost things.'

'So that was like crashing a human computer?'

Tiago rolled his eyes at this simplistic explanation. 'If you like.'

'That'll do for me.' Rick looked round the room. 'Is there anything else we have to fix before we find the girls and Bob?'

'No. Oberon's experts should be able to take it from here.' Tiago tipped the water out of the basin showing the Yankee Stadium on to the floor. 'No point letting Oberon know the full plan, is there? He'd just round up and execute the other rebels. I hope they have the sense to disband before he catches them on the Avalon side of the rings.'

'You're right.' Rick emptied out the images of the Moscow Metro and Tanzanian crater. 'Oops, must've knocked them over in that pitched battle we fought.'

'Yeah, bit of a bummer that.' Tiago spilled the last two basins. 'I know I'm a disloyal Mage, but there's a bit of me that doesn't want to give away everything to Dad's rival.'

'You know, Malduc's idea wasn't so bad, was it? Not the takeover the Earth bit but the challenge Oberon part. I mean, how else is anyone going to overthrow Oberon if they don't get at the source of his power like Arthur and Merlin did? They held out against repeated attack from Morgan and the Fey.'

'Yeah, but even they failed eventually. The Table was defeated.'

'But can't we learn from their mistakes? The professor's already improved on the design. We needn't run it to such a destructive level, only to siphon off enough power so we can defend ourselves.' Rick felt the idea crystallize in his mind—it had been there for some time; he just hadn't realized they might have to do it themselves. It was a big thought, a scary one, like reaching a cliff and knowing the only way forward was by jumping off and hoping to survive the landing. 'You know, Tiago, we were sent to hunt down the new knights of the Round Table and I've come away thinking that we are meant to become them. Are you up for it?'

Tiago's eyes glittered with excitement. 'There's a place for a half-Fey like me at the Table?'

'It wouldn't be complete without all of Team Changeling. Linette too because she's one of us now.'

'Wow, Rick, I don't know what to say! Except, well, yeah, of course. Count me in.'

Rick and Tiago emerged from the Camera to find a crowd on the beach.

'What in Avalon has been going on here?' murmured Rick.

'It's a bloody battlefield. Feybells, I hope Bob and the girls are OK!' Tiago began to run. Their anxiety lessened a little when they saw their friends were still alive. Roxy stood pale and shaken by Linette, who was in tears; the two dogs whimpered dejectedly. Oberon waited, arms folded, legs firmly planted apart on the sand, every inch the king in command of the situation. Morgan hovered at his side, her expression characteristically crafty. Behind this pair was a group of Fey dragon keepers, their reluctant mounts staked to the ground; further off, an army of nixen warriors, ankle-deep in the surge, and a platoon of sycacopter commandos. From the fact that no one was fighting, Rick concluded that these all had to be allies.

As soon as he spotted his master, Bob jumped off Linette's lap and raced towards Tiago, pouring out his mixed joy and fear in a stream of barks that Tiago appeared to understand perfectly. Tiago held out his arms and the dog jumped into his embrace.

'It's OK now,' he murmured into Bob's furry neck. 'We'll sort it out.'

There was no point delaying this interview. Rick led the way as they came to the spot where this impromptu court was being held. He bowed to King Oberon, though his eyes slid to Roxy and Linette in a silent question as to what was going on.

'The rebel Mage?' snapped Oberon, demanding his full attention.

'Sent to the dungeons at Dark Lore, sir,' replied Rick with equal curtness.

'The reactor?'

'Disarmed,' he added swiftly, knowing how Dark Lore depended on this power source. 'We've got it running again on the old power setting but it'll need to be checked for damage.'

The nixen leader approached. 'If I may, your majesty?'

Oberon waved him forward. 'Proceed, Prince Litu.'

The prince gripped Rick's T-shirt by the neck. 'Where is my son? I sent my best warrior to destroy the rebel's armies—did he succeed?'

Rick glanced nervously at Tiago. 'He got sent into the human world by Professor Marmaduke—King Malduc—before he had a chance.'

Prince Litu released his collar and gnashed his teeth together—a horrid clicking sound. 'My boy! We must get him back!'

Oberon's gaze was like a searchlight as it scanned them for clues to their success. 'What happened? Speak quickly, changelings.'

'I'm sorry, sir, but we couldn't stop Malduc sending the nix. It all happened so fast. He was demonstrating how his invention swapped Fey for human, keeping the balance between worlds. He'd already brought Linette over, you see, so had some slack to play with.' That sounded terrible. Rick wished he hadn't mentioned Linette at all. He swiftly moved on. 'When we saw what he planned to do, Tiago and I, we fought him. Between us, we managed to disarm the rebel, send him to the dungeons with his own spell, and then switch off the reactor.'

Oberon clapped slowly—a horrid sound. 'Well done, changelings. You have gone beyond my expectations.'

A fractious dragon tugged at the chains, growling as Fey guards prodded it back to the sand.

Rick glanced at the dragons, amazed to see the creatures so close up. 'Thank you, your majesty.'

'All that remains is for the last of the traitors to be found and eliminated. Where are the armies?'

Rick hoped his face was neutral. 'I'm sorry, sir, I didn't know there were others—we didn't get to hear much about Malduc's plans. Too busy fighting him.' Morgan looked as if she would like to interrupt and Rick felt that would be a very bad idea as she knew him far too well.

'I'm afraid we had to smash his equipment that conjured the portals to make it all stop,' added Tiago. 'There's not much left.'

'Send in your best forensic team,' Oberon ordered Morgan. 'I want every detail I can gather about that traitor's plans. The Wild Ride weren't his only allies; Prince Litu has told us that already. Round up all the drac for a start.'

'Yes, sire.' Morgan picked up a seashell, muttered a charm, and began transmitting her new commands.

Oberon turned back to Rick. 'I suppose you will want to be rewarded for your work?'

There was little the king could give him that he could want. Except freedom for changelings. 'If it pleases you, your majesty.'

'It doesn't, but I reward the faithful as well as I punish the traitorous.'

Rick felt a bubble of hope grow inside him—an insane, fragile dream that they might actually get to leave Avalon if he asked.

'Then, sir, might we stay? On Earth, I mean. Take up our lives again as ordinary humans?'

Oberon's eyebrow flicked up in surprise. 'Why?'

Rick couldn't give the real reasons—that he knew he had been betrayed from the moment he was snatched from his cradle—that he wanted to set up a new Round Table. 'We had no time to get even with the humans. I'd like a crack at that.'

As he had calculated, Oberon understood revenge. 'As long as you do not disrupt my realm, I have no objection. And with your changeling now back on this side, there is no bar to you going, Elfric. Indeed, if you stay you threaten the balance so I would rather see you gone.'

Rick bowed. He was going—he really was going!

'And as for Santiago here—he is a mixed blood so we don't have to worry about him. He is free to leave as well. You two completed the quest I set you so you can go.' Oberon dismissed them with a wave.

*What?*

'Your majesty, what about Roxy? We couldn't have done this without her.'

'But she was out here when you brought down Malduc—and her changeling remains in the human world: for both those reasons she stays.'

'Ask him the rest, Rick,' said Roxy in a hollow voice, nodding to Linette.

'But she's from the other world,' Rick protested. 'What can you want with Linette?'

'As of a few minutes ago, she is a changeling,' Oberon countered. 'The nix warrior was sent in her place—you told me this yourself. I cannot send someone with her knowledge back into the human world—not someone whose loyalty is questionable.'

'Please!' Linette begged, her voice breaking into a sob. 'I have parents—I can't stay here. I can't!'

Rick's heart sank. Fey bargains always, *always* had a sting in the tail. 'She has to go back, sire.'

Oberon raised an imperious eyebrow. 'You dare question my judgement? There is no inevitability. She is like any other changeling now—a burden on my realm. She must enrol in Dark Lore.'

'No, your majesty, she has to go back . . . because I'm staying. I'll be her balance. She'll be useful to you—she's the only one who will be able to sense where the nix warrior is as I guess they are now linked by the exchange.'

Prince Litu clicked his teeth in approval.

'Even if she did say anything,' continued Rick, 'no one would believe her—Avalon isn't real to humans.'

A triumphant smile flickered across Oberon's perilously beautiful face. 'Is that so?'

'If you allow.' Rick knelt, knowing when it was time to turn on the full humble act.

'Please, sire, let the human find my son,' begged Prince Litu.

Oberon nodded. 'I grant your wish, Elfric, Prince Litu. You may thank me later.'

Linette felt sick. This whole experience was plunging from one terrible twist to another like some nightmare fairground ride. First, when she had joined Roxy, the top-fairy-king-person had immediately announced she couldn't go back; now Oberon was manipulating matters so that Rick didn't get his 'get out of jail free' card he had briefly been promised. She felt terrible—like the person stealing the last place on the lifeboat off the *Titanic*.

'You can't do this,' she whispered. Now she'd met Morgan she had a shrewd idea what Dark Lore had to be like.

'It's OK.' Rick gave a brave shrug and hugged Roxy. 'We'll stick together.'

'Yeah.' Roxy hid her face on his shirtfront so no one could see her crying.

'But,' Linette sniffed, wiping her face impatiently: now was not the time for tears. 'But it's not fair.'

'No, it never is.'

'OK, I'm going with her,' Tiago announced, taking Linette by surprise. She had assumed he would stay with his friends, no question. 'I know I'm in the team and everything, but . . . '

Rick nodded. 'Yeah, I get it. You know what we must do?'

Tiago took a quick look over his shoulder. Morgan was approaching, formidable in her bruise-purple leather riding clothes, her boots grinding the stones and sand. Linette flinched back so her spine was pressed against her chair—the commander terrified her.

Rick frowned. 'We have to talk quickly before she sends you back home. We need a distraction. Gordon, Bob?' The two dogs took Rick's hint and bounded up to the nearest dragon. Ignoring the shouts of the dragon handlers, Gordon's plate-sized paws made short work of digging a stake out of the ground while Bob barked his encouragement. The black dragon heaved his front leg free and began creating panic among the nix warriors. Cursing, Morgan diverted to deal with the crisis.

'You mean talk about how we recruit our own Round Table?' Tiago whispered.

'What are you talking about?' Linette was completely at sea.

Roxy had caught on though. 'You think we can do it?' she asked, her eyes sparking with curiosity. 'Resist by forming our own circle?'

Rick nodded once, keeping an eye on the diversion by the dragons. 'Morgan was wrong: no one was recruiting humans; Malduc considered them beneath his notice, but actually it's a brilliant idea. How else are we changelings going to get free if we don't break out of Fey power? I don't know about you but I'm not happy just gaining our freedom for ourselves; I want all the changelings out of that prison and we need something more than wishes behind us.'

'We do it ourselves? But how?'

'I don't know, but there are two people who do: Merlin and Arthur. Looks like we're stuck in Avalon, Roxy, so we make the best of it and go after the king in exile. Tiago, and Linette if she wants, they go and find Merlin in his hiding place on Earth.'

'Not asking much are you.' Tiago smiled wryly.

'Nothing you can't handle, Mage boy. Tell Linette about it when you're safe from being overheard.'

Having directed the recapture of the dragon with a steel link net, Morgan now reached them. 'Whose familiar is that?' She pointed a black painted nail at Gordon.

'Er . . . mine?' offered Linette. Gordon gave her a grateful nudge of his wet nose on her knee.

'Keep him under better control or I will kill both of you next time. So, who is returning to the human world? King Oberon has asked me to create a portal to send no more than two of you back.'

'Linette and Tiago,' said Rick firmly.

'Ah, so I get my favourite warriors back at Dark Lore, do I?' Morgan rubbed a shell between her fingers. 'I've let Magmell and the pixie know. We're winding up this operation—your handlers will return to Avalon.'

Making a last inspection, Morgan's eyes fell on the triskel still bolted to the wheelchair. She swooped and ripped them off. 'You can't have those.'

Linette opened her mouth to protest, but Bob jumped on her knees and Gordon began barking at nothing in particular. If even the dogs knew better than to argue with Morgan, perhaps she should keep her mouth shut, Linette decided.

Roxy hugged Tiago. 'Where are you going to live?'

Tiago squeezed her tight. 'I'll be OK.'

'He'll be staying with me,' said Linette. 'My parents won't have it any other way when I explain he's homeless.'

Roxy next gave Linette a hug. 'Good luck.'

'They'll be so pleased to get me back, they won't care what I ask. But,' Linette tapped her watch—it had stopped working when she crossed the twisty bridge, 'I can't have been gone that long. It feels like for ever but it's probably only a couple of hours.'

'You should times that by a hundred. Time works weirdly here.'

Morgan began the preparations for casting the portal spell. Rick swiftly hugged Linette and then grasped Tiago's forearm with his right hand for a warrior's handshake. Patting both dogs goodbye, the two changelings stood back.

'We won't give up!' promised Linette.

'We'll be seeing you, *amigos*,' vowed Tiago.

The door opened. Without the triskel, the wheels were sinking into the sand and Linette couldn't move. Tiago grabbed the chair handles and pulled her backwards through the gap just as two people passed them going in the other direction. From her position facing backwards, Linette was able to see them arrive on the beach, loaded down with suitcases and other objects.

'Is that . . . is that a painting by Cézanne that Shreddie's carrying?' asked Linette. 'And is Magmell wearing Pocahontas's father's robe?'

'Don't ask.' Tiago parked her on the paved floor just as the portal winked out of sight.

They had arrived on the roof of the new extension to the Ashmolean museum—and the burglar alarm was ringing.

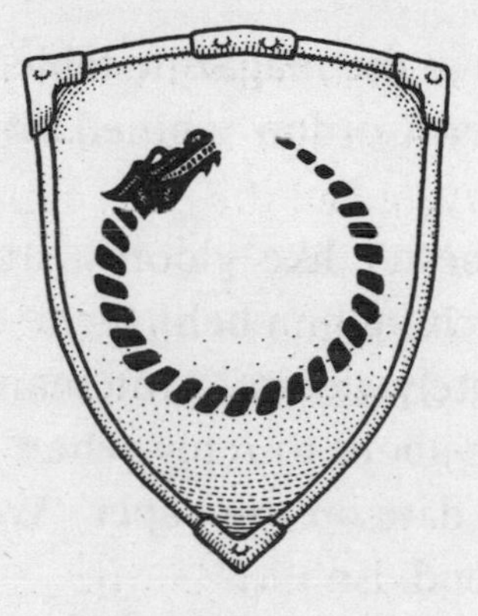

# Chapter 21

The police who apprehended Linette and Tiago couldn't charge them with theft: they clearly had none of the missing items on them and possession of two dogs did not constitute an offence. Linette however was very soon recognized as the girl who had been reported missing and they were whisked down to the station and asked to wait until a responsible adult could be summoned.

'We're too young to be questioned without a parent or guardian,' Linette whispered to the bemused Tiago. 'Just act dumb and nothing will happen to you.'

'That won't be hard,' said Tiago, pulling a vacant expression.

Bob sniffed at the magazine table, dislodging an old newspaper. Gordon whined and hid his face on Linette's lap.

'Gordon doesn't like gloomy stuff,' Tiago explained, scratching him behind the ears. 'And this place is definitely gloomy—too many crooks.'

Linette was about to reply when her eyes were drawn to the date on the paper. 'Wednesday! But it's the weekend, isn't it?'

'Not any more. You've missed a few days—but not many. Rick's missed thirteen centuries—try living with that.'

Linette bit her tongue, but her mind was already wondering what her parents had gone through. Last they knew she had gone for a ramble around college; now she was a national incident. And to think it could easily have been much worse.

'Linette!'

Here it came—the impossible explanation: for her, she'd only missed her parents for a moment or two; for them, they'd had to live with the unexplained disappearance of their daughter for days.

Her parents descended on her—hugging her fiercely, kissing her, asking her over and over if she was all right. She looked helplessly at Tiago.

'Yeah, that professor was a right nutcase,' he began, inventing wildly. 'He took the pair of us into the Ashmolean, promising to show us the . . . um . . .'

'Cape—Pocahontas's cape,' supplied Linette, grateful he'd taken on the burden of making up reasonable lies.

'Yeah, and then abandoned us in a locked store-room when we told him not to nick stuff. We only got out tonight when the dogs found us and brought us the key.'

Bob perked up at this and did his best to look heroic.

'Oh no, how terrible! Have you had enough to eat and drink?' Veronique asked, patting Linette's arms as if expecting them to be reduced to skin and bone.

'*Oui, Maman*. We had plenty. He wasn't trying to kill us. He's just gone demented acquiring stuff. He'd stashed enough food and drink for a few days.'

'But you've been gone over a week!'

Oops. Linette glanced at the headline again—it was a very old newspaper. 'Really? It didn't feel like that. Tiago has been amazing—looked after me.'

Veronique now fell on Tiago, cuddling him and rubbing his hair. He grimaced but courageously put up with it.

Her dad meanwhile was talking seriously to the policeman on duty. 'I don't care a jot about discrepancies in their story! You can send someone round to take my daughter's statement at home but we're leaving and I don't mind how many of your superiors you have to get out of bed to get permission, it is happening now.'

'We can't abandon Tiago here—or the dogs,' Linette inserted quickly. 'His carers have been struck off the social services register, Rick and Roxy have gone to new families, and he has nowhere to go.'

This only caused Veronique to sob even harder into Tiago's hair. 'Oh, you poor thing. *Of course*, you're coming home with us.'

'I can't let you just walk out of here with a minor for whom you have no responsibility,' huffed the policeman.

Linette saw Tiago delve in his pocket and whisper something. While the adults were arguing, he pulled out an official looking letter—at least it seemed to be official but somehow Linette just knew there was magic involved.

'It's OK, officer, I've a letter here from the social services in . . . um . . . Devon giving permission for me to stay with a family approved by my school so as not to disrupt my education.' He turned his soulful silvery eyes on Mrs Kwan. 'I was hoping you might let me stay for a few days until they can sort out something more permanent?'

How convenient. Linette hid her delight, knowing her parents were far from seeing any joke tonight.

Veronique's eyes filled with tears for the lost boy. 'Of course you can stay. I'll demand the headteacher rings the social services on our behalf as soon as the office opens.'

Linette's dad was still threatening to lock the professor up for the rest of his life—which he could never know had already been accomplished.

'Professor Marmaduke just went senile,' Linette said, tugging at her dad's jacket. 'Poor old man probably wandered off and fell in the river or something, taking the stuff with him. He deserves our pity.'

'He deserves secure accommodation—I don't understand what happened to him. To go mad so quickly.' Mr Kwan shook his head in bewilderment.

'Are his rooms still untouched?' Tiago asked, a shade too innocently.

Linette's dad began pushing her out of reception without waiting for permission from the officer on duty. 'Naturally. We have had to leave everything as evidence for the police.'

'Uh-huh.' Tiago's eyes glinted with calculation. He whistled to Bob and Gordon and shouldered the professor's walking stick. 'Let's go, lads. We've got new digs.'

'What have you got today?' Roxy asked Rick as they sat together in a quiet corner of the grounds, facing the newly rebuilt Dark Lore House.

'Feysyks. I'm going to pay much more attention from now on.' Rick watched bitterly as some changelings hurried by talking happily about a football match they were going to play against the pixies later. Morgan had released them from the dungeons, claiming they had cluttered the place up too much now she had a special prisoner to guard. Malduc had one very small cell to endure in solitary confinement, having gambled on two worlds and lost.

Rick sighed. Malduc wasn't the only prisoner staring at his bars. Being back at Dark Lore was harder now Rick and Roxy knew the truth. At least the other changelings had not tasted real freedom and then lost it. Neither did they know they were stolen. It was Rick's and Roxy's responsibility to tell the others the truth and start recruiting for the new Round Table, but it would have to be done carefully or the Fey would get suspicious and any chance of breaking out to find Arthur would be ruined.

Roxy sensed his gloomy mood. 'Don't worry, Rick. Tiago and Linette won't forget us.'

'It's been a while.'

'Not for us. Not even a whole day.'

'How long do they need to find Merlin?'

Roxy shrugged. 'He's been in hiding for centuries; it's not going to be easy. And how are we going to get out of here and find King Arthur?'

'We can't stay this side of the fence but I don't see an easy way to escape.'

'Cheer up, Rick. You're not normally so defeatist.' She tapped his torc. 'Tell him, Aethel, to cheer up.'

The snake unwound from his neck to drape in an amicable fashion over both their arms. Rick smiled, pleased his familiar was now friends with Roxy. 'It's just that I feel as if we've gone full circle, back where we started.'

Roxy shook her head. 'No, you're wrong. It's been a spiral—we've circled but moved up.'

'Don't talk to me about spirals—the last one I tangled with almost ended the existence of two worlds.' At least the Brazen Face prophecy had been meant for the Mage changeling—he was the one who had met with disaster in the Fey power ring, not Tiago or Rick.

'But it's the truth. We know what's really going on now. We have a plan to form a new Round Table; we've got people on the outside helping us; we have each other; Tiago has Linette.'

'Yeah, that's a massive plus. Dark Lore's already more fun with you as a friend.'

'You mean since I dyed Morgan's hair green this morning by switching her bath water?'

'Yep, that's what I mean.' Rick chuckled at the wonderful memory of the commander's shrieks of fury. It hadn't taken her a moment to change it back, but the aggravation had been worth the risk. She still hadn't worked out who had done it as Roxy had made sure they both had good alibis. It wouldn't be long, Rick was sure, before they started causing a lot more trouble for Morgan than a trick or two. Once they told the other changelings the facts, he imagined Dark Lore would rebel.

'You've forgotten one big improvement,' added Roxy.

'Oh?'

'You look way better than before you went to the human world—everyone's noticed here. You're almost cool.'

'Well, thanks.' He tugged his new clothes straight, feeling absurdly pleased to be human. In fact, he realized now, he loved it. He'd choose that over Fey magic any day.

'You're welcome.' Roxy got up and jigged on the spot to restore some warmth in her toes in response to the early morning chill. A spray of turquoise butterflies fluttered from the long grass and fanned around them; silver peacocks sang their musical cries on the green lawns; firebirds flashed gold as they flew overhead into the jade-green forest. Yes, life here promised to be very interesting.

'What do you think about joining that football match later?' Rick asked as he got up to head to the first lesson.

'I think the pixies will win—they always steal the ball.'

He took her hand, swinging their arms between them. 'Ah, but if you're on my side, I think we can take them.'

# CAN'T WAIT TO FIND OUT WHAT HAPPENS NEXT?

## HERE'S AN EXCLUSIVE SNEAK PEEK AT THE NEXT BOOK IN THE YOUNG KNIGHTS TRILOGY

# PENDRAGON

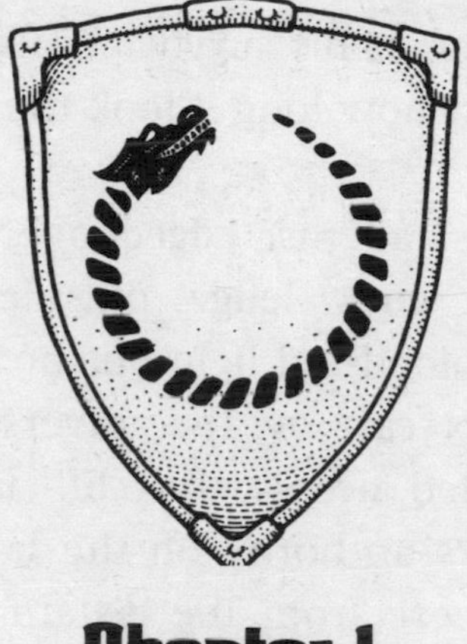

# Chapter 1

The stench of dragon was overwhelming. A burning ache at the back of Rick's throat, a stinging in his eyes—there was nothing else in Avalon that smelt quite like it.

Pausing before the entrance to the den, Rick Halfdane, the Fey king's newest dragon keeper, took a last breath of fresh air. The other keepers, a scarred and scratched collection of Dark Folk, stood in a semi-circle behind him, watching, their amusement plain. All the dragon keepers were little better than outcasts in Avalon: part-trolls, sylph-ogre crosses, disgraced Feys; it pleased them to have a human added to their number, a new underdog to bully. Money was changing hands as they took bets on his survival. His death wasn't in doubt—just how long it took the dragon to kill him.

The sun had just edged over the horizon, flooding the rock ledge outside the dragon stables with blood-red light but no warmth. The long shadows cast by the towers of the royal castle sprawled across the cliff face, stamping King Oberon's authority on the landscape. The northerly breeze from the distant range of ice-capped mountains was cold and dry. White eagles circled above the turrets. Rick tried to make this little moment last: it might be his final glimpse of daylight.

'Go on, then, changeling,' urged Gorth, the veteran keeper, uncurling his iron-tipped whip. A tough part-troll Fey with a gnarled hide and tusks instead of teeth, Gorth had rated a human's chances as very low. 'Sun's up and the king's mount will be really hungry. Waiting will only make it worse.' He spat a hissing droplet of venom on the ground at Rick's feet, his forked tongue flickering. 'And to think I forgot to feed it yesterday; it'll be starving.'

The other keepers laughed. A couple changed their bets to shorter survival times.

He'd been set up. No point risking the only one he loved who he still had with him. Rick tapped the golden torc around his neck. 'Aethel, stay here.'

Obediently, his magical snake shimmered from ornament in to life and slid to safety in a crack just over the rough lintel. Rick had been warned that dragons took offence at any smaller reptiles that dare encroach on their territory.

Deep inside the honeycomb of caves, the beast was already roaring as it sensed the arrival of food. Penned in by the rock, the dragon's claws scraped on the floor and walls, hollowing out a few more inches in the chambers it had already carved in its years of captivity. The noise made Rick's teeth ache, hitting the note that went right to the nerve.

Was there nothing about dragon keeping that wasn't the complete pits for a human? It was the all-out winner in worst job in history, right down there with sewer cleaner.

Casting a last defiant look at his audience of ill-wishers, Rick entered the tunnel and reached for the protective breastplate that hung just inside. A little large for him, it had been made for the previous keeper who had been invalided out after serving this particular dragon for only a week. Next Rick laced up his shin pads and gauntlets, and finally added a helmet to cover his hair. The gear was not much help in the event of the dragon turning on a keeper but it did give Rick the illusion of protection. He breathed through the shivery sensation that rolled inside him. He couldn't think too much or he would never find the courage to face the dragon.

'OK, if I get out alive, I'll get hold of a massive plate of chips somehow and eat every single one.' He had become fond of this human treat during his stay on Earth. Fey cooks hadn't yet discovered French fries so he had no idea how he was going to realize his dream. Still, it felt better to hope than despair. 'So all I have to do is not become a dragon chip first.'

Uniform securely fastened, Rick grabbed a torch and proceeded to the meat dump. No one but the keepers was expected to come this close to the dragons; magical defences were useless as the creatures just ripped straight through them. Brute force and bribery were the only things that worked. The Fey hunters dropped their catch down a specially constructed shoot in the rock. It was Rick's task to drag the carcass the last hundred yards; this was to remind the dragon that it relied on the keepers for every meal—one of the few tools the Dark Folk had to tame the creature's volcanic nature.

Thrusting his torch in to the dark recess at the bottom of the shoot, Rick cursed when he saw that the only offering was a half-eaten chicken. There was no question that this was not a deliberate attempt to sabotage his first day. Rick hooked it off the floor and slung it over his shoulder. He should have expected this. The chances of surviving to eat chips got a whole lot fainter.

'I hate this place,' Rick muttered, words inadequate to describe the deep loathing he felt for his life in Avalon. Painfully lonely, without anyone but Aethel to look out for him, Rick just wished he could be a normal teenager living in an ordinary family on Earth, ignorant that such places as this existed.

Rick turned the final corner to look down on the den in which the Stormridge was stabled. The top of the pit was covered with thick fire-proof bars, long spikes pointing downwards so the dragon could not grip on to them and saw through the steel. That left the creature the floor and walls of its cell on which to vent its frustration. Whitish-grey rubble was heaped in one corner, torn up by claws. The air was thick with dust. At first Rick found it hard to see the dragon as it was almost the same hue as the rock. As a chameleon species, dragons could change colour to suit their environment, but as all of them were kept in dungeons they had lost their rainbow skins. They had become dull, ugly, and vengeful.

Rick peered in to every corner of the prison. Then he spotted his dragon clinging to the far wall, ragged wings flat against its back, tail tucked in to the new gouge it had made in its frenzy. It was enormous—the length of a tennis court, though a good deal narrower with its pinions tucked tightly to its body. Skin pitted and uneven like a dried lava flow, claws sharp as scythes, this old dragon was hideous and mean and would enjoy nothing better than to use his keeper's bones as toothpicks. It wasn't hard to see the parallels between Rick and the dragon's status as Oberon's captives. The dragon hated life in Avalon as much as he did. Maybe more.

'Breakfast is served!' Rick called, throwing the chicken through the bars. It plummeted unimpressively to the ground a few feet from the dragon's tail. The other keepers had already told him he was wasting his time talking to their charges. It wasn't that the dragons didn't have the wit to understand—before Oberon took over, they had once ruled Avalon in their own right and were famed for their intelligence—it was that they just didn't care what usurping Dark Folk had to say. 'Sorry it isn't much. The next thing I'm going to do is hunt down the hunters and make sure you get a decent meal. Double, to make up for today.'

The Stormridge did not move.

'We didn't get a chance to be introduced yesterday,' Rick continued, tone more cheerful than he felt. He was supposed now to lift the hatch in the bars, rope down, and enter the cave to muck out the creature's pen—the idea being that occupied with its meal it would not attack. Some hope. He eyed the pitchfork wondering if he could use it to defend himself at a pinch.

Of course, the sensible thing would be to do this by magic: use a couple of lifting spells to move the dung, zap the floor with a spring charm, and wash the dirt away. Problem was that dragons dampened magic. It was something about their own power that meant no charms worked within a few feet of them.

Rick balanced his way across the bars to drop the rope in to the pit. The pitch fork went next, landing prongs downwards, quivering slightly. He then opened the grill.

The dragon still made no movement—and that was just creepy.

'I'm coming down to clear up,' he continued in what he hoped was a soothing tone. 'To make you more comfortable.'

A curl of smoke wound from the creature's nostrils. A sign of annoyance? Malice?

'OK, coming in.' Rick grasped the rope and quickly slid down. He could feel the unblinking stare of the dragon following his progress. He wanted to hunch his head closer to his shoulders to defend the back of his neck but decided against showing weakness. He smoothly picked up the pitchfork and made his way over to the straw-covered area the dragon had selected for its bathroom, pretending that everything was perfectly normal and he didn't have a one tonne dragon fixing him with a predatory gaze. Don't shake, he urged himself, noticing his legs were in danger of going in to a little jittery dance all of their own. He approached the dung pile. During his induction he had learnt that dragons were fastidious creatures and objected to living in a dirty stable. 'I'll just get rid of this for you.'

That did it. The Stormridge cannoned the short distance between them, its tail whipping the pitchfork from Rick's hands. Just in time, Rick dived behind the heap of rubble, narrowly missing being crispy fried by a blast of flame. Straw blackened and whirled up in sparks, a flock of tiny firebirds. He felt a scorching heat on his face. Hair smouldered. Then nothing.